Christma

Door

STAND-ALONE NOVEL

A Western Historical Romance Book

by

Ava Winters

Disclaimer & Copyright

This is a work of fiction. Names, characters, places and incidents either are products of the author's imagination or are used fictitiously. Any resemblance to actual events or locales or persons, living or dead, is entirely coincidental.

Table of Contents

Let's connect!

Impact my upcoming stories!

My passionate readers influenced the core soul of the book you are holding in your hands! The title, the cover, the essence of the book as a whole was affected by them!

Their support on my publishing journey is paramount! I devote this book to them!

If you are not a member yet, join now! As an added BONUS, you will receive my Novella "**The Cowboys' Wounded Lady**":

FREE EXCLUSIVE GIFT
(available only to my subscribers)

Go to the link:
https://avawinters.com/novella-amazon

Letter from Ava Winters

"Here is a lifelong bookworm, a devoted teacher and a mother of two boys. I also make mean sandwiches."

If someone wanted to describe me in one sentence, that would be it. There has never been a greater joy in my life than spending time with children and seeing them grow up - all my children, including the 23 little 9-year-olds that I currently teach. And I have not known such bliss than that of reading a good book.

As a Western Historical Romance writer, my passion has always been reading and writing romance novels. The historical part came after my studies as a teacher - I was mesmerized by the stories I heard, so much that I wanted to visit every place I learned about. And so, I did, finding the love of my life along the way as I walked the paths of my characters.

Now, I'm a full-time elementary school teacher, a full-time mother of two wonderful boys and a full-time writer. Wondering how I manage all of them? I did too, at first, but then I realized it's because everything I do I love, and I have the chance to share it with all of you.

And I would love to see you again in this small adventure of mine!

Until next time,

Ava Winters

Prologue

Ranger's Peak, Wyoming

1850

The wind outside the train and the baby in Estella's arms were both howling. She could do nothing for the terrible winter weather and even less for the child.

"Hush, Cody," Estella whispered, her voice thin and cracking. She held him close to her body and rocked him. He refused to be soothed, his cries growing louder and more needful. He needed to be fed, which was the one thing she couldn't do for him.

Estella wasn't Cody's mother.

Glancing around the cramped interior of the rumbling train car, Estella saw no one was even looking in their direction. She'd received many dark glares at the beginning of the journey due to Cody's frequent and loud wails, but that was hours ago now, and everyone must have committed to ignoring her.

Or they aren't ignoring us. They're just caught up in bigger problems, Estella thought.

She looked out the frost-covered window at the harsh landscape, the driving wind sending sheets of snow across the hills and valleys. With the sky so overcast and dark, visibility was lowered further until it was impossible to see for any distance. She could pick out only the vaguest impressions of houses and trees amidst the rolling white drifts. Anything out too far past the train tracks was lost in the whiteness.

Estella had known she was taking a risk on this journey in the midst of one of the harshest winters the region had experienced in years. She just hadn't expected the situation to get so bad so quickly. The train had become stuck for several hours due to the snowstorm, necessitating the workers and able-bodied passengers to get out and dig the tracks out of the snow. Some of those who assisted still hadn't warmed up after spending time out there. The inside of the train was frigid even through Estella's many layers, and she sympathized with those shivering men, their lips blue and faces scraped raw from ice crystals flying in the wind.

Cody fell silent abruptly. Estella's heart pounded in the ensuing silence, and she checked the baby, fearing the absolute worst. If they had come so far only for this to be where their journey together ended, she didn't know what she would do. She would have nothing left. She would exit the train and go walking in the storm until the cold claimed her.

Cody's small, pale face was pinched, his eyes shut. His chest rose and fell with short, rapid breaths. Estella adjusted the blankets she had him wrapped in, ensuring he was as warm as he possibly could be. Her heart was still racing, as this was no restful sleep Cody was having. He had cried out all of his strength and was now limp against her.

Every muscle in her body was tensed as she held him and looked out the window. Every extra minute they spent trapped on this train was a minute that the baby suffered. Guilt clawed at her from the inside, wounding her. Not for the first time, she doubted this plan she had made. How could she have ever believed this was going to work?

What if Cody didn't make it to their destination?

But she'd had no other choice.

Her hand had been forced.

Estella had been getting along well enough in the tailor's shop she took over from her late father. She had skilled hands and had spent many, many days assisting her father before he and her mother died, and she was able to keep the business afloat on her own. That she had only herself to care for meant few expenses.

That had all changed when her cousin, Ada, had come to her, seeking assistance after falling pregnant out of wedlock. Ada's father—Estella's uncle—Luther, had forced her out, leaving her with no one else to go. Estella took her in and gave Ada a job doing small tasks in the shop, though her cousin never developed much proficiency with needles and threads.

When Ada took ill late in her pregnancy, Estella cared for her as she would a sister. And she had been the only one there when Ada gave birth, the doctor never arriving. Though Estella had never been involved in any other deliveries, the signs were obvious that Ada's was going wrong. The process took too long. There was too much blood.

In the end, Estella had been left clutching a blood-drenched bundle, huddled over the still, white form of her beloved cousin, Ada's last words ringing in her head.

"His name is Cody. Please protect him."

The whole train shuddered, and Estella broke out of her memories. As she sat up, she thought she saw Ada on the other side of the window somehow, looking as haggard as when she had died. Her black hair was tossed about her head, strands sticking to her sweat-covered face. Her features were drawn and bloodless, her lips gray.

Estella blinked, and it was only her own reflection showing her just how tired and aged she looked, stress adding over ten years to her twenty-one. Rather than black hair, hers was dark brown hair but unwashed and oil-slick greasy, and there were heavy shadows beneath her cornflower blue eyes. Her frown had carved deep furrows on either side of her chin, and her brows were so constantly furrowed together that they might soon become one.

She didn't look like herself.

Perhaps it was for the best. She was about to start a new life. She wasn't Estella, the seamstress, any longer.

She was Estella, the traveler, soon-to-be rancher's wife.

All around her, the other passengers were stirring as the train continued to jitter and groan. The brakes squealed, and Estella recognized the sound from when they quickly had to stop or risk derailing when the snow was blocking the tracks.

"What's happenin'?" she said aloud. "Why are we stoppin' again?"

One of the other passengers spoke while adjusting his hat on his head, pulling it down lower to cover his ears. "We be there, I think. Ranger's Peak."

Estella realized he was right. The snowy landscape outside no longer whipped by so quickly, and the train was slowing rapidly. Through the white haze, she caught glimpses of dark, clustered buildings with smoke going up from every chimney. Spots of wan orange lantern light glowed, fragile bits of warmth and visibility.

Estella shifted her sore and aching legs as the train continued to slow, preparing to stand after being cramped up on the wooden bench for so long. With a final heave and a jerk, the train stopped at the station. A conductor entered the car, ushering everyone toward an exit through which icy, biting wind was entering. Estella grabbed her bag and joined the jumble of others shuffling off. The wind stole her breath, raking right through her layers and turning her bones into icicles.

Cody shivered uncontrollably against her.

Another conductor stood outside the train, helping to assist the passengers as they dismounted into the snow. Estella gripped his arm and felt his strength steadying her as she stepped down.

"Careful now, lass," the conductor said, words streaming in a white plume from his mouth. "Keep yer head above the snow, now."

The teasing comment on her short height would have made her smile if she had been able to feel any part of her face. The cold was turning her into an immobile sculpture, freezing her features into a fixed mask. All she could do was blink to indicate she had heard the conductor's words, and even then, her lashes nearly froze together.

Every bit of strength she had went into making her legs move. She tried to walk where others had already broken the blanket of snow upon the ground, but the cold was the worst, and there was nothing to be done about it.

Lifting her head, she saw the town was like a painting, as unmoving as dabs of paint upon canvas. The only sounds were the crunching footsteps of her fellow passengers moving off and the delicate tapping of ice crystals striking various surfaces: the ground, the trees, and the sides of closed-up businesses.

Where is he?

Estella stopped and turned around, straining to see the person she had come all this way to meet.

Apparently, while she was pregnant, Ada had been exchanging letters with a rancher, making plans to move to be with him. After her death, Estella had written to the man herself, explaining that Ada had died and that she would like to come in her stead. She felt that this was the only way to take care of Cody. She couldn't do it by herself. They needed a man, a family, to provide for and protect them.

That man was supposed to be here to pick her up. But given the train's delay, Estella feared he had already left. She had no money to get a room at an inn or buy food at a tavern.

Her heart sank as she prepared to go door to door, asking absolute strangers for assistance.

A voice rang out, as loud as a gunshot in the wintry stillness. "Estella, over here."

Estella gasped and spun, and a short distance behind her was a wagon drawn by a thick-haired dun gelding. A man sat on the bench, holding the reins with one hand. He gestured for her to come with the other hand.

That must be Christopher Baldwin!

No one other than the rancher would know her name here, so far from home.

Knowing she was nearly at the end of this terrible journey gave her the strength to rush to the wagon, kicking snow the whole way. Christopher got down from the bench, and Estella saw his face for the first time.

"Y-you aren't Christopher Baldwin," she stammered, stumbling back.

In his letters, Christopher had described himself as twenty-eight, with medium-brown hair and very dark brown eyes.

This man before her was nearly twice that age, his hair fully gray and his eyes as pale blue as a high summer sky.

"Ayuh, I ain't." The man looked down at her and gave a small, slight smile. Ice clung to his mustache and beard. "Abe Hudson. I'm the sheriff 'round these parts."

"Mr. Hudson." She was shaking all over from the cold, struggling to think. "I was supposed to meet someone else."

Had she been tricked? Had this man been lying to Ada and then to her to get her to come and be with him?

"I know. I've been writin' them letters in Christopher's stead. I'll bring you to him." Abe Hudson suddenly looked from her face down to the bundle wrapped against her chest. His thin, pale lips pursed together, and his eyes widened. "Seems like we both got somethin' we didn't know about the other. What you have there, Miss Armstrong, is an issue."

Estella's face burned. Her frozen fingers clenched, forming halfway into fists; half was all she could manage. "This is Ada's son. She didn't mention him?"

"No." Abe rubbed his face with his gloved hands. He pulled in a deep breath and lifted his head. "Well, what's done is done now. I'll bring you to Christopher, and we'll see this sorted out. It's a bit of a ride to his ranch. Best we get started now."

Abe moved around to the back of the wagon and stood there, evidently waiting to help Estella climb in. She hesitated, torn between common sense and the need to see this journey through to its end. Truly, she had no idea if this man was telling the truth about his identity, and it would be more than a little foolish of her to get in his wagon.

Cody stirred and whimpered, a tiny, fragile sound that broke her free of the binds of her indecision. There would be

13

a time and place to work through all of this, but that time and place was not right then, right there.

Estella went to stand by Abe, and he gave her his arm to boost her up, then placed her bag in with her. "There's blankets there," he said, "with hot potatoes wrapped up inside. Keep your hands warm."

"Thank you," Estella whispered.

Even if he was a stranger, he seemed kind.

Estella crouched down in the back of the wagon and felt it beginning to move as Abe drove the dun horse. She immediately wrapped the blankets around herself and Cody. The hot potatoes within radiated warmth, and she eagerly tucked one near Cody and held another in her hands. The warmth was almost painful on her skin, shocking even through layers of fabric and gloves.

The ride was long and rough, with little to hear except for the wheels turning and the horse breathing. Estella closed her eyes, feeling her exhaustion in every muscle and bone. Worse, the smell of the potato was awakening her own hunger within her. She swallowed down the saliva that rose in her mouth and huddled more around Cody. She wouldn't eat until he had, and he was far too young for solids, which meant they would both be waiting.

"Just a little while longer," Estella whispered.

Every time her doubts rose again and her control wavered over that bouncing wagon ride, she said it again, until it became like a prayer.

Several times, the wagon stopped, and she would think they had arrived, and then the horse would start moving again at Abe Hudson's shout. With the conditions being what they were, she imagined he was having difficulty finding his way. That gave her a new worry: that they might get lost and be mired in the snow. Would Christopher Baldwin come looking for them?

Estella had so many questions about the rancher, including why the sheriff had been writing letters for him. She was about to raise her voice to ask when the wagon came to another jolting halt. She expected them to start moving again, but then she heard Abe's voice and saw he was looking at her from the rear of the wagon. He had his hands up to help her down.

They must have arrived.

Estella climbed down with the sheriff's help, landing in a large pile of snow that almost reached her knees. Through the snowstorm, she saw buildings: a house and what looked to be a few barns. Lights burned inside the house, pressing a warm glow against each window.

"Come on, now." Abe had to shout to be heard over the wind. "Quickly."

With every stumbling step, she felt the remnants of her old life falling away, like a reptile shedding its outgrown skin. Abe pulled the house's front door open, and she emerged into the glorious, bright warmth of her new reality.

The house was small and neat, with hand-hewn furniture, but she hardly had time to look at anything as Abe ushered her into the sitting room, where a fire was blazing away. Estella cast aside the snowy, damp blankets and her soggy outer coats, then did the same for Cody so they could both feel the fire more acutely. The pleasure of finally knowing warmth after nearly having forgotten it almost brought her to her knees. It was all she could do to stay standing there, her eyes closed.

And then she heard the arguing behind her.

She turned.

Abe Hudson was facing a rather tall and broad-shouldered younger man. The firelight picked out tones of amber in the younger man's sandy brown hair. His eyes were like burning coals, blazing with anger as he jabbed his finger against Abe's chest over and over again to punctuate the point he was making.

"I can't believe that you would betray me like this," the younger man rumbled. "Bringin' these abandons here. Thinkin' that I'll be carin' for them. You must be drunk, Abe."

Abe spread his hands. "I ain't had no idea she'd be bringin' a baby. Weren't the original plan. But what's the harm in it?"

"What's the harm in it?" The other man's voice rose even more. "You think I got the actual to take care of two more people?"

The sheriff seemed hardly bothered by the shouting that was making Estella flinch with every word. "As your friend, I think this is the best thing for you."

"You're an interferin' old man! You don't get to decide what's the best thing for me!" He turned away and saw Estella watching them. His mouth twisted into such a fierce frown that he would have frightened a bear away. "You can't stay here. I don't know why you came, but you got to leave."

Estella rocked back on her heels as realizations came at her like attacks, striking her without mercy. This man was obviously Christopher Baldwin. The physical details fit too well for it to be anyone else. Why didn't he know she was coming?

But she knew the answer to that. For some reason or another, the sheriff had written all those letters to Ada without telling Christopher that he was doing it. She didn't know why that was, and it didn't really matter right then. There was something much more important to do than solving that particular mystery.

She couldn't let this man throw her out of his house.

"Mr. Baldwin," Estella ventured.

"What?" he snapped, impatient.

She flinched back at his sharp tone, astonished that he would speak to her in such a manner. He made an impatient gesture, urging her to talk. She swallowed hard and said, "You can't just throw us out! I don't have anywhere else to go. I don't have any money left."

"You should have considered that before you came out here on a whim," Christopher growled, his shoulders squaring. He towered over her, as she was shorter than even the average woman, his dark eyes glowering down upon her. "Ask Abe to tend to you. I'll not have anythin' to do with this."

Her surprise was turning to anger, sparks of it in her blood. She couldn't believe this man was so willing to just throw her and Cody out. Could he not see that he was being unreasonable?

She wasn't going to let him do this to them.

She was tired of being taken advantage of.

"Mr. Baldwin, I'm sorry that we're intruding," Estella said. "I'm not pleased about it, same as you. I couldn't plan for anythin' else, as I didn't know this would happen. I didn't know that anythin' was planned behind your back. I thought.... Well, there'll be time later for the whole story. Right now, time is short, isn't it? Abe's horse is still outside, and he'll be needin' to get back to town. So, I propose a deal, Mr. Baldwin."

Without meaning to, she was talking with him the same way she would have with a displeased customer at the tailor's shop. And it was working. Christopher was looking down at her, his face red yet silent, waiting for her to go on. At his shoulder, Abe was listening, too.

Estella continued to speak firmly, infusing as much reason into her words as she could manage. "If you send me outside on my own, I'll die. This baby will die. You must wait until the weather is better. I won't be a drag on you, though. I can help out with chores. I can cook. I can...."

She cast her eye around and noticed, for the first time, how dirty the place was. Dishes rested on many surfaces, and dust was in the corners. Boxes were lined up against the wall, so she might have thought he was just moving in, except, judging by the dust on and around them, they had been there for some time.

"I can help you clean this place up. Earn my keep for as long as I got to stay. I swear that we'll be on our way when we can, but for now, we might just need to figure this out and make it work."

Slowly, as she spoke, Christopher's shoulders lowered. He stepped back and turned partly away from her, shielding his face so she couldn't see his expression. When he spoke, it was so low she almost didn't hear him at first.

"It would be the worst thing I ever done if I sent anyone off in this weather with no place else to go." Christopher heaved a huge, annoyed sigh and waved his hand. "Fine. You can stay here. Play housekeeper. I don't care. Just don't make me regret any of this."

Estella gasped out her relief and nodded rapidly. Abe was grinning like he had gotten his way, which Estella couldn't understand. Didn't he know that he had just seriously wounded his friendship with Christopher?

But that wasn't her concern.

"Thank you very much," she said, and Christopher just snorted and swiveled to face Abe.

"I'll see you off," Christopher said, his tone inviting no arguments. "Since you got somewhere else to go. I don't need a third burden."

"I can see myself off," Abe said, striding for the door with his thumbs hooked into his belt.

Christopher followed him outside anyway, without glancing in Estella's direction.

Estella collapsed onto one of the chairs and hugged Cody tightly. In the warmth, he was starting to fuss again, which was a relief and a sign that he still had strength. But, oh, how was she going to feed him? Did Christopher have an animal she could milk?

She had only another few moments to rest, hearing the wagon outside moving away and Christopher's boots crunching the snow on his way back to the front door. She would have to explain everything to him and then work hard to earn her stay, and that still wasn't all.

This was only a temporary reprieve. Christopher obviously didn't want anyone around, much less a woman he didn't know. She wasn't going to become his wife. She had to hope she had bought herself enough time to figure out a new plan, or she might find herself in an even worse situation than this very soon.

Chapter One

"Cody, I don't know what to do."

Estella sat beside the small crate she was using for the baby's bed, having few other options in this disorganized and dirty house. How Christopher had been living there was lost on her, as nothing was in its proper place. He didn't appear to be doing laundry, clothes and bedsheets in jumbled piles on the floor, and he definitely hadn't been washing any dishes. There were more boxes around than those she had first seen near the sitting room, and he appeared to be living out of them, taking what he needed out and tossing other belongings in. She had been struggling to make any progress with the housekeeping meant to be earning her keep, not knowing where she should begin.

Cody was of no help to her.

As she sat there on the floor next to his crate, her face in her hands, he was wailing. When they'd arrived at the house yesterday afternoon, Christopher had a little goat's milk in his kitchen. Estella had fed that to the baby, but it wasn't enough and had run out quickly.

His discomfort made her own eyes burn with the pressure of tears. Guilt was a black rot filling her heart, spreading out through the whole of her chest. There was so much that she was good at, but she did not know how to care for a baby, and she was so tired from the train journey and being kept awake all night by Cody's crying that she could barely think. She knew she was in a terrible cycle of helplessness and did not know how to break from it.

The front door to the house slammed open.

Estella jumped to her feet just before Christopher entered, not wanting him to catch her lazing around. He stepped inside, snow scattering off his broad shoulders and onto the floor. He pushed the door shut against the wind and moved to the sitting room, leaving wet and muddy boot prints on the wooden floor. The fire in the sitting room was still blazing, and he stood before it, staring, his eyes distant. His head was wrapped in a scarf, leaving little of his face to be seen, but Estella had an impression of stillness, as if he wore a mask.

Cody pulled in a gulping breath and let out another ear-splitting wail.

Christopher turned abruptly from the fire. "Ain't you goin' to feed him?"

Estella blinked.

Christopher had barely spoken a word to her since the previous day. He had spent the night in a guest house a short distance away on his land and showed up again in the morning. With how little work she had managed to get done, especially that first night, the breakfast Estella had provided for him was truly pathetic, mainly composed of the remnants of previous meals. But Christopher had not complained about the cold biscuits and tough smoked meat and said not a word about the bitter coffee.

That he was actually asking her a question, particularly about the baby, took her by such surprise that she struggled to find her voice.

He evidently tired of waiting for a response and moved away to the front door. He must have had more work to do and only came in to warm himself a minute.

"Wait." It burst from Estella before she knew she was going to speak.

Christopher turned back, silently waiting. His arms crossed over his chest, highlighting his broad and muscular frame.

Estella asked, "Do you have any more milk?"

"If there ain't any in the house, then I don't got any." He turned away again, and her heart fell. Then, he said, "You want more milk, you're goin' to have to milk the goat yourself."

"You have a goat?" Estella felt her eyes widen. All this time, the solution to her problem was nearby?

"In the barn."

Christopher opened the front door, and lashes of cold wind swept in. He adjusted the scarf around his face and went out. He shut the door after himself, but the sound of the wind whipping against the house was still very loud. Even the windows were rattling in their frames.

Estella left Cody where he was in the crate, disliking it yet knowing it was for the best, and she could move faster without him bundled in a sling on her chest. She stood in the doorway to the kitchen and grabbed the nearest vessel within reach, a jug with a handle, as there was no time to go digging for a proper pail or even a bowl.

With the jug in hand, she went to get some of the blankets from yesterday, the ones Abe put in the wagon for her. She had hung them up, but they were still damp and cold. She wrapped them around herself anyway for whatever small amount of protection they could offer from the elements.

Estella paused to give Cody a kiss on the forehead. "I'll be back," she promised.

His cries were too loud, his distress too great for her comfort to quiet him.

Estella went to the front door, took a breath, and opened it. The wind tore it from her, and the cold came in like a living thing, knocking into her and forcing her to stumble back and grab the wall, lest she fall. Flying ice crystals bit at every inch of exposed skin. She squinted and tried to see through the storm.

The sun barely showed behind thick, low clouds, dropping yet more inches of snow onto the world. The thin light gave her only a faint idea of the buildings on Christopher's ranch.

Closest to the main house was a small barn. Estella aimed for it rather than the larger building she could see. Even if that wasn't where the goat was housed, she could take shelter there on her way to the bigger barn.

The wind fought her every step, trying to push her in every direction except the one she wanted to go in. Her tired, cold legs would not rise above the level of the snow drifts. She had to break her own path, kicking deep furrows in the heavy, wet piles. Her breath rattled in her lungs. Tears leaked over her eyelids and froze on her cheeks.

Finally, she reached the barn and grabbed at it. The door wouldn't budge. A cry of frustration rose in her throat. She looked down and saw all the snow in the way, blocking the door. She kicked out at the snow, panting, tasting the bitterness of her own anger on her tongue.

When she tried the door again, it would only open a small amount. Trying to squeeze into the gap, she discovered it was just enough. With a great shove, she stumbled into the darkness of the barn.

Several animals made startled sounds. She recognized hens clucking, their wings flapping as they fled from her intrusion. She could only just see them in the darkness, their small shapes disappearing quickly into the shadows.

Another animal she had heard was the one she had come to find, that rough ululating call familiar to anyone who spent any time near a farm. Estella stumbled toward the sound as her eyes slowly adjusted to the dark. She made out the pen and the goat inside.

"Please, please, have some milk for me." She entered the pen and crouched down by the goat. Its fur was patchy and sparse in a few places along its flank. It turned its neck to look at her, and she saw flecks of gray on the face and muzzle.

An old lady. Her limited experience with animals was just enough for her to know that. They aged like people did.

Estella placed the jug underneath the goat and petted her, letting the animal nibble at her fingers until it realized she had no food and lost interest. She said a silent prayer and dropped her hands to the udder. It didn't feel very full. She worked the teats anyway and was rewarded with several thin streams of milk going right into the jug. Her hopes started to rise. Even just enough milk for one or two feedings was better than none.

She released the teats and picked up the jug, tipping it to see how much was in there. There wasn't as much as she would have liked, maybe not even enough to fill Cody's belly a single time.

Estella chewed on her lower lip and looked at the goat standing there so placidly. "Just a little more," she decided, placing the jug back down. She reached for a teat again, curling her thumb and second and middle fingers around the fleshy protuberance. She started to squeeze, her ears straining to hear that wonderful sound of squirting milk.

The goat shifted and kicked out, knocking the jug over. Estella cried out and jumped back as milk splashed over her shoes and soaked into the straw. "No!"

The goat made an irritable sound as if swearing at her and moved to another part of the pen, watching her.

Estella got down on her knees and lifted the jug. The handle came off in her hand, broken. Heart thumping, she peered in. A thin scum of white milk clung to the sides and bottom of the vessel. It wasn't even enough for a proper swallow.

She sat back on her heels, her head in her hands. Her breath caught, and she sobbed, beginning to shake all over. Giving the baby nothing would be preferable to teasing his poor, hungry body with a few pathetic sips.

What else could she do? She didn't know if Christopher had a cow. He probably didn't, else he would have mentioned that when she asked about more milk. Was there a way that she could stretch the milk she had gotten? If she added water to it, there would be more. Maybe Cody could be tricked into thinking he had had more to eat, but was it even safe to give a baby water like that?

She didn't know, and all at once, she was standing, swearing, and thumping the side of her fist against the goat pen's wooden gate. She began to pace, raking her fingers through her hair, tearing oily strands loose from her bun to dangle against her cheeks.

If only she hadn't dedicated so much of her time to sewing, spending all her time bent over fabric with needle and thread in hand. If she had been like the other girls who all helped to take care of the younger children and babies in town, she would have had the knowledge she needed to properly care for Cody.

25

I've only ever been preparing to run a tailor's shop. I forgot to prepare for anything else in this life, she thought, mortified.

Another sob racked her body, and she wrapped her arms around herself.

Was there nothing else she could do? Hadn't she at least overheard anything that she could try?

Estella straightened, sniffling. She used the corner of one of the blankets to wipe the cold moisture from her face and took a deep, shuddering breath. If she kept panicking this way, she would never be able to help Cody in the way she needed to. She had to think. There must have been some story or piece of advice for young mothers that she had overheard.

After a moment, it came to her, not so much a story or even an anecdote, just a suggestion of a rumor. She couldn't even remember where she had heard it. She might even have been making it all up in her desperation.

She had to try it.

Estella went to the barn door and pushed against it. More snow had piled up on the outside in the few minutes she had been inside. She leaned her full body weight on it, the wind gusting directly in her face, raking her skin with unforgiving, icy claws.

She managed to slip out and shut the door securely behind her and rushed back to the main house. She thought she saw someone else outside, a dark, bundled figure, but when she turned, there was no sign of them. A figment of her imagination, or Christopher going about his chores in the storm?

There wasn't the time to dwell on it much.

Once she was inside, she realized she had forgotten the jug in the barn. The loss of a thimble's worth of milk was not a great one. She just hoped Christopher wouldn't find it and wouldn't be angry at her for breaking something of his if he did.

Cody was wailing in his little crate, his face as red as a sun-ripened tomato. He waved his fists and kicked his little legs, his feet thumping the inside of his box.

Estella cast off her damp blankets and rushed to him. She held him against her chest. He suddenly screamed louder, and his entire body convulsed, so she nearly dropped him. Heart lurching, she clutched him tighter against her. He continued to screech, flailing his limbs.

I'm cold. Freezing.

She brought Cody into the sitting room, where the fire was burning and would possibly be burning until spring. She started to become aware of her own shivering. Her hands were stiff, weak.

She brought a chair as close to the fire as she dared and closed her eyes, rocking Cody in her arms. After a short while, his crying reduced in volume. Estella sagged back in her chair and sighed. Strange how his cries seemed almost silent now, compared to the previous screaming.

Perspective, she thought tiredly. *Think of the good things. Think of hope.*

As tired as she was of hoping, it was all she had.

Estella rose and moved through the house to the small room she had taken as her own—she wouldn't have dared go into Christopher's personal space. She closed the door and placed the crying baby on the bed next to her.

She shifted her clothes around, then lifted Cody again. She offered herself to him as every first-time mother must offer herself to her baby, with a mixture of hope, longing, and fear, each sharper than the next, like knives in disarray in her chest.

Cody latched onto her. She could hardly bear to look down at his sweet face, his countenance angelic with the dark lashes so delicate against the round cheeks. His lips were on her, his mouth moving instinctually.

And the pain began.

Her soft flesh felt like a towel being rung out while dry, squeezed and twisted with burning friction. She could feel that she was dry, that there was nothing she could give the baby, and yet he was suckling still, expecting milk, growing squirmy and desperate as his desire to feed was once again sabotaged by Estella's inabilities.

Estella could bear the pain no longer. She placed her fingers between herself and Cody. He detached from her and resumed his wailing, begging, pleading with her in his wordless way.

Estella lowered her head and wept with him, her tears falling on his face.

She had thought she had heard of women who could produce milk for infants despite not being mothers themselves. It had made sense to her. After all, why did humans and animals produce milk at all if not to feed babies? Why didn't her body recognize that there was a baby here who needed to be fed?

If she kept trying, would it eventually work?

Had she heard wrong? Did the fault lie with her in particular?

Stomping footsteps outside her room made her suck in her next sob, choking on it.

"Can't you keep that darned baby from airin' his lungs?" Christopher's voice came through the door. She could see his shadow underneath. "I thought you were goin' to feed him."

"I...."

The shadow left her door as he moved away without waiting for her response.

Estella wanted to scream herself. She hadn't done anything wrong, yet Christopher seemed to have such disdain for her. Could he not see that she had been tricked even worse than him? He was here, at his home. She had given up everything for this.

Yet Abe didn't seem to notice how angry and ornery Christopher was being.

They must have been friends for Abe to think it was a good idea to write letters in Christopher's stead. How anyone could be friends with such a grouchy man was lost on her.

Unless he hadn't always been this way, which begged the question of what had happened to turn him sour.

Estella couldn't devote any time to thinking about that. She had already spent too much time sitting down. The house needed cleaning, and this baby needed feeding— somehow.

Chapter Two

The snowstorm broke with an abruptness known only to the natural world, the clouds clearing away in minutes to reveal the dull gray placidity of the sky. The afternoon sun seemed to be a limpening flower, losing all its vibrancy to the cold.

The wind continued howling, and clouds were gathering again at the horizon, but visibility was good, and the conditions were tolerable enough for Christopher to get some actual work done. He was tired of chores, mucking stalls, and checking equipment. He needed to engage in his true purpose.

He went into the larger of his two stables, where his mares and younger horses were kept, including a rowdy yearling who was even now kicking repeatedly at the stall door. Christopher walked in front of the stall and stood there in front of the horse, hands on his hips, observing this behavior. The yearling snorted, nostrils flaring, and turned his head to regard Christopher with a wild, dark eye.

"Y'know, I like that fire you got," Christopher said. The yearling's ears swiveled toward him to listen. Some of the other nearby horses were doing the same. "Ayuh, burns bright. Maybe too bright. We'll see."

"Talkin' to the horses again?" The barn door swung open, swirls of snow blowing around the approaching figure's boots. "They talkin' back yet?"

Christopher looked on at his foreman with genuine surprise. "I wasn't expectin' that you would come today."

Jackson Sinclair, Christopher's foreman on the ranch, led his own horse into the stable and grabbed a blanket to dry him off, scattering yet more snow onto the barn floor. "If I ain't come in, I ain't get paid, right?" He chuckled.

Christopher also managed a chuckle. "That's right. Well, I'm glad you're here, even if it's just for a short while. I'm goin' to take this one out for a trainin' session. He needs to be learned, and if he's goin' to be learned, best do it on a day he's too uncomfortable to disobey."

Jackson moved to stand beside him, and they both looked at the yearling, who was now trotting around the perimeter of his stall and tossing his head. "He's a beautiful animal," Jackson remarked, his voice soft.

Christopher grunted his agreement.

When he moved from the town to this ranch three years ago, he had purchased a number of horses and began breeding and training them. Some of those original horses he had sold again when they would not breed or produce unideal offspring. This yearling was by far the best colt his breeding attempts had resulted in, born to his best mare after a young and inexperienced stallion somehow managed to get to her after she had refused all the other males.

The yearling's coat was a rich, warm brown without a speck of any other color in it. His golden mane and tail were already impressively long. He was tall and powerful, with a musculature that would continue to deepen and mature with age. He would be an excellent addition to Christopher's breeding stock...if all went well, that was.

"He's got the spirit to be a good breeder." Jackson voiced Christopher's own thoughts aloud.

Christopher nodded his agreement. "That's just what I was sayin' before you came in." He shot a look at his foreman, his most trusted partner and good friend, and gave a small kick in his direction. "Horses don't talk back to you 'cause they don't like you none."

Jackson snorted and dodged the kick easily. "They don't got to like me. They got to respect me."

Again, Christopher nodded. The yearling was watching them, a keen intelligence in his eyes. "That'd be the issue. This one doesn't have no respect for his handlers. He's wild. If he's goin' to be a good breeder, he's got to have the right temperament, and he ain't showin' that."

Breeding and raising horses to sell was a very long-term commitment, and it had to be done right to make a profit. Anyone looking to buy a horse expected quality, and they expected their horse to come trained, or at least tamed and ready to be worked with. It was Christopher's job to tame and train. If he could not get this yearling in good condition, he wouldn't be a breeder, and no one would want to buy him to be used as a breeder. He would be relegated to life as a working animal. That was fine, though a waste of good stock, but no cowboy wanted to work with an unruly animal.

The pressure of time was upon Christopher to make the right choice to ensure a good future for his anima. A profitable future.

Jackson spoke. "You're thinkin' about gelding him."

Christopher nodded. "I can breed his sire and dam again, get another with his quality if I have to. If he's gelded and loses some of this spirit he's got, he'll bring in a good amount of actual. I'd prefer not to. It just might be what's best for him."

"Well, let's see how he is today. I'll get the gear." Jackson moved past Christopher. Christopher continued to stand there and look at the yearling, sighing heavily.

He had quite a bit of debt following him around, particularly after what had happened three years ago when he needed to restart his entire life. He couldn't afford to just throw aside all the time and work that had gone into this animal by gelding him and handing him off to any old cowboy. But he couldn't keep around an animal that might grow to be a terror and hurt the other horses.

His shoulders felt heavy, slumping down as his thoughts piled up.

As if he didn't already have enough worries, and now that woman and baby were here, living in his house, consuming his resources....

Jackson returned with the gear and handed Christopher a rope. Christopher tied a loop at the end of the rope and tossed it easily over the yearling's neck. The young animal's whole body tensed, his muscles flexing and twitching.

Christopher bided his time, letting the yearling get used to the rope before he gave it a tug to tighten the loop. "You ready, Jackson?"

"Ayuh." Jackson held a bridle in hand, ready to slip over the horse's face.

Christopher undid the latch on the stall door. His own muscles were tense, readied.

The yearling kicked the door open and lurched forward, bucking out with his back legs. Christopher held tight to the rope, not pulling, simply letting the horse feel its grip around his neck. As his head came up, Jackson swooped the bridle over his face. The yearling squealed out and wrenched away, too late, an instant after it was secured in place. Bowing his head to the ground, he brushed at his face with his forelegs. Christopher and Jackson tightened their respective grips, Christopher's on the rope and Jackson's on the reins.

Still, the yearling fought his bounds, kicking out with his rear hooves and wrenching his head. Christopher dug his slick, wet boots against the hay to prevent himself from unbalancing. The sheer force behind the yearling's movements stunned him, though he had plenty of experience with horses. He had been working with them since before he moved out to the ranch. When he lived in town, he had worked as a blacksmith. Shoeing horses had been a near-daily event.

Gradually, the realization set in for the young horse that he would not be able to fight his way out of this situation. He stopped jerking and pulling and stood in place, though his head was up, his ears alert, eyes rolling in their sockets. He stamped his hooves and swished his tail, intimidation behaviors.

Christopher stayed relaxed and was not intimidated. Horses were very attuned to the emotions of the humans around them. If he allowed his nerves to show, the yearling would sense his weakness and renew his fight.

"What you want to do with him now, Boss?" Jackson asked.

"Let's just hold him here a while," Christopher replied. "He's still got that flight in him."

Young herd animals tended to be skittish and were liable to believe they were about to become prey. Christopher hoped a period of patience and calm where no harm came to the yearling would show him he had no reason to fight them so hard.

"When he's calmed a bit," Christopher continued, "we'll take Nippy out with us. Might be she can help us learn this young one his lessons."

Hearing her name, the mare called Nippy lifted her head and whickered at them over the wall of her stall. Christopher clicked his tongue to her, and she banged on her stall door, just once, politely.

When Christopher purchased Nippy, she had been named Honey. Her habit of biting the other horses when they fooled around and disobeyed her had earned her a name change. She was the leader of Christopher's herd of horses, the matriarch, and she expected order amongst her ranks.

"Don't know why we haven't tried to bring her out to help us sooner," Jackson said. He raked his fingers through his damp, reddish hair.

Christopher made no reply. The truth was that he had been hoping to do this on his own. With his back to the corner and his options slim to none, he was having to reconsider.

"Chris." Jackson was looking at him, his green eyes narrowed. "I know this ain't none of my business...."

Here we go. Christopher clenched his teeth together. "Then maybe you shouldn't ask."

"I wouldn't, if you was only my boss. But seein' as we're friends, I'm inclined to take the chance to satisfy my curiosity." Jackson inclined his head slightly, indicating a bare space on the barn wall. Christopher knew he was really motioning to what was outside in that direction.

The main house.

"I was ridin' up, and I saw...well, a woman through the window of your house." Jackson shook his head. "I thought I was mistaken, but then I heard somethin'. I don't know how to say what I thought I was hearin', Boss. I never been married once in all my near-forty years, but I been around, and I know I *wasn't* mistaken about that sound comin' from your house."

"You're dancin' around it like someone's shootin' at your boots," Christopher growled.

The yearling horse was still watching and listening, absorbing what he was feeling, only this time, he was unable to help the worries and frustrations as he thought of the situation he had been put into by Abe Hudson.

"Alright." Jackson frowned, the wrinkles on either side of his mouth crinkling to form deep burrows. "I heard a baby, Chris."

"Yes, sir, you did, and it's entirely Abe's fault."

"The sheriff?" Jackson exclaimed. They knew each other through Christopher, though they were not as close as he was with the two of them. "What's the law got to do with this?"

"Not the law. Just Abe." Christopher held the rope so tightly he felt the fibers pricking into his skin. "He done decided to go barkin' at a knot. You know, I had an idea he was keepin' something from me. He was actin' sort of funny lately. It turns out that he was sendin' letters on my behalf to this woman, posin' as me, to get her to come here. I guess the plan was for her to be my wife."

Jackson was staring at him, clearly taken aback by what he was hearing. Christopher took this as proof he hadn't been in on it. He didn't know what he would have done if both of his closest friends were plotting against him.

"This woman, she didn't know she wasn't talkin' to me. She showed up here yesterday, rode on a train, I guess, with Abe to escort her. She was as shocked as I was to find out all of this had been Abe's doin'."

"And the baby?" Jackson prompted, his voice quiet.

"Abe indicated it wasn't mentioned."

"Well, ain't this a situation." Jackson scuffed the toe of his boot in the hay. "You said she came in yesterday, in the middle of all that snow? She must have been mighty desperate."

Christopher said nothing in response. The woman's situation wasn't his concern. She wasn't even supposed to be here. "The weather's too harsh to send her off by herself again. She says she's got nowhere to go. We made a deal. She cleans the house, and I let her stay until other arrangements are made."

The yearling was calmer than before, his breathing slowed. Jackson relaxed his grip on the reins. When the horse made no move to take advantage, he let go of it. Still, the yearling remained where it was, relatively docile, and Jackson moved away to get more gear for Nippy.

He spoke from the other side of the stable, a soft aching in his voice that was only a mere echo of the pain in Christopher's heart at this subject. "It's decent of you to let them stay. Considerin' your past."

Christopher stared down at the floor, his eyes burning. He almost felt like riling up the yearling, anything to cause a distraction that would get him out of this conversation.

He tried not to speak of this. He tried not to even think of it, like ignoring a bullet lodged inside him, a wound that had never healed right.

Jackson walked back over and stood beside him. He put his hand on Christopher's arm and leaned close. "Abe might be an old fool, but he's only tryin' to do what he thinks is right. Could be he thought...a new family...."

Christopher wrenched away from the other man. He rounded on him, and now the yearling was tugging at the rope, snorting, agitated, though there was no fear of it breaking free when Christopher's hands were such tight fists they might never open again.

"I don't need no new family!" Christopher snapped. "I love Bonnie. I love Troy. They're gone, but they're still in my heart. There's no room for anyone else."

The fire that took his wife and six-month-old son was a tragedy that he would never be able to forget. Rather than try to rebuild his burned house, he had forsaken all of that and moved to put distance between himself and the past.

Now, thanks to Abe's meddling, he was being forced to feel all this pain and loss once more.

"Anyways, the woman, Estella, she ain't a very good housekeeper. And that baby is a nuisance, never stops cryin' so far as I can tell. I don't want them around any longer than they got to be."

If only he could believe that this break in the winter storms would last. But he had seen the oncoming clouds and knew it was far from over. It was only November, after all.

Can I handle having them around through Christmas, into January? Longer than that?

Surely, he wouldn't have to wait that long. Someone in town might be willing to take this responsibility from him.

"Do you think that you might give them a chance?" Jackson stepped away to Nippy's stall and let her out. She stood very primly, her dappled gray coat glossy even in the low light, and allowed Jackson to slip the bridle over her head. "It might be good for you."

"I'm not talkin' about this anymore. I'll send you home if you try, and then you'll have wasted your time comin' all the way here and back with no pay." Christopher turned to the stable doors. "We've wasted enough time. Come on."

"Yes, Boss," Jackson said in a vague, sarcastic sort of way.

Christopher stormed past him. The rope around the yearling horse's neck stretched taut as the young animal dug in his hooves and refused to move.

Nippy let out a low whicker, her tail swishing.

The yearling made a low grumbling and moved to follow Christopher.

This just might work out, he thought, but any enjoyment he might have gotten was well diminished by the thought that he could not stay outside and work with the horses forever. He was going to have to go back to his house and face that woman again. And her baby, too.

Chapter Three

Twice more, Estella tried to feed Cody herself, and each time she made the attempt, she was forced to stop due to the pain his suckling caused her. She felt the pulling deep, deep inside of herself, and she so badly wanted to provide for him. Her body simply refused to produce milk, and the pain made her balk each time she considered trying just one more time. She thought that maybe if she kept at it, her milk might start. She knew it was that way for animals and people, that sometimes there was difficulty at first, but she could not change the fact that the process didn't seem to be working for her.

When Cody had to be pulled from her without any satiation, he screamed so fiercely she felt she might die with the guilt. That, too, dissuaded her from any further attempts. She kept tempting him and then leaving him hungry. His little body didn't understand. All he knew was that his one caretaker was failing him.

Her worries were becoming honed into true fear. She could no longer even think of cleaning anything. She burned dinner and failed to sleep at all during her second night on Christopher Baldwin's ranch. She just paced her room while Cody wailed and the wind howled until morning came, and she was expected to prepare breakfast in that filthy kitchen, using pots and pans that had not been cleaned in ages.

Her brief perusals of the food supplies gave her even more to be concerned about. The flour had mold in it, the potatoes were blackening, and a good deal of the smoked meats smelled suspiciously rancid, as if they had gotten damp at some point. What meal could she make with rotting food?

How was she supposed to do *anything?*

In the end, she salvaged the un-blackened portions of the potatoes and fried them alongside eggs and lumps of cheese that looked bad but smelled okay. She served the food and then sat at the table across from Christopher. Her plate was untouched before her, the unseasoned, suspicious foods eliciting no hunger from her.

"Coffee's better today."

Estella jerked her head up, taking a moment to understand Christopher's low grumble. She clutched at her dress over her knees. "Thank you."

He lowered his mug and shoveled potatoes by the forkful into his mouth until the small, greasy mound was gone.

From Estella's room, Cody began to cry yet again.

Christopher flinched, his wrist knocking against his mug. Hot coffee splashed across the table and dripped off the floor. Estella jumped up in alarm and ran into the kitchen to grab a towel. When she returned, Christopher was dabbing at the mess with his sopping napkin. She crouched and scrubbed at the floor with her towel, her heart skittering as she felt him glowering down upon her.

His chair squealed as he pushed it back, and he stood and walked out of the dining room. She heard the front door open and slam shut and a quick series of footsteps crunching through the snow before he was too far away for her to hear anything more.

She dropped the towel and buried her face in her damp hands. Coffee continued to drizzle from the tabletop onto the floor, brown flecks of the stuff splashing onto her dress.

I can't do this, flew through her head. *Nothing is right, and I can't do this.*

41

Cody just kept crying and crying. Estella staggered to her feet and went to him, picking him up from the crate and holding him in her arms. He was lighter than he used to be. She had been trying so hard not to notice that. He was just too delicate now, too small. If he became ill, he wouldn't have the strength to survive.

"What can I do?" Estella whispered to him. She pressed her lips to his forehead. "What haven't I tried yet?"

His screams gave her no answer. She asked herself the same questions and searched, searched hard. She could try milking the goat again while being more careful. Perhaps regular milking sessions would increase its supply again over time. If only she had the time and didn't have a baby on her hands—her nephew, her own flesh and blood—who was starving before her very eyes.

Had Christopher been almost anyone else, even an outlaw, she would have asked him for help. His demeanor and especially his recent reaction to the baby crying gave her no hope that he would find enough kindness in his heart to assist.

"To the goat, it is." Estella rested her cheek against Christopher's and closed her eyes. Then, she put him down and bundled up to venture out into the cold.

The jug was in the pen where she had left it the last time. She put it aside to bring back into the house with her and went over to the goat. The animal eyed her warily on her approach and bleated.

Estella kneeled down beside her and stroked her fur. "I'm sorry," she whispered. "I just need to try again."

The goat shook her head, ears flapping.

Estella placed down the bowl she had brought with her and rubbed her hands together to create any fragile warmth that she could. There was a bitter humor in the fact that she was shivering and bone-weary, and it was the goat's comfort she worried about.

She touched the udders, and the goat shifted and settled. To Estella's inexperienced touch, it didn't seem to her as if the goat had any more milk in her than the other day. Hoping she was wrong, she wrapped her fingers around a teat and squeezed.

Nothing.

Her heart lurched and began to pound. She tried again, squeezing quicker and with more purpose. A small quantity of milk fell into the bowl, more of a dribble than a squirt.

"Please," she whispered, hardly aware of it.

She squeezed again, and the goat kicked at her hand. She hardly felt the pain, though tears were in her eyes and leaking coldly over her cheeks. She gave the second teat a try, and that was better, but her efforts were still mostly in vain as the goat quickly ran dry, like a well without any water.

The goat wandered away to nibble at some feed in a trough, leaving Estella to look at the sip of milk she had collected. She knew she would need to boil it and that there was always less liquid left at the end of boiling. And what about tomorrow? And the day after that?

There was a presence at her back, solid and dangerous. She didn't know when she had become aware of it, but it was there, watching her. She felt like a fawn in the gaze of a mountain lion, absolutely vulnerable.

"What are you carryin' on about in here?" The presence behind her spoke in Christopher's gruff, accusing voice. "That baby's back in the house, makin' a noise they can hear all the way in China."

Estella stumbled to her feet and turned to face Christopher. He looked down upon her from his greater height, the harsh lines of his face starkened further by shadows. He had no sympathy for her, no care at all.

"Why are you usin' a bowl for milkin' instead of a bucket?" he asked.

"Because I don't know where to find one."

And she began to weep openly, the tears flowing with the suddenness of a flash flood. Her shoulders shook, and she put her hands over her face, sobbing into them.

"Estella?" Christopher's voice lowered as he spoke her name.

That only made Estella weep harder, all of her worries and fears and stressors pouring out of her in a tide of endless tears. Had she at last elicited sympathy from him? She must be truly pathetic to break through and surprise him. She *felt* truly pathetic. She had failed at everything, in all ways. There was nothing left that she could do.

Something scratchy prodded at her hands. She flinched back and saw he had extended his handkerchief to her. It was hardly more than a thin bit of rag, the edges unraveling into loose threads.

"Take it," Christopher grunted.

Estella held out her hand, and he dropped the handkerchief into it. Even just by holding it in her hand, she felt how worn the fabric was in many places. The fibers were on the verge of snapping and creating holes that would only continue to widen; within a few months, he would have a handful of scraps instead of a handkerchief.

She dabbed at her face with the cloth, feeling how quickly her tears soaked through, so she could feel wetness on her fingertips.

Christopher was staring at her, his expression somewhere between unreadable and perplexed. She knew he had no idea what to make of her. How was she the same person who had so quickly convinced him to let her stay, this sobbing mess?

"What's wrong with you?" he demanded abruptly.

"It's too much," she whispered. "All of this is too much for me. I can't."

"What you mean, it's all too much?" He shook his head. "Far as I can tell, you've hardly done any work since you showed up here. The house looks the same. You don't take care of that baby, either. He cries all the time, day and night. I thought that we had us a deal worked out, but it seems like you've forgot to hold up your end of it."

He thought she was useless or, worse, manipulative, a no-good crook who took advantage of the kindness of others. She searched for the words to tell him how she really felt and what was really happening. Her mind was too scattered, refusing to cooperate. "I can't think. I can't sleep."

He just kept looking at her in that infuriating way, and with the abruptness of a fire springing to life from an unseen spark, her chest was full of anger. How could he not see that there was more to this than any perceived laziness or unwillingness to work?

She wrenched her hand back and threw the handkerchief at him. The scrap hit his arm and tumbled harmlessly down to the floor amidst all the dust and bits of hay. Christopher watched it fall, then glanced back up at her. Her breathing came in shudders and sobs. She clenched her hands into fists by her sides.

"You...you don't know what I've gone through to get here," Estella said, and images flew through her mind of her bloodied cousin's body, the weeks afterward, her uncle's cruel face.... A wave of despair nearly rocked her off her feet. Only just barely did she remain standing. "You don't know. The baby. Everythin' I've been doin' is for the baby, but I can't help him. I can't feed him. This goat of yours doesn't give hardly any milk at all."

Christopher folded his arms over his chest and frowned. "I got to ask why you can't feed your baby yourself."

She hadn't realized that he might not know her full situation. Thinking back on it, there was little time for him to be told anything. He would only know what Abe Hudson, the sheriff, had managed to tell him that first day when he was too angry and surprised to listen properly. They hadn't discussed it any further since then.

Estella tried to reset herself mentally. "Cody isn't my baby. He's my nephew."

"Then why you got him? He's not much more'n a month old. Should be with his dam."

She was surprised he would have any idea about babies. Most men didn't. "Ada passed givin' birth to him. I'm all he has. But I'm scared that he'll die if I don't get him some proper milk. Would you be able to think clearly and get work done if you were me?"

Christopher looked at her and then gave a single, slow nod. She had a feeling he wasn't actually answering her question and was more just acknowledging what she had said. He turned away and left the barn, disappearing into the crystalline whiteness outside.

Estella bent, picked up the bowl of milk and the dropped handkerchief, and stood again. She had trouble making her legs move, and it was perhaps best to wait a little while to put distance between them before she also went out. She couldn't wait too long, though. Cody needed her. He needed this milk, however small of a quantity it was.

She wiped her eyes on the threadbare handkerchief again, took a long, shaking breath, and let it out again. She felt no better for having cried, only worse. Her talk with Christopher had also not helped. She had just told him a baby might die, and he'd had no reaction.

He'd asked what was wrong with her. She should have asked *him* what was wrong with him, to be so callous as to just walk away when she and Cody were in need.

Chapter Four

A pounding on the front door jolted Estella out of the fugue she had been in. She looked up and around, almost surprised to find herself in Christopher's house, his handkerchief spread out on her knee. She had washed it, trimmed off the unraveled edges, and then folded them under to prevent them from unraveling again. Even when not really paying attention, her stitches to hold the folded hems in place were neat and precise. She should really add some reinforcing fabric to the back to minimize the chances of those thin spots turning into real holes.

Or make him a brand-new handkerchief. That's all I'm good for: sewing.

The pounding came again, and Estella set aside her sewing. Cody was awake in his crate, unmoving, staring blankly up at the ceiling. She turned away from him, unable to bear the sight of his hollowing cheeks, and went to the front door. As she was opening it, she wondered if she even should be. Christopher wouldn't knock on his own door, and any visitor would be looking for him, not her.

It was too late, the wind catching the door from her hand and yanking it open. A bundled figure not much taller than Estella looked in upon her, the face almost entirely obscured by scarves and hats. The eyes peering out from the layers were moist and pale gray. Looking into them, Estella was struck with a sense of shrewdness, as if this mysterious person knew everything about her after a single look.

Something beside the figure moved. The stranger held a rope that looped around the neck of a rather large gray goat. The goat stood awkwardly, hind legs slightly splayed to accommodate a very large, full udder.

"I heard someone here could use a good milking goat for an infant?" The figure's voice was swift and businesslike, though not unkind.

Estella briefly stammered, then gave up. She was too tired and overwhelmed to know what to do or say.

"I'll invite myself in, shall I?" The figure stepped inside, brushing past Estella. "Shut that door, dear. You're letting all that dreadful cold in."

Estella shut the door and turned around. The stranger pulled off the scarves wrapped around their face and neck, revealing a woman in her mid-forties with blonde hair in very fashionable curls. The woman shivered and looked around. "Oh, dear. I had no idea things were quite so bad. I would have been here well before now. But you know Christopher's ways by now."

Estella shook her head, utterly confused. "I'm sorry, I don't understand."

The woman looked at her with those shrewd, pale eyes. "Oh, he didn't tell you that I was coming? That man. My name is Vera Cassidy. I am the local dressmaker, seamstress, and knower of many things."

"It's nice to meet you, Mrs. Cassidy," Estella said politely. She was still hopelessly lost, but at least she could remember her manners.

"Oh, my dear, you can just call me Vera. And your name?"

"Estella Armstrong."

"Estella, that's such a beautiful name." Vera looked around again. "Where is the baby?"

Estella motioned her over to Cody's little crate, where he lay without fussing, without doing much of anything at all.

"May I?" Vera asked. Without waiting for an answer, she pushed the goat's lead into Estella's hands and bent down to the crate. She scooped up the baby, one hand carefully behind his head to support it, and lifted him into her arms. She tilted her head from one side to the other, birdlike, then let out a heavy sigh. "The poor thing is starving."

"I know he is." Estella felt a burning in her eyes, and the tears came. She had never been so quick to weep until now.

Vera bent her head and pressed a kiss to Cody's forehead, then placed him back down in the crate. She turned to Estella, her expression serious. "But there's still time. All is not lost if we start acting now. I'll need your help, Estella, and you'll need to learn so that you can do what needs to be done yourself."

Estella nodded, brushing the tears from her face. Vera handed her a beautiful handkerchief with rose floral details embroidered on two adjoining edges, just enough to add prettiness without sacrificing function.

"There, now," Vera said while Estella wiped her eyes. "You look exhausted. Whatever you've gone through, it must have been very difficult. From now on, you know my name. You can come and find me whenever you need anything. I promise you that."

"You.... Are you an angel?" Estella croaked. "How did you know that I need a goat?"

"Why, Christopher came to me at my shop earlier today." Vera sounded surprised that she didn't know this. "But we can talk while we work. Pull on your coats, Estella, and take me to the barn so we can get this nanny here settled in."

Estella nodded and moved to the foyer at the front door, pulling her coats and gloves off the hooks on the wall. She dressed quickly and then led the way outside.

Snow still blanketed the ground in a thick layer, with huge, dense drifts pushed up against the sides of buildings. Tracks now crossed the snow in many different directions, though some were already filling in as the wind pushed loose snow into the depressions.

"How did you get here?" Estella shouted. She saw no sign of a horse or wagon.

"Christopher took my horse to the stable as soon as I arrived," Vera yelled back.

Now Estella was even more confused as to the sudden goodwill Christopher was showing her and Cody. He had seemed not to care at all earlier in the day, and now he had sent her a goat and a kind woman to help her.

Estella pulled the small barn door open, and they went inside. The goat that was already in there turned at their approach and bleated out. The new goat bleated back and strained toward the pen.

"Oh, no, you don't, Apple," Vera admonished gently. She led the goat over to the adjoining pen and walked in, pulling it in after her. "You'll want to keep these two separated for a time, Estella, or they might get into a scuffle. With a wall between them, they can get to know each other without getting at each other. You don't want to know what it sounds like when goats fight. You'll think that you've got drunken, angry men in your barn. Now, do you have a pail?"

"I...." Estella looked all around. She had not yet actually looked for a proper bucket in which to gather the milk.

"I see some shelves over there. Why don't you go look?" Vera stroked Apple's head between her ears.

Estella hadn't noticed the shelves. She silently cussed at herself as she went over to them and quickly located a milking pail. What had she even been doing before this? Had she not managed to think clearly for even a second? Although, a proper pail would be no more useful than a broken jug when a goat had no milk to give.

She brought the pail back, and Vera indicated for her to close the pen. The middle-aged blonde kneeled in the straw and placed the bucket beneath the nanny goat. She started milking, and the sight of the thick, creamy streams going right into the bucket was almost enough to make Estella weep again.

"Now," Vera said, while her hands were busily squeezing, "why don't you tell me how it is you and that sweet baby in there have wound up on this ranch of all places? And sit down while you do it. You look liable to collapse."

Estella lowered herself to the floor of the pen as she watched Vera milking. She felt that she could not give Vera an abbreviated version of the story. She owed this woman the full truth.

"My parents died in a robbery," Estella said, and her heart ached. "I would have died too if I wasn't at a barn dance at the time."

"You're an orphan, then. How long ago was this?"

"Just about two years," Estella replied. "I took over my father's tailoring business."

"I thought I saw that someone had been sewing in the sitting room there. Very nice work, too." Vera lifted her head and smiled. "I would know."

Somehow, Estella managed to smile back, though it quickly faded from her lips. "My uncle, Luther, forced my cousin from his home after she became pregnant. I took her in, and I cared for her. When Ada gave birth, she...she only lived long enough to name Cody and ask me to care for him."

"I'm so terribly sorry for your loss," Vera whispered. She stopped milking to rub Estella's arm.

"I wanted Ada to have a proper burial," Estella said, "but Luther was forbidding it. He called her an embarrassment and said that she was undeserving. I tried to reason with him. There was only one way. I knew he had always planned to ask my father for the family business, our tailor's shop, so I offered it to him. I told him he could have it if he would give me permission to bury Ada the proper way."

Vera had finished milking and was looking at her, her gray eyes soft. She seemed to be listening without any judgment toward Ada's unexpected pregnancy and the actions Estella had taken to lay her to rest properly.

Estella had already become so used to Christopher's gruffness that she had no idea how to respond to such gentle treatment. She just kept talking to fill the silence.

"As I was making arrangements to bury Ada and give Luther the family business, I came across letters Ada had been writing to a local rancher. Or so I thought." She explained that the letter-writer had actually been Ranger Peak's sheriff, acting in Christopher's stead. "I wrote another letter explaining Ada had died, but I would like to come in her place. I know now that Ada never mentioned the baby, and I didn't think to because I thought she had already done so."

Vera shook her head and clucked her tongue like a disapproving mother hen. "What a jumbled mess of misunderstandings."

"When I came, we were all confused because of all the things that hadn't been communicated properly." Estella looked down. "I managed to convince Christopher to let me stay until the weather gets better."

"Well, I don't foresee the weather improving until well after Christmas," Vera declared. "So we had best get you set up properly. Let's go back to the house now, and I'll show you how I treat the milk and store it."

Estella led the way back to the house. Cody was crying, a weak fussing in stark contrast to his typical wails. She held and rocked him in her arms as she followed Vera into the kitchen.

Vera swept several items on the counter to the side and placed the pail of milk on top. Cringing, Estella knew that Vera must be judging the state of things. She was a woman in a house, and it was her job to maintain cleanliness—and that was before she had made a deal to do so.

"I've been so exhausted and worried about Cody," Estella blurted out. "I haven't been able to focus long enough to do anything else."

"You don't have to explain yourself to me." Vera lifted a pot and then placed it on the stove, evidently finding it clean enough to use. "I know what it was like to care for my daughter when she was a newborn. I had so many fears, I forgot how to breathe sometimes. Bring that milk here."

Estella fetched the pail, and Vera poured the contents into the pot on top of the stove. "We're going to heat this nice and slow until it boils. It's best for babies to have their mother's milk, but this is what we have to work with. Boiled is best. It's safer, like boiling water from a river before you drink it. But we won't boil it too quickly or too long. That makes it less wholesome."

Estella leaned her hip on the counter, rocking Cody slowly as he continued to whine. "I don't care what it is or how long it takes. I just need to feed him. I've been strugglin' to get him milk. Prices are up right now, and I didn't have much spare money to begin with, and then I gave my shop away to Luther. I've been so desperate, and I fear for him."

"Hush. No more fears. You can have that goat, and if you milk her twice every day, you will have plenty for that baby and to cook with, too." Vera smiled. She used a wooden spoon to slowly stir the warming milk.

Now that she had started talking and sharing herself with the older woman, Estella found it hard to be quiet. "Christopher's goat wasn't givin' me anything. And I tried to nurse Cody myself. I heard of women who can nurse babies who aren't their own. I wasn't able to, though."

Vera chuckled. "It can happen, but rarely. I only personally know of one woman who managed it, and that was back when I used to live in New York."

"You aren't from the area?"

"Oh, I moved way out here to Wyoming when I was a little older than you. Can't you tell I was a high-society lady?" Vera laughed again. The smell of warm milk was filling the kitchen as she stirred and stirred. "I got plumb tired of that fast life and came out here."

Vera's voice had clearly gained the right accent over time, but now that she was listening for it, Estella picked out a trace of something else that must have been New York.

"You shouldn't be feeling guilty about not being able to produce, Estella." Vera smiled at her. "You surely love Cody like your son. I can see it in the way you hold him. And love shows through in how much we worry about someone, too. But even the actual mother who gives birth to a child can have trouble feeding him. We can have low production and dry up, same as any cow or goat. You've done your best, and that's what matters."

Estella let out a sob, rushed to Vera, and put her arm around her. "Thank you. Thank you so much for doin' this. If there's anythin' you ever need from me, please ask. I need to repay you somehow."

Vera put her free arm over her shoulders and squeezed gently. "Christopher said the same thing, more or less, when he came and asked me to get him a good nanny goat."

"I don't understand why he's been so ornery with me up until now. We were both tricked into this."

"Christopher is ornery with everyone," Vera said. She gave Estella another squeeze before releasing her to focus on the milk once more. "He didn't always used to be that way, but that's not my story to tell."

Vera's voice turned heavy as she spoke vaguely of Christopher's past. Estella's mind prickled with curiosity that was nevertheless easily ignored. She couldn't be bothered to learn about the man right then.

"Since you're liable to be in the town for a while, I hope that you'll come and see me again at my shop." Vera changed the subject, and Estella was happy to let her do so. "I have a daughter that's about your age, Clementine. You need to meet her. And I don't know how much of your personal belongings you were able to bring when you came out here. You're welcome to use some of our supplies for your own sewing."

"I couldn't. I wouldn't be able to repay you," Estella said, although a large part of her wanted to accept the offer.

She had been able to bring only the most basic of her supplies: her favorite needles, her mother's scissors, measuring tapes, and thimbles. That was really all she would need while she was here. She suspected Christopher's clothes would have plenty of rips and holes needing mending—once she finally managed to look through them for the laundry. As much as she might enjoy some idle embroidery, she didn't know she would have the time for it and didn't need the temptation.

"Kindness doesn't need repaid," Vera scolded her, speaking firmly. "If you won't accept donations, fine. But you wouldn't be able to turn down a gift, would you?"

"Vera...." Estella sighed. "No, I wouldn't. It'd be impolite."

Vera nudged her and laughed. "I know too much. You can't outsmart me. Now, look here; this is starting to simmer. We want it to boil, so it will be a little longer yet."

The conversation turned idle between them as they waited for the milk to boil and then boiled it for the appropriate amount of time. Vera did most of the talking, regaling Estella with information about Ranger's Peak and its yearly holiday events. She had missed all the fall festivities, but the bakers were making seasonal desserts, and the shops were full of candies and trinkets. And there was the Christmas Fair that would be happening next month, shortly before Christmas Day.

Will I even be here that long? Christopher might not allow it.

At last, the milk had boiled long enough. Estella trembled with anticipation, wondering if Cody could sense that it was getting close to the time for him to finally eat a full meal and if he picked up on her excitement. She watched Vera, observing her technique as she slowly poured the milk into a few other containers and then into a bottle.

"Here." Estella held Cody out to Vera. "You feed him. You're the one who did all the work. You deserve the honor."

Vera held up her hand. "No. Thank you, but you're the one who deserves it. Take this bottle, Estella. Feed him and know peace."

Tears in her eyes, Estella nodded her gratitude. She took the bottle and offered the nipple to Cody. He only lay there, still and dull.

"Squeeze some onto his mouth," Vera instructed, putting an arm around her. "He needs to know that there's milk for him."

Estella did as she was told, pinching the nipple to squeeze a drop of milk onto Cody's lips. His tongue flicked out between them. His eyes flew open, and he started to suckle with the same urgent need as he had at Estella, only now he was actually getting what he needed. He drank and drank until Estella feared he might choke, he was taking the milk in so swiftly.

Then, his movements started to slow. His body relaxed into Estella's, yet this limpness did not disturb her the way it had been. Some deep and rooted part of her recognized this as relaxation rather than exhaustion.

The bottle slipped from Cody's mouth. He rested his head over, his eyes sliding shut. He slept, and at least it was a restful sleep. Had he ever known such a sleep before?

Estella held him closer to herself, her cheek to his forehead. He smelled of milk, as she was certain a baby should.

"All of your rests from now on will be sweet," Estella whispered to him. He made a small sound and nestled closer.

Vera rubbed her arm. "Well done. Look here." She pulled Cody's blanket down. "He's got a nice round belly now."

Estella looked on upon that smooth, milk-filled belly and felt a thrill of pride. She had needed a great deal of assistance to make it happen, but it had happened all the same.

Vera neatened Cody's blanket again. "You'll find he'll act much like a roostered old man now, waking to paint his nose and falling asleep again. And you'll be changing his diaper more often."

Estella laughed. "Anything. As long as he is fed, I will do anything."

"You'll be a wonderful mother to him."

Estella rocked the sleeping baby in her arms and considered that word: mother. That was what she was to this baby. She hadn't felt like much of one until right then.

It was a welcome thing, to be a mother, to have a purpose.

Chapter Five

Christopher walked into the house and paused as an unusual sound came to him. It was a sound he had known well, like an old enemy, up until two days ago when that woman arrived with the baby. How quickly he had forgotten it amidst all the crying.

It was the sound of silence.

He listened through the stillness that was thick and deep as the snow outside and managed to pick up on the faint crackling of a fire. He shed his outer layers and went to the sitting room where the fire burned low in the hearth, shadows dancing over the furniture and shelves. If he unfocused his eyes, he could almost see his Bonnie sitting before the fire as she used to when it was dark and she wanted to continue knitting.

I used to tell her she would catch her yarn on fire, doing that.

He stepped into the room, and the shifting of the shadows revealed that there *was* someone sitting in the room after all. A small form was nestled in the corner of the sofa, buried beneath blankets.

Christopher moved around to stand before the fire, looking at her. Her lips were slightly parted, her breaths soft and even. Her face was peaceful, all the wrinkles of stress smoothed out. She was almost too pretty to look at, and he averted his eyes lest he start seeing similarities between her and his deceased wife. After all, they both had dark hair and the same slight form, though Estella was perhaps a touch thinner and her face was narrower, her chin coming to a delicate point. She seemed to be made of gentle angles, like a paper doll.

There was a crate on the floor beside Estella's feet. The baby she had brought with her was in there. What was his name? Cody.

He had helped Mrs. Vera Cassidy when she showed up riding on her horse, leading that nanny goat on the ground beside her. Her horse needed to be warmed up and given some water and oats while Vera did whatever it was she needed to do to assist Estella. He would have assisted Vera again with putting the tack back on and seeing her off, but she had turned down this offer, stating she could do it on her own. There hadn't been much of a chance to ask her anything about how things had gone with the goat, if he had even wanted to ask anything in the first place.

The new goat was in a pen in the small barn—he had seen that—and now that he was standing here and looking at the sleeping baby, he had no doubts that the goat was a good milker and the baby had at last been fed.

The peace and quiet are well worth whatever favor Vera eventually asks me for.

The baby made a small snuffling noise in its sleep. Christopher's eyes flicked to Estella. She didn't so much as stir, even as the baby made another slightly louder sound. She was deeply asleep. He felt bad for her that she had been going through so much, even if he didn't know the full extent of her situation. She had obviously been exhausted. Travel was not easy, and he was a large man that no one dared to pick fights with. She was a woman, vulnerable, liable to be preyed upon by bad men. And to endure her travels not just as a lone woman, but a lone woman with a child that didn't even belong to her....

He sighed and rubbed his face. Maybe he needed to be gentler with her. Though, they did have a deal. She had spoken like a businessman when making that deal with him.

He would hold her to that deal like he would with anyone else.

The baby's eyes were open. Christopher stilled as those eyes filled with the light of the fire until they seemed to be full of burning from within, as if from an inner source of life and vibrancy. They roamed almost lazily over the ceiling, then glanced over Christopher. They paused, a brief focus, Christopher held in their grip for but an instant that seemed like an eternity, before wandering off again.

He hadn't realized he was holding his breath. He let it out and leaned over to get a closer look at the boy. The color of his eyes was ambiguous in the night and firelight. He was small and slighter than he would have been when he was born due to what Christopher now knew was a long struggle to feed him properly. His cheeks were somewhat hollow, the sockets around his eyes a bit too pronounced. The fuzz of hair on his head was dark, patchy.

Christopher's heart gave a great and terrible tug, and his body shuddered all over. He felt like there was a rope binding him, the end of it being yanked upon, leading him toward the baby, Cody.

His own son, Troy, had looked nothing like this. Troy had had Christopher's sandy hair, and he had been much older at six months. He had been vocal, babbling constantly, and was able to roll over and over and over again until Bonnie feared he would never learn to crawl and would simply roll everywhere he wanted to go. Christopher used to laugh at that, until she would also start laughing. Then she would swat at his chest and tell him how mean he was, speaking it with a smile.

At that point, he usually kissed her, and following the kiss would come things he didn't dare think of now that she was gone and he would never have her again.

Abe and his men had never been able to come to a conclusion as to how exactly the fire in the house had started, nor why it had burned so swiftly. The best estimation they had was that Bonnie had been cooking and spilled some oil and that the wood used to build the house was cheap and old and easily consumed by the devouring flames.

Christopher did not know how Bonnie and Troy were found. He had begged Abe not to tell him. As much as it might have soothed him if there was evidence Bonnie and Troy had been taken unaware, the risk of pain was too great. He feared he would be told Bonnie used her last moments of life to try and save Troy and that she had been unable to. His mind would break if he had to consider the fear and desperation his beloved wife had felt as she succumbed, knowing their child was not saved. And his poor, poor son, unable to understand what was happening to him.

Christopher shoved the thoughts away, a moan rising up in his throat. He shoved his hands into the crate and lifted Cody, blanket and all. The child fit easily in his hands. He looked at him, a lump of sorrow in his throat. It was *wrong* to have another woman, and especially a child, in his home. He had tried so hard to move on and not think of the past, and now they were here. It was a betrayal to Bonnie and Troy.

How could he endure having them here?

And yet, he could not send them away. There was no place for them to go. Bonnie would have been furious with him if she was still around, and it would not be the play-anger she showed whenever his jokes strayed too far.

"Christopher?"

He jerked his head up. Estella was sitting up, pushing her blankets aside. She rubbed at her eyes with her fists.

He stood and thrust the baby into her arms. "I was just seein' how you two were gettin' along in here before I retired."

Estella pulled Cody against her, cradling him so gently in her arms. She bent her head and rubbed her lips on Cody's forehead, and he nuzzled at her with a faint coo. "He's much better now that he's gettin' his grub. That goat Vera brought has so much milk. Thank you for organizin' this. I was so worried."

Christopher turned away from her, shifting his feet. "It was the right thing to do," he grunted. He did not want her to think that he was having any sort of feelings for either of them and added, "I was sick of hearin' all that hallowin', day and night."

"So was I." She gave a pinched little laugh.

He clenched his jaw. "Ayuh. Well, now you can get him to sleep, you can start cleanin' the house, as was agreed."

"Yes, I meant to. I was just.... I fell asleep." Another tight laugh, this time with an edge of guilt to it.

He waved his hand and started to walk out of the room. "You can wait until the morn. I'd suggest startin' with the kitchen."

"Yes, of course." Her soft voice followed him out.

Christopher stepped outside and shivered in the cold air, though he had already been shaking even before walking out there. He lowered his head and trudged on to the guest house, taking his time to perhaps clear his mind so he might manage to get some sleep that night.

Chapter Six

Another snowstorm blew in and held the world in its grip for two full days before breaking, leaving an even thicker layer of snow and ice on the ground and atop every building. Estella was already in an unfamiliar place, and the constant shifting of the snow piling up and blowing around did not help her get her bearings. She felt quite distinctly as if she was in a dream even during her waking hours, her surroundings constantly vague and moving.

She did manage to make some progress on cleaning the house for those few days, as Cody was sleeping much longer than he ever had before. She began with the kitchen, as Christopher had suggested. She would have started there anyway, desperately needing counter space and vessels to begin making proper meals. There was at least plenty of fresh water to be used for washing. All she had to do was go outside and fill pots with snow, then melt it on the stove.

As she had more room to work in the kitchen once the dirty dishes were fewer in number, she had a chance to organize and take appropriate stock of the food situation. She discovered a bag of old but edible oats, some dried fruits, and a jar of honey with the contents mostly solidified. With these new finds and the seemingly endless supply of milk from Apple, the goat, she was at last able to make some pancakes and biscuits and porridge to eat.

On the morning that the snowstorm broke, as she was serving Christopher his coffee and honey porridge, she brought up the food situation to him. "We have a little more than I thought, but it won't last for long. Maybe you should take a trip to town to get some more supplies before the weather takes another turn and we find ourselves having to eat your boots?"

Christopher stuck his spoon in his porridge and grunted. "When I've finished the morning chores, I'll get the wagon ready."

"Thank you."

He grumbled again and began to eat. She left him alone to have her own breakfast and then cleaned up the dishes after the meal. Then Cody was awake and whining for his bottle, and she took him to the sitting room to feed him. Now that she actually could give him the milk he needed, sitting and giving him his bottle was pure delight. She felt so close and connected to him as she held him and he suckled, so wholly dependent upon the nourishment she was at last able to provide. He was so happy to eat and then so peaceful afterward. He was not yet smiling, but his eyes did it for him.

I hope that Ada can see us now and that she is proud of us for coming as far as we have together.

When Christopher came in later to fetch them for the supply trip into town, Estella had them both ready. She followed him outside and stood by the wagon as he guided a horse over and hooked them up.

"It's goin' to be a long trip," Christopher said over his shoulder. "You still sure you want to come?"

"Of course, yes," she replied.

He stepped back from the horse and said, "Then get in the back, and let's be on our way."

Estella did as he said, climbing into the back of his small wagon. Christoper called out a command to the horse, and they were off with a lurch.

It was a long journey, as Christopher had indicated, as the horse had to pick its way through the deep snow. On a few occasions, Christopher dismounted to help guide the horse around some obstacle or other. Estella's offers to assist were turned down, and she stayed waiting in the back. Cody slept easily in a sling against her chest, bothered little by the cold with Estella there to shelter and warm him.

The wagon wheels hissed and crunched through the snow. From the land around them came other sounds, the sources of which Estella was uncertain, given that she had been in a wagon both times she took this journey and knew not what lay on either side of the road. She did hear branches creaking and little thumps and snaps that might have been twigs falling or animals moving around. A singular crow seemed to be the only bird left in all of Wyoming, and it followed them for quite some distance, letting out dull, throaty caws every so often.

As they came closer to town, the horse had less difficulty pulling the wagon, as other wagons and people had been moving around and creating their own paths. Someone, somewhere, a group of children was laughing, but they seemed too far away.

Christopher commanded, "Woah!" and the wagon came to a stop. They must have arrived.

Estella rose and climbed down from the wagon, landing on the paved bricks of what appeared to be a market square. All of the stalls were currently unmanned, almost unrecognizable beneath all the snow.

Estella turned and took in the town, seeing it properly for the first time without all that wind and falling snow to obscure the sights. Everything was blanketed in a layer of glittering white, as if the snow was instead many tiny pieces of diamond. The houses and businesses looked like cozy little safe havens, with warm, fiery glows showing through the windows and smoke lifting up from the chimneys.

The children she had heard were running by at the end of a street, tossing handfuls of snow at each other, a small dog barking at their heels. Their laughs came in puffs of white smoke.

"How do you like Ranger's Peak?"

Estella flinched as Christopher spoke from behind her.

She turned and looked up at him and gave a small smile. "It looks like a picture in a children's book," she said.

She was thinking of one book in particular, an item she had picked out in anticipation of Cody's birth. It had been a collection of very short tales centered around different holidays. Above the story about Christmas had been a picture of a boy all bundled up, running through a snowy town with a spotted dog at his side.

She felt the same gentle feelings when she looked at this town as she had when she saw the drawing and imagined that fictional town where children could run rosy-cheeked on snowy streets.

This place was real, and she knew it would have its flaws, just as any other place did, but to look at it was a pleasure.

Christopher's mouth twisted, and that was the only response he gave her, which seemed unfair, given that he had been the one to ask her the question. Why ask if he didn't care for the answer?

"General store's that way," Christopher said, pointing at one of the larger shops with a porch out front. Some graying old pod sat in a chair on that porch, rocking slowly back and forth. "I got an account opened up there. Get what you need. If it's too much to carry, they'll have a wagon you can pull."

"What about the tailor's shop?" Estella asked. Christopher frowned, and she continued. "Your clothes need repairs. I brought my own supplies, but I need a few things there."

He motioned to another store a few down from the general store. A large sign over the door was mostly covered in snow. Judging by what bits of the letters were still visible, Estella thought it said "dressmakers."

"Be quick." Christopher got back on the wagon bench. "I want to get home in time to finish my work."

"I won't be long," Estella promised.

She hurried off, going straight to the dressmakers as she didn't want to have to worry about toting a wagonful of supplies behind her, as she would if she went there second.

She picked her way along using the trails and tracks that others had left behind when they came before her, and then she cut sharply through the snow to reach the front of the store. The snow around the door had been cleared away, and there was nothing to obstruct her as she let herself in.

The inside of the shop was well-lit, with a burning hearth and many supplemental lamps all around. Dresses on stands filled the front of the store, placed strategically before the windows to catch the wandering eyes of shoppers. The vibrancy of the colors used surprised Estella, and she reached out to lift the ruffly hem of a red dress. It was a lustful color, red, and she had not worked much with it herself. Still, it was a beautiful piece of clothing, excellently made. The pale yellow one beside it, patterned with white spots, was even prettier with all the lacy trims and ribbons.

"Hello, hello, who's in the store?" a familiar voice called out from the back of the shop behind a protruding wall.

Estella crept around shelves of fabric and sewing bits and bobs, picking her way to the wall. She peered around and saw a tailor's workstation, an organized chaos of fabric samples and half-sewn dresses. A blonde woman perched on a stool was applying pins to a dress form and then marking down measurements on a sheet of paper. She paused and glanced over her shoulder; pins bristled from between her legs.

"It's me, Vera," Estella said. "Estella Armstrong."

"Estella!" The pins dropped from Vera's mouth, and she rose to her feet. She swept across the floor, her full checkered skirt billowing out around her, and embraced Estella tightly. "How wonderful of you to visit. And so soon! Would you like a cup of tea? Oh, my, and this is our dear Cody. Look how plump he has become after only a few days!"

Estella laughed and hugged Vera back, turning sideways to avoid smooshing Cody between them. "Yes, he's doin' so much better. Sweet as a lamb."

"Wonderful." Vera leaned back, her warm smile suddenly dropping into a frown. "What are you doing all the way out here in town? You aren't leaving yet, are you?"

"No, Christopher drove me to get some supplies. I just wanted to thank you again. I brought you this." Estella reached into her pocket and pulled out a small handkerchief with roses and graceful curving vines embroidered onto it. "I had made this shortly before I left Gatty, where I lived. I would like you to have it."

Vera took the handkerchief and held it up to one of the lanterns. "Such delicate, exquisite stitching you've done here. Your control is masterful. Clementine, come and see our visitor! Look at what she's gifted me!"

From a side door that was likely a supply closet, a young woman around Estella's age emerged, carrying a box overflowing with fabric scraps. "Mother, you've dropped pins all across the floor!" She set the box aside and swept over, moving in the same graceful, fluttering way as her mother, and kneeled down to gather the fallen pins in her hand. She glanced up and smiled at Estella. "Hello! I'm Clementine. You can call me Clem."

"I'm Estella." Estella motioned to the sling with the baby inside. "And this is Cody."

"Yes, Mother has told me about you both!" Clementine straightened and pushed the pins into a nearby pincushion already bristling with them. She glided to her mother's side and took the handkerchief. "You made this, Estella? It's so pretty."

"You know that you don't have to give me anything, however," Vera said.

Estella smiled at her. "I think we established that it's impolite to turn a gift away."

Vera laughed. "Speaking of that. I put aside some things for you. And would you like that cup of tea? Clem, keep our guests entertained while I put the teapot on."

Vera was already on her way out of the room, brushing skirts with the dresses on their stands. Estella called after her, "Christopher is waitin' on me! I shouldn't dally for tea."

But Vera had already gone.

Estella looked at Clementine, meeting her bright blue eyes. "Do you think that she heard me?"

"She did. Whether she listens is another thing entirely." Clementine laughed. She folded the gifted handkerchief and placed it aside next to the dress form Vera had been working with. "My mother says that you're a seamstress, too?"

That's what she wants to ask me about? Of all the things Vera probably told her about me, my past, and the baby, she wants to talk trade?

Clementine looked at her and tilted her head, waiting.

"I-I owned a tailor's shop," Estella stammered. "Before I came to Ranger's Peak."

"What was your specialty?"

"It used to be my father's business. I worked with men's clothes."

Clementine brightened, standing straighter. "Then, you don't know how to make dresses? I'll have to come callin' on you one day and show you how it's done. You're stayin' out on Christopher Baldwin's ranch, right?"

"Yes, I am." Estella put her hand on the sling, stroking Cody's sleeping form. "I don't know how much he would like visitors. Especially right now."

Clementine touched her arm. "I know you're afeared of word about you and Christopher getting' around, but you don't really need to. People already know, probably. They saw you comin' into town and Abe pickin' you up and takin' you to the Baldwin ranch. You'll get some looks and judgment, but most will acclimate to it. And if they don't, you don't need to give them a moment of your time. You've already met people who are kind and acceptin' of you. That's Abe, me, and my mother. Christopher, too, in his own way. We'll watch out for you."

The kindness from yet another stranger brought tears to her eyes, blurring her vision. She sniffed and said, "I need to make another handkerchief to thank you now, Clem. I'd do more, but...."

"Let me come call on you one day when things are slow here in town." Clementine leaned in close and lowered her voice. "Tell you the truth, I wouldn't mind the chance to get close to one of those ranch hands. Mother's tellin' me it's about time I give someone the mitten...."

Estella put her hand over her mouth. Clementine looked at her and giggled.

Vera reentered the room, holding a small bag. She pressed it into Estella's hands. Diminutive as the bag was, she felt it was stuffed full. "Here you are," Vera said. "No tea today, but come some other time. I have this wonderful herbal brew my sister back in New York sends me every year for Christmas."

Estella put the bag over her shoulder and nodded to these wonderful newfound friends. "I hope to be back some other time, yes. I wish I could stay longer, but there's groceries to be had."

Clementine gave her a hug, and then Vera pressed a kiss to her cheek. Her lips were wrinkled and dry. "Love on that nipper for me, every chance you get."

Estella promised she would, and then Clementine walked her to the door while Vera went back to work.

There was no sign of Christopher on the wagon bench, Estella noticed, as she made her way the short distance between the dressmakers and the general store. He must have gotten in the back to keep warm while he waited on her.

The general store was even more brightly lit than the dressmakers, barrels and stacks of goods cheerily lit. The candies Vera had previously spoken of were piled into crates—brightly-colored bits of boiled hard candies, squares of fudge, caramels, and candied nuts—and toys for children and other trinkets nearly toppled off the edges of every shelf. Estella turned her attention away from those and such delights as fur mittens and sweet-smelling oranges and walked up to the counter to speak with the attendant about what she needed.

The man's eyes went to the baby in the sling and then up to her face. He seemed to give a mental shrug. He had probably seen stranger than this, Estella reasoned, what with the train bringing so many through every year.

"What all can I get for you, ma'am?" he asked.

"You might want to write it down," Estella said. "I've got a bit of an order. For Christopher Baldwin's account?"

Again, he paused, then moved on. He rested his arms on top of the counter. "Ain't needed to write an order down since I was seven, so we'll see. What you need?"

Estella began to list off the items she would need to fill Christopher's barren pantry shelves. Flour, beans, rice, and oats were the most important, but she also requested salt, pepper, sugar, cinnamon, coffee, and a few of the jarred fruits and vegetables from the shelves behind the grocer. He nodded along the entire time she was speaking.

"You expect you can carry all that?"

"I'd prefer to borrow a cart of yours, if you have one to lend." Estella turned and pointed out the window. Past a number of signs proclaiming the store's current offerings, the market square and Christopher's wagon could be seen. "I've only a short ways to go, and then I'll bring it back."

"I've got a wheelbarrow."

"That's just fine."

Estella lingered beside the counter while the grocer busied himself. She watched, curious whether he would actually recall everything she had requested. And he did, including the right quantities, too. When he finished, the wheelbarrow was quite full, but Estella thought that she would be able to push it just that short distance.

"All ready for you, ma'am." The grocer dusted flour from his hands. "I'll make the appropriate charges to Baldwin's account, and we can square up next time he comes to town."

Estella nodded her thanks and grasped the wheelbarrow handles. She pushed hard, and it moved forward. The grocer moved to hold the door for her, and she thanked him again and walked out onto the porch.

"It's 'bout time you finished." Christopher's gruff voice came from her side on the porch. She flinched, a squeak emerging from her mouth, and turned to see him standing there. "Rattle your hocks. I want to get home."

"Yes," she stammered, "of course."

She turned and resumed pushing the barrow but was quickly halted by the steps going down from the porch. There were two and not very tall, though as she stepped to the side to judge how she might get her wheelbarrow down them, they seemed as high up as mountains.

Christopher grumbled and stepped over to her. He bent and lifted the barrow, the muscles in his arms and chest pushing against his clothes. Then he set the barrow on the ground again at the bottom of the steps and took over, pushing it all the way to the wagon. Estella followed after, and when he began to stack everything up in the back, she reached out to help.

He motioned her away. "Just get in."

She climbed in and was moving to her previous spot when her knee bumped against something hard and crate-like. Flinching back at the pain, she saw what the new, mysterious object was, and her hand flew to her mouth to stifle a gasp.

It was a beautiful cradle, a little old and scratched but otherwise just as perfect as anyone could ask for. The wood was dark and glossy, and the edges were sanded smooth.

"What is this for?" Estella looked back and forth between Christopher and the cradle. She almost wouldn't have believed it was there if her knee wasn't still throbbing.

Christopher heaved a sack of oats into the wagon, not looking at her. "The baby can't sleep in a crate. It ain't proper."

She just kept looking at him until he finished unpacking the barrow, then wheeled it away to bring back to the store. Then she looked at the cradle again, and her heart could not have been more confused. This was his second significant act of kindness toward her.

Curiosity grew in her, taking up some of the space previously occupied by all her stress over Cody. What exactly was this man's story? Would she ever find out?

Chapter Seven

That very evening, the clouds came again, and this time, it was not snow they brought. Freezing rain fell, turning to ice on contact with any surface. Christopher simply gave up on his chores, as his tools kept freezing to the ground and then to his icy gloves. He visited his horses to make sure they were warm, stopping at each stall to give an apple or handful of oats.

He stopped before the stall with the yearling. The horse snorted and tossed his head.

Christopher's shoulders slumped. He dropped the apple into the straw inside the stall. "Alright," he said. "I gave you my best effort."

The yearling twitched his ears and snorted again. He dropped his head and snatched the apple, crunching it.

"I still got plenty to learn, myself," Christopher said. "I couldn't make you the best you could be. And this winter hasn't helped. Soon as I can get a vet here, you'll be gelded. We'll all be better off that way."

The yearling sniffed at the spot where the apple had been, searching for more.

Christopher moved away and went to the main house. He decided he would tell Estella to make an early dinner, and then he would retire. *The extra sleep will be a treat—if I can manage it.*

He removed his outer layers and headed for the sitting room to warm up before the fire. The crackle and orange glow were enticing, drawing him in. As he was stepping through the doorway into the room, a soft voice caught his attention, and his eyes flicked in that direction. Estella leaned deeply back into a chair, the baby wrapped up in a blanket and settled in the crook of her arm. She had one of the bottles and was feeding Cody. He suckled greedily, his hands and legs moving inside the blanket. He was much, much stronger than he had been at first and not nearly as pale, less like a child's neglected doll and more of a thriving baby.

Estella's face was soft as she looked down upon Cody while feeding him, her eyes halfway closed, her lashes long and highlighted in gold by the fire. A small, idle smile curled the edge of her lip. Her posture was relaxed, comfortable.

Christopher jerked back into the hallway before she could sense him, look up, and see him. His breath heaved in and out of his chest, ragged. His shoulders jerked with it, his whole body jolting as if being struck again and again.

Estella still looked nothing like Bonnie, and Cody was not Troy. But the pain was as terrible as if he had seen his wife and son sitting there together because he knew that they could not be. The illusion was a lie. If he went in there, he would be forced to see it was all a farce, and his heart would break.

It was best not to go near them. He wouldn't even look at them.

Christopher turned away from the room. Being in his own home wasn't worth it. He should leave and go to the guest house. Never mind dinner or the comfort of the fire. He would rather be isolated.

Although, there would be no reprieve in going to sleep early. His dreams would plague him. Strangely, they were hardly ever dreams of fires and burning houses. Christopher wasn't particularly imaginative; he knew that about himself. He would rather leave that stuff to the poets and authors. Still, if he thought about what dreams a man should have in the aftermath of a house fire, he would assume those dreams would be about flames and destruction, the ruination of one's life and possessions by an intangible force he could not fight.

Only rarely did a blaze feature in his nightmares. Most often, he found himself in some forgotten place—a forest, an overgrown field, a mine tunnel—and he would be pursuing the sound of a woman's voice calling to him, calling his name. His dreaming mind said the woman was Bonnie and he had to find her, even though he had now gone so long without hearing her voice that he couldn't quite remember exactly what she had sounded like. And that was its own terrible source of pain.

When he awoke from these dreams of pursuit, never having found the beckoning woman, he would feel as sore and tired as if he had actually been running all night.

Christopher's hands became fists.

Was there no reprieve for him anywhere? He couldn't be in his own house because of Estella, and going to the guest house would be no better. What should he do, then? Where was he to go? Outside once more? And for what purpose?

He was so lost, so confused, frozen in one place where he was sure to eventually be discovered by Estella. He had no desire to talk to her and face her inevitable questions.

His body moved of its own accord, his mind still in the grips of confusion and doubt. He moved in the direction of the bedrooms, stopping before he fully arrived to linger in front of a very small and unobtrusive door. Estella was sure to have found that door herself and would know it was no supply closet. Had she gone up, looked around? Christopher supposed he would know if he saw disturbances in the dust.

His body was still moving mostly without his guidance. He watched his hand lift to settle upon the knob, twisting and pulling the door outward. A set of tight, narrow steps led very steeply upward.

Christopher ducked away to grab a lantern and lit it. The whole time he performed the task, he was telling himself that he didn't have to do this. He could stop at any point.

With the lantern casting its light up the narrow steps, he climbed. Even as he came to the final step before the landing, he was still telling himself that he could stop and turn around.

He stepped up fully into the dark attic, and the feeble excuses he had been telling himself at last fell away.

There was little in the attic. He'd had little to bring with him when he moved out of town and only bought what he thought was absolutely necessary to furnish his home. As such, he hadn't needed to shove anything into the attic to make space. There was a single broken chair, a stack of old clothes and blankets, and a small assortment of boxes.

The dust on the steps and floor of the attic seemed undisturbed, with no obvious footprints. Christopher walked to those boxes at the back of the attic, which were covered with a layer of undisturbed dust. Estella hadn't been up there.

Don't, Christopher silently begged himself.

But he couldn't stop.

There was something wrong with him, and he couldn't stop, only watch his own hands stretching out to lift up the smallest box from the stack. He crouched, placed it on the ground, and set his lantern nearby. Bits of fluff and dust drifted in the dancing glow.

His heart racing, Christopher reached into the box. His fingertips brushed something so small and delicate, and he lifted it out in the palm of his hand. It was a baby bootee, knitted in soft blue yarn.

He groaned deep in his chest and rocked on his heels. He put the bootee aside and reached back in, pulling out its pair and then a little tin baby rattle he had fashioned himself one day while working at his blacksmith forge. The grains of rice he had placed inside the rattle before sealing it up were still moving around as he put it aside, softly clattering. How very hard he had worked on that rattle. It hadn't come out very well. He worked mostly with iron, not tin, making the process just different enough for the quality of his work to suffer. Still, it had been functional, and he had been so proud of it.

Next to come out of the box was a ragdoll horse with button eyes.

Christopher clutched the toy in both hands and groaned once more. It had been three long years since he looked at the contents of any of these boxes.

After the fire had stopped burning, he had been invited to sift through the wreckage for anything salvageable before it was all cleared away. He hadn't been able to stomach the idea of looking so closely at his ruined life. Abe had done it for him, trawling the ashes, finding just enough to place in these few boxes.

Christopher couldn't understand how anything had escaped the fire, especially not in such good condition. His only thought was that it was a small act of God. He wasn't on such good terms with God, didn't know how he felt about Him any longer. He didn't know if these salvaged fragments of his past life were meant as a blessing or punishment.

What did I do to be punished?

He asked himself that as he crouched in the dark. The bootee, the toy horse, and the other bits and bobs of his life all smelled strongly of smoke, stinging his nose and eyes.

And if it's a blessing, why does it hurt me so?

"Christopher? Are you up there?"

He jumped to his feet, his leg knocking into the boxes. He grabbed at the one now on top and felt many light objects moving around inside. He snatched his hands away again as if they had been burned and marched over to the top of the stairs. Estella's face, small and shadowed, peered up at him from around the cracked door at the bottom.

"What do you want?" Christopher demanded. He didn't want her to see him in this vulnerable state. He wouldn't want anyone to see him like this, and certainly not her, a stranger.

She flinched slightly as his booming voice carried down to her. "I didn't hear you coming inside the house."

He ignored her and demanded again, "What do you want?"

"I thought I'd ask if you felt like an early dinner. It seems to be very bad outside, and I don't know how much work you could accomplish—"

"Fine," he snapped.

Estella moved away, and so did he, putting everything back into the box and placing it on the stack once more. He grabbed the lantern and went downstairs, pushing the attic door shut behind him.

Estella was moving around in the kitchen, clattering pots and utensils. Christopher gritted his teeth and moved to the kitchen to watch her as she drifted idly around. The baby was in a sling on her chest, apparently sleeping.

Christopher held onto the doorframe, and suddenly, there were words escaping from him before he even knew they were coming. "You shouldn't assume I ain't getting any work done today," he said, his voice dark.

Estella looked back over her shoulder at him, frowning slightly, her brows knitted together. "Pardon?"

She clearly had no idea what he was talking about, and he wasn't even all that sure, either. There was just this urge inside of him to make sure she didn't get comfortable with assuming things that weren't her right to assume. She was a guest. *He* was the one who should be telling her what was to be done and when.

"And you should have started supper hours ago. Don't you know that's how this works? You cook well ahead of time, so it's ready whenever the men are hungry." Christopher's voice was rising. "Your mother must not have taught you the proper way."

Estella put her hands on her hips, still holding a pot in one hand. "Well, she did try. I was mostly too busy helpin' out my father with the family business. Not every woman is the same, you know."

She had a good point, and that made him more upset, that she should be right and he should be wrong. "Maybe if you had spent more time at home, you'd be better at cleanin'. This place is still in a state. You're supposed to be takin' care of all this."

Her face flushed with pink. The baby was beginning to fuss, so she put her hand on him and patted him through the sling. "You can't expect me to work my way through *years* of grime in such a short time. I'm workin' hard, Christopher, but you haven't exactly made it easy on me."

"Then work harder!" he exclaimed. "Otherwise, what's the point in even makin' an agreement with you? This isn't charity. We had a deal."

Cody began to wail. Estella set the pot down with a thump on the counter. "Now, look at what you've done. Now I need to stop him from fussin' because you can't stand that, which means supper will take even longer. I hope that you're happy with causin' more problems than before you started in on scoldin' me."

Estella rushed out of the kitchen, making soothing sounds to Cody. Christopher stared after her, astonished at how she had spoken to him. The shame that came was black and bleak, shadowing him. She was right, of course. He had not helped at all.

He wasn't even sure why he had gone after her and said such things. She was clearly trying her best. He just...hadn't wanted this situation to start feeling normal and okay. He wanted her to be upset with him.

Having a happy coexistence with another woman and a baby would betray the family he used to have. Even if it caused him pain and made him seem like a bad man, he could not allow that to happen.

Chapter Eight

Estella was just leaving the barn with the chicken eggs she had collected when she saw riders coming through the snow. She stopped and put her hand over her eyes, trying to focus, but she couldn't make out who the riders atop the horses were. She would have thought they were ranch hands, but she had begun to understand that Christopher hired very few people. The foreman, Jackson Sinclair, and one other were already working, and she didn't think two more were needed.

But what do I know about running a ranch? And keeping house? she thought bitterly.

It had been two days since Christopher had been so unkind to her, and she was still smarting from his words. She couldn't understand why he showed her kindness through his actions, but his words were so mean. He had not apologized, and they had hardly spoken since then, not that they talked very much in the first place.

Estella resumed walking to the house and pushed the door open. The wind sent a swirl of snow inside, heavy white flakes landing on the floor and immediately melting. She started to push the door shut when a familiar call had her turning around and stepping back outside.

"Estella! Hello!" One of the riders approached the house and dismounted. They pushed back their hood, and Estella saw Vera's shrewd pale eyes and dignified face.

"Vera?" Estella looked to the other rider. "Then Clem, is that you?"

Clementine pushed back her own hood and smiled at her. "We told you we would come calling, and here we are."

"Oh, my," Estella exclaimed, suddenly remembering the eggs she still held. This wasn't an opportune time for a visit, but she was very excited all the same. She liked the stately Vera and her enthusiastic daughter. "Come in, please. Get out of the cold. I'll take care of your horses while you warm up by the fire."

Admittedly, she knew little about horses. Jackson or the ranch hand would have to help her.

"Oh, I'll do it," Clementine said. Vera handed her the reins of her own horse. "You just point me in the direction of the stable."

"Are you certain?" Estella asked, but Clementine was already moving away. Estella waved her in the direction of the stable building, then turned to Vera. "Come inside. I'll make some tea."

Vera rubbed her arms and shivered. "Tea sounds lovely."

They both went inside and shed their snowy coats. Estella went straight to the kitchen, and Vera followed after her. Between the two of them, they soon had a pot of tea brewing.

Estella went to a cupboard to find cups. "I can't believe you two came here through the snow."

"There wasn't much business to be had in town, and we thought to surprise you." Vera smiled. She took the teacups Estella found and placed them on a clean-enough tray. "How are you fairing out here?"

"Well enough."

Vera gave her a suspicious look. "You don't sound so sure. Well, Clem and I will do what we can to cheer you up while we're here."

"I truly appreciate it." Estella lifted the tray with the tea cups. "Cody is in the sitting room. Let's go sit, and you can see how well he's doing. He's completely changed ever since you brought the goat."

Vera clapped her hands together. "I would surely love to see him."

They went into the sitting room where Cody was in a basket Estella had begun using for him. The baby couldn't be in the cradle or her sling all the time, and Christopher was right that a box wasn't proper, so she had been happy to find the basket.

Vera immediately swooped down upon the baby, lifting him into her arms and pressing kisses all over his face. Cody had been sleeping until he was abruptly lifted, and his head wobbled as he tried to focus on Vera.

"Look at how much stronger he is," Vera said, marveling. She stroked Cody's cheek and the patchy tufts of hair on top of his head. "You'll have a hard time with him when he learns to walk and talk. He will be quite the little man, I'm sure."

"I'll be happy no matter how he grows." Estella sat on the sofa, her voice soft.

She had no idea where the two of them would be in a few months, much less by the time Cody was moving around on his own and talking.

Her heartbeat started to quicken with renewed anxieties.

The door to the house opened, and Clementine entered. She peeked into the parlor and found them. She held bundles wrapped in brown paper, tied with twine, like meat from a butcher's shop. She walked over to Estella and deposited the packages onto her lap.

"We brought you gifts!" Clementine announced.

Estella furrowed up her brows and looked down at the wrapped bundles. "Gifts?"

Clementine flopped down onto the couch beside her and put a hand on her shoulder. "Early Christmas presents," she said. "Since we don't know if you'll still be around or have moved on by then. Mother and I figured we shouldn't wait."

Estella looked over at Vera, who was nodding along. Tears sprang up into her eyes at this kindness, and she removed her handkerchief from her pocket to dab the moisture away. "I don't know how to thank you for this."

"Open them," Clementine said. "That way, you know what you're thankin' us for."

Estella nodded. She picked up the first package and tore at the paper. Her fingers trembled with excitement. She knew it was selfish, but she was glad to celebrate Christmas even in this small capacity. Now, if she had to spend her actual holiday alone and uncertain, she could hold onto this memory and still be happy.

From the first package she pulled out a number of rag diapers, all new and very nicely sewn. "These will be put to good use," she said, laughing.

"Open this one next." Clementine pushed another packet into her hands.

Estella tore the paper off and found a number of miniature shirts in bright colors and patterns, all of them perfectly sized for a baby of Cody's age. "These are so very perfect," she said, in awe at the craftsmanship that had gone into the clothes. "Are you sure that I can just have these for Cody? So much work went into these."

"Of course, they're his," Vera said. She held Cody easily in one arm while reaching to pour the tea. She was much better at doing things one-handed than Estella was. "I knew as soon as I saw him that I wanted to make clothes for him. He'll look so handsome."

Estella rushed through fixing her own cup of tea to resume opening the presents. There were a few fabric toys for Cody to play with when he was a little older and a pair of miniature mittens.

And just when she was beginning to think that these gifts were just a clever way of giving her supplies for the baby, she smelled something delicious and discovered she was unwrapping a slab of fresh fudge. The sweet treat was studded with nuts and dried fruits. Clementine fetched a knife from the kitchen, and they all had a small piece as they sipped their tea. The texture of the fudge was silky, the nuts and sweet raisins a divine addition.

The last present she opened was a heavy one, though of a small size. When she saw what it was, she could only marvel at its perfection: a pincushion like the high-society ladies might have, made of pure silver with a magenta velvet cushion on top. It was more like a wedding present, something so beautiful she couldn't imagine actually using it.

"I-I can't accept this," she stammered. "I don't have any use for this."

"Nonsense," Vera said briskly. "Every lady should have a precious item to make her feel special. Mine is a gemstone-crusted hand mirror."

"Mine is a tortoiseshell comb," Clementine said. "I don't use it, but I like to take it out and look at it sometimes."

Estella closed her hand around the precious trinket, feeling the cold, heavy silver. "Thank you," she whispered. "I will cherish it forever."

"Hopefully, you *will* get some use out of it." Clementine cleared away the brown papers and pulled out yet another packet from her pocket. "I brought these. They're copies of some of the dress patterns we use. And there's some fabric that I left in the hallway. I would love to see what you can do with these."

Estella was dizzy from being treated so kindly. She had never really had many friends due to being so focused on her work. She hadn't known how special of a feeling it was, to be cared for by people who liked her for who she was. These two didn't want anything from her. They just wanted to be with her because they enjoyed her company, and she enjoyed theirs.

Opening the last packet from Clementine revealed the dress patterns. At just a glance, Estella understood most of the techniques and terminology from making men's clothes. Some parts were more confusing than others, however. The clothes she was used to working with didn't have so many complicated parts. The fabric was taken in and let out again, and there were so many different types of ruffles.

"I hope that I can figure out how to use these," Estella said.

"Don't you want to challenge yourself?" Clementine's bright blue gaze was sparkling. "If you're anythin' like me, you won't be satisfied with not knowin' how. Why don't you tell me and Mother what parts look confusing to you?"

Cody started to fuss in Vera's arms. Estella reached to take him from her, sighing. Vera waved her off and stood. "You two get started. I'll take this nipper and change him, feed him, and put him down to sleep."

Estella knew that she could trust Vera to take care of the baby. She had raised a daughter successfully and still showed considerable skill with children. She thanked Vera and told her where to find everything she needed.

Vera headed off, making cooing sounds to the whining Cody.

Clementine was laughing softly as Estella turned back to her. "She loves babies. I think she always wanted to give me a sister or two, but it wasn't meant to be."

"Well, if it makes her happy, it's a fair shake to let her take care of Cody," Estella decided.

She resolved not to feel guilty any longer about accepting help from these two. There were so many more things for her to worry about. She needed to save her energy and apply it to the right things.

Clementine spread out one of the dress patterns on the sofa between them. "This would be a good one for you to start on," she said. "It's simple enough. But you look it over and see if there's anythin' you want me to explain."

Estella leaned her head over to get a good look at the pattern. "I could probably do it," she said, and a little doubt crept into her voice. "There's just so many parts to sew together. I worry I wouldn't do it properly."

"Oh, Estella, it couldn't be easier. Just don't think of it all as different parts." Clementine touched a marked seam on the pattern. "Just focus on each seam as you do it. Think of it as just attaching lace to a handkerchief. It's just a straight line. You'll just be attaching one part to the other following these simple lines. You know you can do that."

"When you put it that way, I do suppose it sounds easy."

Estella tried to visualize the pattern that way, focusing on even smaller parts, and that did give her confidence. She was a tailor's daughter, for goodness' sake. She knew there was no mistake she could make that couldn't be undone and fixed.

"The hardest part might be finding time to do anything," Estella said. "Now that I can feed Cody, I can get work done. I need to really focus on cleaning up this place. I've started, but it's apparently not enough to make Christopher happy."

And what would make him happy?

She scoffed internally, feeling herself grow tense and frustrated.

"I'm sure you'll find time," Clementine said. She nudged Estella with her shoulder. "You won't be able to resist. You will make time."

Estella nudged her back. "I think you're probably right. I do wish that Christopher would go easier on me. He's a strange man. I can't figure out how to make him happy. I would say it's almost like he wants to be grouchy."

Clementine clasped her hands together and lowered her head. "Knowing what he went through, there are reasons for his gruffness."

"What he went through?" Estella echoed. "Do you know something about him that you can tell me? Vera said it wasn't her story to tell."

Clementine glanced around to check that Vera wasn't on her way back. She spoke quieter, leaning even closer to Estella. "I can tell you quickly. It will help you understand him. Just don't tell Mother that I told you. She wouldn't think it was proper."

Estella's heart thumped. "I swear, not a word."

Was there actually a good reason for Christopher to behave like he did? What could he have gone through?

Clementine pulled in a short, quick breath. "It was three years ago. He used to be a kind gentleman. He was friendly and funny. His wife, Bonnie, was a friend of mine. We weren't very close friends as we didn't spend much time together, but I did know her."

Did she say wife?

Christopher had had a wife? He had been married? He hadn't said any such thing that would indicate he had been married, and she had seen no sign of any other woman in the house. But if this story took place three years ago....

What had happened to his wife?

"Christopher would work as a blacksmith, and Bonnie would stay home to take care of their son, Troy." Clementine paused again, and Estella found herself looking around, fearing the time wearing down. If Vera came back, she would never get her questions answered. She had more than before.

She couldn't imagine Christopher being a *father* to any child, not with the way he acted around Cody.

"No one knows for sure why it happened," Clementine whispered. "But while Christopher was at work one day, his house burned down with his wife and son inside. He has been changed ever since."

Estella's hand flew to her mouth to smother her gasp. Through her fingers, she whispered, "No. How awful."

Clementine bowed her head, silent.

Estella leaned back, her hand still covering her mouth. Everything she had been confused about was now clear, like the aftermath of a blizzard when the wind had died down and the sun glared off the white of the snow. She could see too well, and it hurt her eyes, making her want to turn away so she would have to look and hurt no longer.

It was no wonder that Christopher acted so gruffly. He must have still been in agony from his losses. He was missing his wife and child, and here had come Estella, bringing Cody, no doubt confusing him endlessly. When he looked at them, did he see his lost family?

Of course, he wanted Estella to be gone so he didn't have to face his hurts.

At the same time, of course, he was helpful when it came to Cody. His fatherly instincts made him do these kind things, like finding a milking goat and a cradle, but he wouldn't be able to carry out these tasks without a great deal of pain.

Estella's heart squeezed in her chest, and tears rose in her eyes. She hurt for him, that he had to endure what he did. He must have moved out to this ranch not long after the fire that took everything from him. She might have done the same when her parents died if it hadn't been for the tailoring business. She had clung to that as all she had left of them, but Christopher had been robbed of even that small comfort.

Vera walked back into the room without Cody. She was smiling, apparently oblivious to the mood in the room. "I thought you two would have the fabrics in here by now. We chose such pretty ones for you, Estella."

Clementine stood. "We were carried away with jibberin'. I'll get the fabric. You enjoy your tea, Mother."

Estella busied herself with refreshing Vera's tea, taking the few moments to breathe deeply and steady herself. She would think about all of this business with Christopher later on when she was alone. Right now, it was best to focus on the gifts she had been brought. She didn't want to get Clementine in trouble for telling her Christopher's secrets.

But they aren't secrets, really, are they?

Her stomach twisted inside of her.

Everyone in the town must know. Not just the mother and daughter but every single person would be aware of Christopher's past and the deaths of his loved ones. They must have witnessed it and attended the burial.

He could not have enjoyed dealing with anyone in town, seeing the pity for him on their faces. Just another reason for him to isolate himself and live his life alone—until Abe interfered to bring a new woman into his life. Surely the sheriff was smart enough to know this wouldn't have gone well?

Just more questions that she had no answer to.

Chapter Nine

Christopher stomped into the house, knocking ice from his boots. He was hot inside, his blood simmering after spending hours out in the cold looking for his horses. How three of them had gotten out of the stable, out of their *stalls,* he couldn't understand. Jackson wouldn't be so foolish. Could it have been the ranch hand? Christopher had sent him home without pay for the day, which had seemed the right thing to do at the time. He was no longer certain of that. This harsh winter weather, the wind—it could do strange things. Maybe it was no one's fault that he and Jackson had had to walk around and find the horses—two mares and one stallion—before they froze to death. Maybe he was angry for nothing.

He wouldn't admit it, though. He didn't want anyone to see him doubting himself. His men had to think that he was certain of everything he did and said, or they would start to doubt him, too.

It was nearly suppertime, and he could smell something meaty and savory cooking. He hoped it was stew, thick and rich, served with crusty bread. There was little better to eat to warm a man's soul and relax him.

Christopher moved to the kitchen to investigate and was pleased with not only the simmering pot of thick stew on the stove but also the general state of the room. The floor had been mopped, and all the counters were wiped clean. The cobwebs were gone from the corners of the ceiling, and no dishes were waiting to be washed.

Christopher looked around for Estella and thought he heard her somewhere else in the house. He went to the pot on the stove and dipped his finger in to taste the sauce. It was richly flavored by vegetables and strongly peppered, exactly how he liked it.

He left the kitchen, figuring he would find Estella and compliment her on her work. He didn't enjoy being unkind, and he believed in acknowledging when someone had done the right thing. He was glad she was finally upholding her end of their deal.

A quick check of the sitting room showed that she wasn't there. He heard her again, and she seemed to be in the hallway by the bedrooms. He stepped into the hall, and there she was, the baby in a sling on her front as she fiddled around with something on a small side table.

Christopher noted the assortment of empty boxes nearby, which Estella must have also organized. He nodded his approval to himself. He had been more or less living out of those boxes instead of putting the items where they belonged. Estella would need to tell him where she had decided to put things.

"Estella," he said, turning to her.

She froze and turned to face him. "Yes, Christopher?" Her expression was guarded, her lips pursed.

His eyes flicked down to the table she had been fiddling with, a slim decorative thing he had picked up for cheap in town about a year ago. He had thought he might find a use for it and never really had. Estella had placed a few decorative items there, including a small mirror and a carving of a rearing horse. The most prominent of the decorations was a beautiful white vase, rounded at the bottom and narrowing to a tall cylinder with a flared, almost flower-like opening.

Christopher stared at that vase, a lump knotting up his throat. He wasn't aware of stepping back until he struck the wall. He grunted, reaching behind to push away from the wall, stumbling upright again. Through it all, he couldn't look away from the vase. His heart beat like hummingbird wings.

"Christopher?" Estella was reaching out to him, her fingers passing through the empty air between them.

He moved back before she could touch him. With a great effort, he jerked around to face away from the table and the offending vase. "Why is that vase there?" His voice came out a low, rough growl.

Estella didn't answer for several long moments. He could feel her confusion. "Why shouldn't the vase be there? It's very pretty and unique."

There was no way that he could give her a meaningful answer. He wasn't going to tell her of his wife, not now, not ever. He wasn't going to say that Bonnie had picked out that vase as a wedding present to herself, only to later pawn it when times were hard and they needed quick money. How it had pained her to let go of that vase she loved, though he himself had never much liked the design.

Christopher could not tell Estella that, after the fire, the shop owner who purchased the vase had given it back to him for free, helping him to have just another small piece of his former life.

Aside from a locket Bonnie had been wearing at the time of the fire, that vase was all he had left of her. He had kept it in one of those boxes at the bottom, where he would never have to see or think about it.

"It shouldn't be there," Christopher growled out.

He turned and left the hall, needing to get away. He found himself back in the kitchen, surrounded once more by the comforting scents of bubbling stew. His stomach twisting, he was hungry no longer.

I went to see her to be kind to her, and all I have now is this pain. Nothing will ever be right as long as she is here.

"Christopher."

The soft voice behind him made his shoulders tense up. Estella had followed him.

"Can you look at me, Christopher?"

He didn't want to. He didn't want to look at or speak with her. He wanted to eat his dinner and then leave the house.

"Fine, then."

He heard her moving away.

He groaned inwardly and turned to her, not wanting to act too much like an insolent child. "What is it that you want from me?" he demanded.

Estella lifted her head. There were still shadows under her cornflower blue eyes, but her gaze was clear and gentle. "Does that vase remind you of your wife? Was it hers?"

It was as if she had taken a knife and stabbed him directly in the heart. He was bleeding internally, the terrible agony of loss invading all that he was. He couldn't breathe.

How? How does she know?

Vera and Clementine had visited. One of them must have told her. He would guess the culprit to be Clementine. Vera was a busybody and loved to know everything about everyone, but she was at least discreet.

Estella clasped her hands together and bowed her head. "I am so terribly sorry for your tragedy."

Christopher struggled to speak around the pain filling him. "Yes," he managed to choke out. The effort left him weak. He fought for control, refusing to let himself be seen this way by someone who wasn't even supposed to be there. "The vase. You need to put it away."

Estella nodded. "I will. Right now, I will. I'm so sorry, Christopher."

He couldn't answer as she walked away. He scrubbed at his face with both hands and sighed.

There had been such understanding in her eyes, a depth of empathy that went past just pitying an outsider. She wasn't just looking at his pain. She, in some capacity, knew what it was like to be so hurt. If only he knew more about her.

He pushed *that* thought away as soon as it came. He didn't need to know more about her. She might be kind and hard-working—now that she wasn't so distracted—and she might be wonderfully gentle with that baby that wasn't even hers, but there was no reason for him to get closer to her. She was going to leave soon. He would *not* allow a stranger's departure to hurt him.

The pain inside him soured into anger, a different sort of knife, one that he turned on himself. How could he even be thinking things like that about Estella? None of it mattered. He didn't care that she was so pretty with her big blue eyes and pink lips and thick, dark hair like chocolate, not at all. Everything beautiful faded in time. Best not to start admiring now when, in the end, it would all be worthless.

Estella returned to the kitchen without looking at him. "Supper will be just another minute," she said, her voice even.

Christopher left to go to the dining room and sat at his place at the table, his hands folded. When Estella came shortly with the food, he said nothing, only nodded his thanks.

Not another word passed between them the rest of that night.

Chapter Ten

Estella held her own wrist in her hand, watching the blood dripping from a gash on the back of her forearm. The large gray nanny goat, Apple, stood a few paces away, nostrils flaring, tail flicking irritably.

Estella wiped at the blood with her coat sleeve to see how bad the cut was. There wasn't much pain, and she was relieved to see the cut was rather shallow. She dropped her hands to her knees and looked at Apple, who stomped her back hooves irritably.

"Please, Apple," Estella said. "I need your milk. Please."

The goat bleated angrily and stamped her hooves again. Her udders were swollen with milk, no doubt uncomfortably so.

The past few times Estella had tried to milk her, Apple had reacted with pain and anger, finally culminating in a fierce kick Estella had been unable to dodge. She had no idea what was going wrong, as the nanny goat had been relatively calm and patient up until then. She had only a little bit of milk left for Cody and had been trying to stretch it out as long as she could, leading to him becoming hungry and unsettled once more. All the progress she had made was slipping away from her, and her heart clenched at the idea of ending up right back where she had started.

I can't endure that again. I can't. Cody can't.

Estella picked up her milking pail and moved to Apple's side again. Apple bleated at her and snorted.

"It's alright," Estella said softly. "I'm not goin' to hurt you. Can I just look at you?"

Apple grumbled and bent her head to nibble at the hay-strewn floor, keeping a watchful eye on Estella. Estella reached beneath the goat and touched her udder, feeling the swollen, tender skin bursting with milk that needed to come out. She thought that the udder seemed to be strangely hard. Was it just from a lack of milking, or was there something else occurring that was causing pain to the animal?

Estella bent lower and took a proper look for herself. Her eyes widened as she saw the typically pink udder had turned red and shiny around the teats, the veins visible and swollen-looking. The goat had an infection of some kind.

Estella sat back, biting her lower lip. How was she going to fix this? She didn't know enough about animals and treating wounds, and she certainly didn't have money to afford a veterinarian...and that was if a veterinarian could even be brought to the ranch in such poor weather.

But Cody needs *milk,* she thought. She stood and paced the pen, Apple and the other milkless goat watching her. *What if I just leave Apple alone? Will she get better or worse?*

Tears sprang into her eyes.

She wanted to cry.

If only crying could solve her problems.

There wasn't anything she could do, and she feared making the situation worse by trying. She left the barn and returned to the house, hearing Cody screaming with hunger from inside. Estella went to his cradle and lifted him in her arms, rocking him. He refused to be soothed, his face turning red as he cried. She began to pace the house with him.

"What am I going to do?" she whispered.

Things had seemed to be going so well, too. Was she doomed to live this life, always fearing that her joyful times would end in sadness?

"What's going on?" Christopher looked out at her from the kitchen doorway. He had a lump of cheese in his hand. He must have gotten hungry and come inside for a bite before going back out to work. His eyes were narrowed as he watched her.

Estella held Cody closer to her body, hoping desperately that Christopher wouldn't become angry with the baby. It wasn't Cody's fault that she was once again failing to take care of him.

"What's he cryin' for now?" Christopher pressed. He stepped closer, looking down at the baby. "Does he have that fussin' disorder?"

"No, it's...." Estella clenched her teeth. How she wished this was as easy to solve as fussing. If Cody was feeling illy in some way, at least she could have tried to treat his discomforts. Unfortunately, the only thing that would help him was milk.

"Then what is it? What's gone wrong now?"

She rounded on Christopher, her throat and eyes burning. "I can't feed him again! That goat Vera brought has somethin' wrong with it and won't let me do anymore milkin'."

Christopher pressed his lips together.

"I know what you're goin' to say!" Estella exclaimed. "And you're right. I can't care for him properly. I'm not a good enough mother. I should have found someone to take him. Or given him to an orphanage. At least an orphanage would have the resources to care for him!"

Christopher looked down on her and seemed calm in spite of her anger and raised voice. "What's wrong with the goat?"

Estella shook her head. "I don't know. The udder is swollen. She seems in pain. She kicked me, see?" She held out her arm to show the cut. The blood had dried to a thin, cracking crust around the injury.

His lips moved slightly. She couldn't tell if he was holding back words or sneering at her. She turned away and resumed pacing, and he lingered at her back for a short while before leaving.

She deserved his judgment. His wife must have been perfectly capable of feeding their child. Estella hadn't given birth to Cody; she wasn't suitable to be his mother, no matter how she truly loved him like her own.

Eventually, Cody ceased his crying and sank into a restless sleep, his eyes moving beneath the thin lids. She placed him back in his cradle and stood over him, chewing her lower lip and twisting part of her dress in her hands until she worked a hole in the fabric. Her legs weakened by anxiety, she sank onto her bed and rested her head in her hands.

Sometime later, though she wasn't sure how long, she heard the sound of a throat clearing. She lifted her head. Christopher stood outside the open door to her room, a milk pail down by his side. He lifted it and tilted it slightly, and she saw it was full of fresh, creamy-white milk.

She was on her feet and over to him before she knew it. "How did you do that?" she exclaimed. "How did you milk that goat? She was savage when I tried! Didn't she kick you?"

Christopher waited until her flurry of questions had finished. "Do you want to keep askin' me questions, or do you want to boil this milk?"

"You don't even have to ask me that!"

She grabbed the pail and took it to the kitchen to boil the contents as Vera had shown her. She stumbled as she walked and froze, fearing that she might spill the milk and make the situation worse. She took a moment to remind herself to be calm. Cody was asleep. There was time to get the milk ready. She didn't have to be rushing.

Moving much more slowly this time, she went to the kitchen and got the milk warming on the stove. She felt Christopher's presence at her back, and she turned to him. "I didn't give you any proper thanks," she said. "I don't know how you managed to do this, but I am in your debt. Again."

Christopher waved his hand, his head turned slightly away so he wasn't looking directly at her. "It's nothin' much," he said. "I took a look at the goat. I know how to fix what's wrong with her."

"You do?"

"Ayuh," he said, nodding. "Same problem happens to mares sometimes. They kick at their foals, and I got to go in and get the milk to feed the babies myself."

She closed her eyes in relief. He was so very knowledgeable on many things. She really should have focused on learning more than just a single trade. "But what *is* wrong with Apple and those mares?"

"A sawbones could probably tell you better than I."

Christopher walked over to the pot of milk on the stove and stirred it with a wooden spoon lying nearby. Vera hadn't said anything about stirring the milk while it heated, but Estella felt it would harm nothing and had been stirring what she collected. And stirring gave her something to do while she was just standing there at the stove.

"Do you see a sawbones here right now?"

Christopher looked around as if he might actually see a doctor had come into the kitchen and chuckled slightly. "I suppose not. From what I know, any woman or milkin' animal can have it happen to them. Some kind of infection. You were right about the swelling, and it causes them pain. You just got to be quicker about the milkin'. You can't hesitate or try to be gentle. It hurts 'em whether you're gentle or not. Just be confident and get the job done fast."

"And if you get kicked?" Estella looked at her arm again. The cut was really starting to sting.

"You'll get kicked. It's just part of it. You clean it up later on, and I mean later on. If you back off, you let the animal know they got their way, and it'll make them more ornery." Christopher put his fist in the palm of his hand, a firm gesture. "Just let 'em kick and finish up on your own terms. You will want to boil that milk a little extra long to make sure it's clean for Cody."

"Will the infection clear up on its own?" Estella looked up at Christopher.

"It should. I know some tricks to help." He lifted a finger and went to a shelf, grabbing a bottle. He turned and showed it to her. Whiskey. "A splash of nose paint in the drinkin' water helps to dull the pain. And if there's any garlic, you can feed that to Apple next time you go out. I don't know why, but garlic is good for helpin' infections."

"I'll remember. Thank you, Christopher." She smiled at him, her chest warm.

Was this a glimpse of the man he used to be? This kindness? She could see how a woman could fall in love with him if that were how he had been before.

Not her, though. She hadn't fallen for any man before, and she wasn't about to fancy him, even if he was kind, even if he spoke in a firm, confident manner that made her feel as if she could be confident, too.

"Sure," Christopher said, his tone suddenly brisk. "Tend to that cut before you go handlin' the baby's milk."

He turned away and left the kitchen, leaving her to her tedious task.

When the milk had boiled for what she judged to be long enough, she took it off the heat to cool. By the time Cody awoke and began to fuss again, she had a bottle ready for him. She sat on her bed and held him in her lap, watching as he suckled eagerly. There really wasn't anything like the deep satisfaction of being able to provide for him. It just felt *right,* as perfect as watching a sunset. There was just a peacefulness, a meditative quiet. She didn't have to think about anything. She could just sit there and watch him.

Christopher appeared in the doorway to her room, watching her. No, she saw, his eyes were on the baby, full of such an aching longing that she decided she would break the rules of convention. Who was to say what was proper anymore when she was living in his house with a baby, not her own?

Estella looked at him until he realized it, and she inclined her head at the spot on the bed beside her.

He hesitated, and she could feel him fighting with himself from even across the room. Then, he stepped forward and sat beside her, leaving space between their bodies so they didn't touch. His weight compressed the mattress, and Estella had to lean in the opposite direction to avoid tumbling against him.

They sat there in silence as the baby drank his milk. She kept sneaking looks at him, and he was watching the baby every time with that same longing.

What is he thinking? He must be missing Troy.

Estella considered offering for him to hold Cody and decided against it. She didn't want to presume too much.

Cody finished the bottle, and Estella moved him to her shoulder. She gave him brisk, gentle rubs on his back.

"I thought you were supposed to pat 'em," Christopher said.

Cody's body jerked as he let out a long, loud belch, the sort a roostered old man might make as he stumbled home from the tavern.

"Never mind. I guess you know what you're doin'."

Estella looked up, and Christopher met her eyes. Then, he laughed, and Estella started laughing, too. Something passed between them then as they sat there laughing over the silliness of a baby's loud burp. Estella couldn't even begin to name it, wasn't even sure if she wanted to, but it was nice to be sitting there with him right then.

It was best not to question the moment, just to enjoy it.

Chapter Eleven

The pale brown mare stood at the back of her stall, her legs quivering as if she had run a hundred miles. Her head hung low, her nose touching the straw bedding. The pieces of straw swayed with her rapid, uneven breaths. Her flanks were heaving.

Christopher stood by Nippy, the matriarch of his herd, and worried for her as he had never worried for another horse. He had dealt with sick and injured animals before. That was just part of being a rancher. He had long since lost count of how many scrapes he had patched up and sprains he had bound in bandages. Bouts of indigestion and respiratory issues, difficulties with birthing; he had seen it all.

But this...this was new.

Because horses were herd and prey animals, they tended to hide their injuries and sicknesses. A rancher had to know exactly what to look for when it came to his animals. He had to know the smallest signs of an illness to begin work on curing it right away, giving the animal the best chance of recovery. Christopher had seen the progression of many illnesses, and he took pride in his keen eye for spotting potential problems.

Nippy had not been showing signs of a progressing illness. Her behavior had not changed, nor had she lost weight, had a fever, or lost appetite. She had been perfectly fine a day ago.

Now, she looked as if she had been sick for weeks. She was weak and had difficulty breathing. She hid at the back of her stall, leaning on the wall, her behavior nervous and defensive. When Christopher looked at her eyes, they were dull. An inspection of her mouth showed pale gums. Her tail hung limp and motionless behind her. Whatever was wrong, it had happened fast.

"What do you think, Chris?" Jackson said. He stood by Nippy, rubbing her behind her ears. She showed no pleasure in being petted. "You got any idea what's goin' on?"

Christopher crossed his arms. "I wish that I did," he said shortly.

Jackson snorted. "You must have some thoughts."

"Fine," Christopher snapped. "I'll talk, and it won't help. I swear to you, I'm as clueless as a baby right now. I wish I weren't. I wish I had some idea. Could she have been gettin' sick for days, and I didn't notice? Possible. Not likely. She's not showin' typical signs of a winter sickness, anyway."

"Her breathing," Jackson pointed out.

"But her breathing isn't rattlin'. She doesn't have any fluid in her lungs or nothin' like that. Doesn't seem like she's got a stomach upset, either." Christopher kicked at a very normal piece of horse dung. "It almost seems like she's truly tuckered out, like I worked her so hard she ain't got any energy left. I can't figure it out."

"Maybe somethin' spooked her last night?" Jackson suggested, and Christopher knew he was just reaching for any reason, however thin and implausible. "She didn't get any shut-eye and is just tired?"

Christopher didn't even bother with responding to that. "Let's move the other horses so there's an empty stall between her and them. If what she's got can be spread, then we need to stop that from happenin'."

Jackson nodded his agreement and stepped out of the stall to the neighboring one, looping a length of rope around that horse's neck to guide them to a new spot. "I really hope we don't lose her."

Losing the matriarch would disrupt the whole herd. His other mares might take to fighting to try and assert dominance and become the new leader. While some skirmishes were expected amongst herds, the risk of injury was always present. Even though he knew how to treat injuries, something could easily become too serious for him to handle, and then he would have to somehow find the money to pay a veterinarian.

"I ain't heard you talk about the bank in a while," Jackson said as if reading Christopher's mind.

Christopher spat on the ground. "Same story as always. They want their money. Darned bankers don't care that everyone's havin' a hard time and no one has the tin to spare."

Those wolves at the bank had been more than happy to give him a loan to set up his ranch. He had been late on some payments, and now they were coming after him, wanting the rest of what he didn't have.

They took advantage of me when I was in mourning, he thought, clenching his hands into fists. *Talked me into taking out more than I could feasibly pay.*

The truth was that he was coming ever closer to losing everything he had built out on the ranch. He wouldn't say so out loud to his ranch hands, especially not to Jackson. Adding their worries to his would do no good.

Jackson returned after shifting the horses around to make empty spaces on either side of Nippy. "I, uh, I ask because I ran into Otis Ryder in town the other day."

Christopher growled at the mention of Otis Ryder, the owner of a small mining empire in the area. "What did he want?"

"He wanted to know when you were goin' to sell your land to him."

"Ayuh, I figured that was it. And what did you tell him?"

"I told him that he would have better luck charmin' honey from bees. And he just laughed and said he knew it was possible, then walked away." Jackson held up his hands.

Christopher growled wordlessly. As if the pressure from the bank wasn't enough, Otis Ryder was nagging at him from the other side.

No one liked Otis, but no one could pin down what was wrong with him. The man just had a way about him, a wolflike sneakiness. He was always up to something.

Otis had been born into a poor family and worked his way up to his current position of wealth through sheer hard work. When he was only twenty-three, he founded his mining company, Orion Mining, digging up large quantities of nickel and gold. Now forty, he was rich but never satisfied. He was always looking to make more money.

That was why he was looking at Christopher's ranch.

"You're a stronger man than me," Jackson said. He offered Nippy an apple, which she did not take or even sniff at. "I would have sold ages ago just to get him to leave me alone. And make some profit at the same time. Why *don't* you want to sell, Boss?"

"It's the principle of things." Christopher refused to elaborate. He didn't want to talk much more about this.

About a year before Christopher bought the land, one of Otis's surveyors found gold in the stream that ran through the property. He hadn't been able to get his hands on it, and then Christopher bought it. Ever since, Otis had been hounding him to sell the land so he could use it for mining purposes.

Had things been different, maybe Christopher would have happily sold. He could have charged Otis for every so much of the gold he found and made a continuous profit off it.

But things weren't different.

This land was his shelter against the nightmare of his past. If he sold it, where was he meant to go? Not back to town. He couldn't bear it. Was he meant to start up another ranch, start over from the beginning again, his fragile peace disturbed?

He would not sell. He would not fall victim to one of Otis's schemes, like so many had. He could see into that man's heart just like he could look past the guise of health his horses presented to see what was wrong with them.

Most of the time, anyway, Nippy being the exception.

"How are things goin' with Estella and the baby?" Jackson asked. He stroked Nippy's mane, teasing out tangles with his fingers.

"You sure are full of a lot of questions, aren't you?" Christopher grumbled.

Jackson just looked at him, waiting to be answered.

Christopher sighed and gave up. "They're fine, I suppose," he said. "The baby's mostly settled. Some trouble with the goat Vera brought to provide milk, but that's fine now, too."

When Cody was fed and quiet, he was quite the sweet little nipper. Christopher didn't say that aloud. Nor did he mention Estella, not wanting to talk about her in case some of his private thoughts slipped into his voice. He didn't want Jackson to get the wrong idea about all of that.

Jackson was grinning, though, his thoughts apparently already heading in that dangerous direction in spite of Christopher's hopes to the contrary. "You know that you could ask her to jump the broom with you. That was why Abe brought her here in the first place. It'd benefit you both. And she's purty, which is always a bonus."

Christopher snorted, beginning to feel that this talk was headed in a direction he didn't like. "Tarnation, no! I ain't gettin' married to anyone ever again. Once was enough for me."

Jackson chuckled, frustratingly refusing to be deterred. "But why not? She's sweet. And I've had some of her cookin' by now. She's got a nice touch with spices. She's capable, too. I heard that she ran her father's business before comin' here."

"Where you hearin' all this?"

"Vera and Clem." Jackson lifted his hands. "Estella's gotten pretty friendly with them, hasn't she? Seems like if she was able to settle in the area, she'd be happy here. You could give her that."

"It's not goin' to happen!" Christopher suddenly shouted, having had enough of this. He grabbed his foreman by the shoulder and shook him, breathing hard. "She don't belong here. She was brought here on a lie. That's a bad foundation. She needs to go on and find somewhere else to be and leave me *alone.* I don't want to hear anythin' else from you about this; you understand me, Jackson? Or I swear I'll demote you. Enjoy gettin' paid like a common ranch hand."

A third voice spoke from behind them. "Now, what in the Sam Hill is goin' on in here?"

Jackson pulled away from Christopher and went to stand by Abe at the stable entrance. The sheriff's shoulders were crusted over with snow.

Christopher kicked his boot at a clump of hay. "Great. Now I got to deal with you, too. What you want, Abe?"

Abe hooked his thumbs in his belt. "I got some reports of trespassers on land a bit north from here. The McVey property. Thought I would stop by and see if you had been havin' any of your own troubles. Seen anyone loiterin' around?"

"No." And thank goodness for that. Christopher didn't need anything else to worry about.

"Alright." Abe paused, rubbing his gray beard. "I heard that Otis has been expressin' interest in your ranch again."

"Great," Christopher said sourly. "I'm so glad that everyone in town is so interested in me." Why couldn't he just be left alone? That was all he wanted.

"Can you give us a moment here, Jackson?" Abe nodded to him.

"Sure." Jackson chuckled, and Christopher aimed a frown at him. "I'll just stop by the house, see if Estella's got any hot coffee. You two take as long as you need for your secret meetin'."

Jackson trudged off through the snow. Abe leaned around and watched him go until he was out of hearing range, then turned back to Christopher.

Christopher shoved his hands in his pockets and waited for what he was sure was going to be some unpleasantness.

"Chris," Abe said, voice low, "I can lend you some actual to get the bank off your back. If you get in good standin' with the bank, Otis won't have reasons to go after your land so hard."

The offer made Christopher curl his lip. "I know you don't have that kind of spare money."

"I can find it if you truly need it." Abe stared at him.

Christopher turned away. "No."

"Chris, think about this."

"I did, and I'm done thinkin' about it," Christopher said shortly. "I am not puttin' you in debt to then put myself in debt to you. Don't you say another word about it."

"Fine." Abe turned away from him. "I just want you to be taken care of."

"Well, I appreciate it, but if I'm getting' out of this mess, it'll be of my own accord."

Abe clicked his tongue. "You are somethin' else. I just don't know what. Well, I suppose I'll go and see about some of that hot coffee myself, then be on my way."

"You do that. Thanks for stoppin' by."

Abe walked off, leaving Christopher alone with his thoughts and a sick horse.

He crouched down by Nippy and stroked her, murmuring soft words to her. He hoped that she couldn't feel how worried he was about what he had just heard. It seemed to him like

Otis Ryder was up to something if he was going around and talking about Christopher's ranch, but what?

Can't get too caught up in that, he thought and pushed his worries to the side.

He had too much on his mind already. He would only worry about Otis if the man actually came to talk to him. Otherwise, he would keep on doing what he was doing, forging forward.

Chapter Twelve

Estella stood in the final room of the house where she had finally finished cleaning and organizing, hands on her hips, admiring the shining floor and lack of cobwebs. At long last, her side of the bargain had been fully upheld.

Her chest was warm, and she found herself standing tall, though there was a painful tightness in her side; that pain always made itself known when she worked extra hard and moved around a lot. It came from an old childhood injury, one that she had almost not survived. While she hated that injury and the scars it had left her with, she was pleased to have another sign of just how much of an effort she was making to transform this home into a clean and tidy space suitable for living.

But as she stood there, she was struck by the idea that something was missing. Frowning, she mulled over what that could be. There wasn't anything else for her to clean for the moment. She hadn't touched Christopher's room or office, and she had a feeling that she shouldn't mess around in the attic too much.

She didn't need to be preparing a meal, and Cody was fast asleep in his cradle when she last checked on him. So, what could possibly be nagging at her?

Puzzled, she went to the nearest window and looked out at the fields of whiteness. Her mind wandered. She had started work on a gown using the patterns Vera and Clementine had brought her. Could that be what was on her mind? She examined the idea but felt no particular urge to get back to the gown at the moment. The pattern she had chosen was tricky, as she had wanted to really test herself and grow her skills, and she knew she needed to pace herself to prevent frustration.

It really was so nice of them to give me that pattern as an early Christmas present....

Suddenly, she knew what was missing. The house was missing something. It was almost Christmas, and there were no decorations! Christmas used to be such an important time of year for her and her parents. And when she was taking care of her pregnant cousin, she and Ada had had all sorts of plans for Cody's first real holiday...not that he would remember any of it.

I should make this place more cheery, Estella decided.

She hadn't seen decorations of any kind when she was emptying those boxes, but Christopher had been living out of those. He didn't need decorations on the daily, which meant that if he had any, they should be stored somewhere out of the way.

Estella moved and found herself in front of the narrow door leading up to the attic. And here she had just been thinking about how she shouldn't go messing around up there.

If she only took a quick look, she wouldn't cause any harm, would she?

She fetched a lantern, lit it, and climbed up those narrow, dusty steps. The only signs of recent use were a set of large bootprints going up and back down. She stepped where Christopher's prints were but could not stop the hem of her dress from whisking more dust from the steps to drift in the air.

The attic was mostly empty, though a small stack of boxes drew her eye. She went over and looked inside them. She was too afraid to paw through the contents very much and only examined the top layers. Finding nothing in each of the larger boxes, she picked up the smallest one to look inside.

Right on top were two knitted baby bootees, a matching pair crafted with extremely neat and even stitches.

Tears burned Estella's eyes as she saw those tiny bootees, the perfect size for little feet. She could imagine Christopher's son Troy wearing them and kicking his legs with them on. She wanted to take them out and look at them closer but knew that that would be a very bad idea. These things were not hers to touch and hold.

She put the boxes back where she had found them and moved back down the stairs, again trying to stay where Christopher had previously stepped. She put the lantern back where it belonged and checked on Cody—still asleep.

Well, she couldn't look in Christopher's bedroom or office for Christmas decorations. She would just have to improvise.

She pulled on a coat and scarf, grabbed a basket, and stepped outside. Snow came down lightly from the overcast gray sky, a fine sprinkling that melted upon contact with her hands. She stood for a moment and looked around, wondering where she should go, as she hadn't really explored the ranch before. All she had really done was go back and forth between the barn and the house.

There were plenty of trees around, dormant oaks and thriving evergreens, and she set off for the nearest stand. She could smell the pine sap as she approached, that bright, citrusy aroma. There were bushes around the tree trunks, with bright red berries growing amidst pointy green leaves. Estella felt like a little girl as she scurried amongst the trees, gathering berry springs and evergreen branches. Whenever she found a good pinecone, she picked that up as well. Her thoughts leaped ahead of her as she thought of how she would display the pinecones in a nice big bowl and where she would put a vase of the holly berries. She imagined snuggling up by the fire to sew a banner for the front entry hall, a cup of pine needle tea nearby.

The cold nipped at her fingers and nose, but she didn't mind. She was smiling as she did her foraging, filling her basket until the evergreen branches were overflowing the edges.

She brought it all back inside and began to enact her plans without even waiting to warm up or clean the sticky sap from her skin and clothes. The bowl of pinecones went on a table in the entryway, and she arranged berries and bright pine fronds into two vases to go on either side of the fireplace mantel. She brought more of the greenery into the kitchen, lining the windowsills with it.

She stepped back and once more surveyed her work with her hands on her hips, a smile on her cold lips. Yes, it was a good start. Oh, but she was only getting started. She had picked up a number of sticks with cracked bark. How wonderfully rustic would those look if she bound them up in little bundles with some string and wove sprigs of holly and pine into them? She could make several strings and hang them from the ceiling.

Her fingers itched to get crafting.

Christopher entered the house. She recognized his heavy walk. After a few steps, he paused, and she held her breath, wondering if he had noticed the decorations and what he would think of them.

She thought she heard him grumble something under his breath, and then his footsteps resumed. He walked into the kitchen, carrying the bowl of pinecones in one hand. His brows were furrowed. "What is this?"

"It's decorations," Estella explained. She pointed out the decorated windowsills. "And there's more! I made up some vases for the mantel over the fireplace, and I'm going to sew a banner."

"Absolutely not!" Christopher's voice rose. He set the bowl down with a thump. "You need to get this stuff out. I don't want to see it."

"What? Why not?" She was confused. "It's so close to Christmas! I've lost track of the days a little, but it's time. It's past time! Don't you want to celebrate?"

"I don't celebrate Christmas." His voice was as sharp as a knife, cutting right through her hopes and plans. "And this is my house, so we do things my way. No decorations of any kind."

Estella shook her head. "Why don't you celebrate?"

"It ain't none of your business, is it, woman?" He made to leave.

She grabbed his arm, shocking herself with her own bravery...and also shocked by the solidity of his muscles. He wrenched around, and she immediately let go of him, but now she was upset with him yet again. "I'm not askin' you to put in any effort. But I *did* put in all this effort. It isn't fair to me to make me get rid of everythin'."

"Then, you should have asked me beforehand." His nostrils flared, and his brows were low, casting his dark eyes with deeper shadows. "You wasted your own time, and you ain't got anyone else to blame."

"You told me to fix up your house, and that's what I'm tryin' to do. I didn't know you wanted this place to be so cold, like an army base. No, I'm sure the soldiers have much more Christmas cheer than you." She knew she was crossing a line. He was still in mourning. But he wasn't the only one who had lost people!

Putting up decorations and celebrating the season didn't mean leaving their loved ones in the past. It was a way to honor them. Surely, Bonnie wouldn't want Christopher to spend the rest of his life in darkness, never enjoying anything. She would want him to partake in the festivities and have fun with his life.

Estella was searching for a way to explain her thoughts when Christopher just walked right out of the room. "Hey, wait!" she cried and rushed after him.

He ignored her and stomped outside, leaving the door wide open for the wind and the snow to get in.

Estella burned inside.

She grabbed the bowl of pinecones, brought them to the door, and cast them all out into the snow. "Are you happy?" she shouted. "I'm doin' what you want, Christopher! Does it make you feel good?"

There was no response from Christopher, but Cody began to cry inside the house.

Estella rushed to get Cody and held him in her arm. Onehandedly, she took all the other bits of greenery and brightness she had brought into the house and threw them outside. The snow landed on them, and she figured that if the weather stayed the same all night, all signs of her hard work would be covered up by morning.

She went back inside to get Cody a bottle, and as she sat feeding him, she thought about Christopher.

Would he ever allow himself to heal from his tragedy?

She knew it had to be hard, but he wasn't even trying.

Her heart took a long time to slow down. She lingered with Cody even after he had finished his bottle, cooing to him as he drifted off to the restful sleep they both deserved, but only he could have.

Chapter Thirteen

Ranger's Peak was as beautiful as the last time Estella had seen it, even more so with the addition of some Christmas decorations. As she rode through on the back of the horse she borrowed from Christopher's stable, she glimpsed a tree inside the post office, all wrapped in gold and silver ribbons. The general store had green pine boughs on the porch railing, and the barber had mistletoe and holly sprigs around the front entrance.

Estella guided her horse to Vera and Clem's dressmaker shop. She knew how to ride a horse thanks to her father, although she wasn't the most skilled or confident rider by any means. Christopher was evidently a wonderful horse breeder and trainer, the mare beneath her responding swiftly and calmly to all of Estella's cues. The quality of the horse made her feel that she was a better rider than she actually was, which was both good and a little frightening. She had a baby in a sling on her front. She didn't want to forget to be careful.

Red triangle banners embroidered with stars draped from the dressmaker's roof, flapping in the wind. Estella left her horse out front, covered with a blanket to keep her warm, and walked inside.

The shop was much warmer inside and smelled of sweet cinnamon spices. There were lit candles all over and more sewn banners, plus strings of dried oranges, red berries, and cinnamon sticks. At the back of the shop, a Christmas tree stood tall, upwards of eight feet, and covered with bead strings, little ornaments, and satchels that must have held a piece or two of candy each.

"Clem? Clementine, are you here?" Estella called out.

Clementine let out a wordless shout of excitement from the back room and rushed out. "Estella!" She threw her arms around her, and they embraced tightly, maneuvering around the baby sling to do so. "How wonderful to see you here! We didn't expect that you'd come calling. Here, take one of these. Take two, one for you and one for Christopher. They have Mother's homemade candies inside."

Clementine took two of the satchels from the tree and pressed them into Estella's free hand. Then, she seemed to notice that Estella had something in her other hand. "What's this?"

Estella's mood lightened as her friend's enthusiasm rubbed off on her. It was hard to be upset about Christopher when she was experiencing such good cheer, standing amidst such pretty decorations. "I brought the gown that I've been workin' on."

Vera appeared, gliding forward with her hands clasped together. "You've found time to work on a gown? Oh, I would love to see what you've done so far. Here, come to the back, and let's have you put it on one of these dress forms so we can get a good look."

Estella followed Vera, and they set up the gown on a dress form. "It isn't quite finished yet," Estella began, but she was cut off as Clementine clapped her hands and squealed out.

"It's beautiful, Estella!" Clementine cried. She ran her hand over the layered details of the bodice, then grasped either side of the flared, ruffled skirt and spread it out. "You really have such wonderful, even stitches. Little ducklings all in a row, right where they should be. And look at the work on this bodice, these darts. They're so very even, aren't they, Mother?"

Vera used her hip to brush Clementine out of the way and took her place. "I really am surprised that you chose this pattern to work on, Estella, but I am also very pleased! You took on the challenge, and you are excelling. Of course, you're good at dart work from your time as a tailor."

Estella patted Cody through the sling, feeling as if she was standing on air from all the praise. Her stomach was full of bright, tingling sparks. This was like coming home, finally, to the place where she belonged.

If only she could actually stay here forever, if she actually belonged.

She pushed those thoughts out of her mind and focused on only the good parts as best she could. "I've never had to do so many. Men's clothes don't need quite so much adjustment. Oh, but those ruffles. I'm still not done with those. I worry I'll *never* be done with the ruffles."

"You will," Vera said, laughing. "You'll get faster with them, but they never are the quickest part."

"Some days, I set aside just for that kind of work," Clementine added.

Estella smiled at her friends. "I really am happy you think it's coming along well. I'll continue to work on it. Maybe next time, you can wear it for us, Clem."

Someone came into the shop as they were talking and walked up to them now. Spurs jangled. Jackson removed his hat, approached the three of them, and gave them each a smile and a nod. "Seems I might have caught you busy," he said to Clementine.

Clementine's cheeks were slowly turning a brighter shade of pink. "No, no, we aren't too busy. Well, I mean, Estella, was there anythin' else you wanted to show off?"

Jackson held his hat in both hands before himself. "I didn't realize you was ridin' to town today, Estella," he said. His eyes flicked to Clementine and then back.

Estella swiftly judged what was occurring. Clementine had hinted at meeting the ranch hands when she came to the ranch, and she must have done exactly that. Why else would she have such high color? Why else would Jackson be there, unless he was suddenly wanting to wear dresses? No, it was clear that the two of them had started to fancy each other, and Jackson had come calling on Clementine, not knowing there would be anyone else around to witness it happening.

"I just had to pick up a few things from the store that Christopher suddenly wanted," Estella said, to which Jackson nodded. "And I thought I might visit while I was here."

Jackson shifted where he stood, his body moving ever so subtly closer to Clementine's. He was more than ten years her senior, but if they fancied each other, that didn't matter much. They were both of age and free to fall in love with whomever they desired.

How wonderful for them.

Estella thought of her scars and held back a sigh. Even if she happened to get out of this situation and into a better life, no man would want to be with her once he found out that one whole side of her body, from shoulder to hip, had been disfigured. And she couldn't blame anyone for that. She wouldn't want to buy a book that had had the cover damaged so terribly. The contents of the pages might be fine, but no one would be enticed to read such a book when it looked so ugly on the shelf.

Bonnie was probably perfect.

Where that thought came from, she wasn't sure. It seemed to fly out of some dark crevasse like a startled bat, wicked and biting. Was she jealous of Christopher's dead wife? That really wasn't like her at all.

"You look like you've got something on your mind," Vera said.

Estella protested, but Jackson and Clementine were looking at her with such concern now. And Vera was too shrewd to be swayed.

There wasn't any reason for her not to talk with them. They were her friends. Perhaps they could help her to feel better.

She quickly told them how she had tried to make up some Christmas decorations. "But Christopher told me to take them all down. He said he doesn't celebrate. I think it's more than that. I think that he hates Christmas."

Jackson rubbed his face. He slumped, his tall back bowing. "Chris ain't wanted to be part of any shindig since he lost his family. You know about that by now, I'd reckon."

That was what Estella had figured out for herself.

"Bonnie was very much into Christmas," Clementine said, giving Jackson a friendly and agreeable look. "She loved any reason to have a party, but Christmas was her favorite. No doubt he's reminded of her."

Estella's heart ached. She felt simply awful. She was exactly the wrong person to come into this man's life, at exactly the wrong time. It wasn't her fault, and she couldn't help it, though.

Vera let out a sudden snort, and Estella jumped. The seamstress's lips were twisted. "It's about time he started celebrating again," she said, her voice as tart as an unripe orange. "The trouble with that man is that he holds onto everything. He never lets anything go. He doesn't need to forget, but he does need to move on."

"Mother, it's not so easy," Clementine admonished. "If I lost you so suddenly, why, I don't know that I would ever get out of bed again! It's a wonder he's doing as well as he is."

"He's hiding, is what he's doing. From the world, from his own pain, from all the good things that could be his if only he would try just a little harder." Vera turned and started to gather up Estella's work-in-progress dress from the dress form.

"I've tried," Jackson murmured. "He wants to wallow in his grief. It's familiar to him at this point."

Estella took the dress back from Vera. "I should go do my shopping."

"Of course, dear." Vera gave her a kiss on the cheek, and Clementine hugged her. Estella said her farewells to them and Jackson, then went outside. Her horse was waiting for her, idly pawing at the snow.

Estella took the reins and walked the horse over to the general store to tie her up there while she went in and shopped. The store was very busy, and she had to wait her turn in line. Many of the people in front of her were purchasing decorations and large amounts of food to serve for the holiday dinner.

Would Christopher allow even that? Would he let her bake a ham and a potato casserole and spiced cookies? What if she wanted to roast chestnuts and whip up some thick, delicious eggnog? Those were all things that she used to do with her family, who all loved Christmas. It was a time to cherish each other and one's self by going just a little bit further to make life rich and extravagant.

Even if she left the ranch and found somewhere else to live, she wouldn't have the means to make a proper holiday by herself. And she wasn't going to be able to leave. It just wasn't feasible. She was there until the weather improved, for better or worse.

"Are you cold, miss?"

Estella looked around at the young girl standing in line behind her, a shopping list in hand. The girl removed her scarf and held it out. "You can borrow this if you need it."

Estella realized she was shivering, though not from any outside cold. It was the sadness getting to her, overwhelming all else that she felt. She longed for her father's warm and comforting embrace. She ached to hear her mother's voice again.

She wished that her life had turned out differently. If only she could wake up and find that she was two years younger, comfortable and warm and safe in her childhood bed with her parents in the next room over.

The girl was still waiting for her to say something. Estella pulled herself out of her sadness and put a smile on her face, although it didn't feel as genuine as she would have liked. "I'll be fine. You keep that for yourself."

"Alright," the girl said and put her scarf back on. "You'll warm up soon anyway. It's nice in here."

Estella's smile gentled. "Yes," she agreed. "It is nice and warm in the store."

Think about the good things. Get through this as best as you can. There's nothing else to be done.

Chapter Fourteen

"Here's the mashed potatoes." Estella set the large bowl down on the dinner table next to the roasted chicken breast and buttery biscuits. She lifted the serving spoon and placed a large dollop of potatoes on Christopher's plate. She served herself a smaller portion, then took her seat across the table from him.

Christopher watched her as she lifted her fork and poked at her meal. Everything looked delicious: the chicken was golden-brown and seasoned well with salt, pepper, and onions, and the biscuits were tall and flaky. Unfortunately, he had no appetite for any of it. The scents were turning his stomach.

Estella picked up a biscuit, broke it open, and swiped butter on the cut halves. Her every movement was slow and reluctant, as if chains were wrapped around her body, weighing down her limbs. Her lips were turned down into a constant frown, and the shadows under her eyes were darkening again when they had been so close to fading only a short while ago.

She had been so close to being happy once she was finally able to feed Cody. Christopher had ruined that. He had made her sad by being so unstable. She must not ever know where she stood with him, whether he was going to start up another argument. That wasn't proper. He should be better.

He didn't know how to be better.

But there was one thing that he could do to help a little bit.

He folded his hands on the table and spoke while looking down at the cooling food on his plate. "Estella."

She flicked him a look. He felt her uncertainty, saw the tension in her muscles.

"If it means so much to you...you can decorate the house."

Estella sat up straighter and set her fork down. Her lips pressed together. "No. I...I don't think that I should. Not if it pains you."

Christopher massaged his temples to stave off the beginnings of a headache, one that he had brought on entirely by himself. "I can't have you bein' miserable, too. That's my job."

Estella let out a startled little laugh. "Christopher...are you sure? I really would like to, if you're alright with it."

"I am. You go ahead and find more of those nice things like before. I won't change my mind and make you get rid of them again." He kept his head bowed. His eyes were burning. "My wife, Bonnie...she loved Christmas."

His voice choked.

He couldn't do this.

He could have the decorations, but he couldn't talk about it.

Estella rose from her seat and moved around the table. She sat down beside him and held out her hand. She paused, hand still in the air, then seemed to reach some sort of decision and touched the back of his arm. Her fingers were very warm and surprisingly callused. All that sewing she did must have hardened her skin, just as when a man played the guitar for years and years.

"I don't know anything about her," Estella said softly. "It seems like she was a very good person."

"She was." Christopher stared at her hand on his, finding himself amazed by the contrast of her long, delicate fingers and hardened fingertips. "You put all your effort into sewing, learnin' how to be a tailor. Same as me, before all this. I was workin' at the blacksmith forge almost as soon as I could walk. Bonnie weren't like us."

Estella tilted her head, listening in silence.

"Bonnie...she had so many different passions." Every word hurt, yet he discovered that he wanted to keep talking. He used to love jawing about Bonnie to anyone who would listen.

His voice low, he allowed himself to speak through the pain. "She was always wantin' to do so many different things. One month, she would embroider. Then she was learnin' how to bake all sorts of different breads and pies. She learned some Spanish once, when there was some Mexicans stayin' in town for a time. I even taught her a little bit of smithin'. She was just so bright, all the time. But Christmas...that's when she was brightest."

Estella reached over to her plate and moved it to her new spot. She started to eat her biscuit while watching, listening.

"The last Christmas we spent together...the one before I lost her...she made this bread dish. It looked like a wreath, a big circle of bread all wrapped around the inside of spinach and mushrooms and cheese and tomatoes. Well, she was plannin' on servin' it for the Christmas dinner the next day, but we wound up eatin' it all ourselves that night. And we darn near made ourselves sick. But it's still the best thing I've ever eaten."

Christopher blinked a few times to fight back the moisture creeping into his eyes. He picked up his fork and stabbed at the chicken and mashed potatoes.

"I could make somethin' like that," Estella said. "It doesn't have to be for Christmas. Why, I can make that for dinner tomorrow."

His heart trembled in his chest. "Ayuh? You think you could?"

"I don't know that it would be as good as hers. And we don't have any mushrooms right now."

"So it won't be exactly the same. That's alright." That was ideal, in a way. He ate a little, mulling over his thoughts while chewing. He wasn't sure where to go from this point.

Estella spoke up. "Your talkin' about Bonnie reminds me of my cousin. Cody's mother."

Christopher was relieved to be given something new to focus on. "What was her name?"

"Ada."

"What did she used to be like?"

Estella seemed to mull over his thoughts in the same way that he had. "We weren't much closer than ordinary cousins until she fell pregnant. My aunt and uncle and the rest of her family rejected her. She came to me, I think, as I worked in a men's tailor shop. She may have thought I would think differently from other women. And she was right. I felt for her. I took her in. And so quickly, we became like sisters. We were spendin' every moment together. She always had some new idea on how to make money for us, although she never carried out those ideas to their fullest. She was skilled, but she never really dug in like she could have. But so long as she was happy, I was happy, too."

"You did a good thing, takin' care of her when her own parents wouldn't." Christopher couldn't imagine how frightened that young woman had felt, all alone, abandoned by the ones who should have loved her unconditionally.

"She was so excited to have Cody, in spite of everythin'." Estella used her handkerchief to dab at her eyes. "I saw how much she loved him, even when she was dyin' just from havin' him. Protectin' him is my way of honorin' her. It's why when he's uncomfortable and I can't help him, I feel like I'm such a failure."

"You ain't a failure," Christopher growled. He thumped his fist on the table. "You done more than could ever have been asked of you. You're remarkable, Estella."

She looked at him in surprise and let out a laugh, breathily uncertain. "You don't mean that."

"Of course, I do." He put his hand over hers, briefly, squeezing before letting go.

Her smile was fleeting. "If I'm so remarkable, I'd have found a better way to handle everythin' that happened after she died."

He tilted his head. "Well, what all happened after she died, then?"

And she told him how she had been unable to give Ada a proper burial without permission from her family. The only way to get permission had been to strike a deal with the uncle, giving him the tailoring business, thus letting Ada be put to rest but placing Estella and Cody in a perilous position.

Christopher looked at Estella, and suddenly, it was as if he had new eyes and was seeing her for the first time. She had gone through so much and struggled so greatly, and her current position was still one of uncertainty, and yet she was right here before him when so many others would have given

137

up. Everything she had sacrificed had been for the good of others, first her cousin and then the baby.

The shadows underneath her eyes were battle scars.

Her infrequent smiles were a hallmark of her strength.

Estella lifted her eyes to Christopher's, and it seemed they became locked together. He couldn't look away. In fact, he discovered he was leaning in closer to her until he could see the tiny, fine wrinkles at the corners of her eyes and mouth. He could smell her, sweet goat milk and harsh soap vapors.

His stomach was opening up wide inside of him. Not only his stomach, but his chest, the emptiness inside him fully realized. And there she was. He recognized her as the perfect fit to fill that emptiness.

No, not perfectly sized, but good enough. Just right.

If only.

He leaned in a little closer to her, and she was doing the same. Her eyelashes lowered, shuttering her pretty cornflower eyes.

Still, there was some space between them. If only he could bridge that gap. Bring her into himself. He wouldn't be whole again, but nearly so. And perhaps in time, he might find that they had adjusted to each other to fit just right after all.

"You're so brave," Christopher breathed.

Estella looked at his mouth. Her shoulders lifted and fell in a series of rapid shudders.

He reached for her hand again to ask her if she wanted to, to see if this was *really* what he wanted, too.

A warbling cry from elsewhere in the house was a wall thrown up between them. Estella jumped back so swiftly that she nearly knocked over her chair. If Christopher hadn't reached out and grabbed it, it would have fallen over.

"I'll go check on Cody," Estella gasped. She rushed away, her footsteps receding rapidly. Shortly, Cody ceased crying.

Christopher sat back in his chair, stunned as to what had just happened to him. It was like he had forgotten who he was and how things were for just long enough to be dangerous.

He couldn't kiss Estella. He couldn't fall for her, no matter how wonderful and brave she was. He could not open himself to her when, eventually, she was going to leave.

She would take his heart with her if that happened, and he didn't think he would survive losing his heart another time.

He needed to be so much more careful from this point on.

Chapter Fifteen

Apple gave a little kick as Estella started to milk her. It was just a little warning, and her hoof didn't make contact.

"Yes, you're as savage as a meat ax," Estella said, not flinching. "Now, hold still, and let me finish."

Apple gave a little grumbling bleat and stood still, allowing herself to be milked without further fuss. Using Christopher's tricks, she had healed up plenty and was easier to manage again. Her udder was still a little red and swollen, but milking her did not seem to cause pain so much as occasional discomfort due to lingering tenderness.

As her hands did the task she had become so accustomed to, to where she did not have to think about it at all, her mind wandered to her dinner interaction with Christopher the previous day. A tight knot of mixed, unidentifiable feelings formed in her stomach, an unwanted Christmas present all wrapped up with a bright ribbon of fear.

She couldn't believe that she had come so close to kissing him! Why had she even allowed that to happen? Had she been so overcome with emotion while thinking of Bonnie and Ada and their losses that her defenses lowered to such a point where she was no longer in control of herself?

Or was it his compliments? And she was so desperate to please him and have their temporary situation be a good one that she was willing to act in a way completely foreign to her?

Though she had never really fancied any man before, she had kissed a few boys on the cheek when she was much younger before she knew how really improper it was. She even kissed one on the lips very quickly and briefly. They had been only ten or so, not understanding what they were doing, what they felt, and why. It had never been talked about between them, not before or after, and he had gotten married several years later, at sixteen. Most likely, he had forgotten about that kiss long before that point.

All that to say that even with her very limited experience, she hadn't felt anything like what she experienced last night. There had been a *pull* inside her, an instinctual tugging in Christopher's direction.

Estella finished the milking and brought the pail back to the house to boil what she had collected. She stood there and stirred, looking at her pale reflection in the simmering pot. She wondered if Christopher had been seeing her or his dead wife when he was leaning in so close that she could smell the animal aroma of horses on his clothing.

It didn't matter. None of it mattered.

She could not allow herself to fall in love with him, as he would never fall in love with her. He was still too heartbroken, too caught up in his losses. Besides, he would just change his mind anyway whenever he discovered her scars.

She took the milk off the heat and made up a bottle to bring to Cody in his cradle. Passing the sitting room, she caught a glimpse of something on the sofa that hadn't been there before. It was a box, and there seemed to be a number of things inside the box.

Curious, Estella walked over to it and saw a note on top of the box's contents. The handwriting was stiff, the letters blocky and large.

"Abe's wife had a load of ornaments she didn't want no more. Thought you might use them to decorate. And give the rattle to Cody."

The note wasn't signed, but there could only be one author.

"Rattle?" Estella murmured and looked inside the box. Laying right on top was a tin rattle that she thought she recognized, though she wasn't sure where she would have seen it.

Then, it came to her. She had seen this when she was up in the attic. It was in the same box as the baby booties.

Estella picked up the rattle, felt its contents sliding around inside, and heard them, like a brief burst of rain on a tin roof. She held it close to her chest and smiled. Obviously, this was Troy's rattle. Cody was not yet interested in his environment, but she thought he would be soon, and he might like to shake the rattle around.

And did Christopher say ornaments?

She looked back into the box and gasped as she saw that the contents were exactly as promised: a jumble of mixed Christmas decorations. She set the rattle and bottle of milk aside and started taking things out to get a better look at them. There was a string of dried oranges and cranberries, thick paper stars, bundles of cinnamon sticks, and fake pinecones with a snowlike frost crusting them. She took out a number of porcelain angels, each with a hook to be hung from a tree branch, all white and gold and dainty.

She hadn't been certain if he had actually meant it when he said she could decorate. Now she knew that he was. She couldn't wait to hang up the stars and set out the pinecones again. And she would need to go back outside and fetch more pine branches.

I'll take a saw and cut off a very large branch. I can set it up in a pot in the sitting room and hang the paper stars and angels on it.

Oh, but a Christmas tree wasn't the same without presents. She needed to secretly prepare some cookies or fudge to place beneath it. Perhaps she could make Christopher a new handkerchief or a scarf, something quick and easy and useful.

Her thoughts stuttered to a halt as she thought of how much it would bother him if she did put up these decorations. He was such a kind man beneath the grumpy exterior. He was...vulnerable in a way that he would probably never admit, not to her, not to himself.

What if she didn't put up the decorations? That would hurt him, too.

Estella chewed on her lower lip before putting almost everything back in the box except for the string of dried fruits, the cinnamon bundles, and the paper stars. She would start by putting up these and see Christopher's reaction. If he seemed okay, she would set up more of the blatantly holiday-themed decorations.

Pleased with her compromise, she went at last to bring Cody his bottle. When he was fed and happy, she placed him in the sling to keep her hands free and got to work on bringing a touch of cheer to the house.

Chapter Sixteen

Lifting the ax, Christopher brought it down on the piece of wood, and the two halves fell off the chopping block. He placed his last piece of wood on the block and let the axe fall again. The sharp blade cleaved through the grain of the wood, leaving two more-or-less even halves. Letting out his breath in a puff of frosted air, he lowered the axe and rested it on top of the stump.

He started to gather up the wood he had chopped, bringing it to the pile leaning against the side of the house. He could see Estella moving around inside through one of the kitchen windows; she was making up a dough, a cloud of flour surrounding her as she kneaded. He smiled slightly and turned away to fetch more of the wood he had been chopping.

He hoped she had seen the decorations he had brought. An early morning visit to Abe's house in town had given him more than he would ever have thought to ask for.

"Don't be afraid to come back if you need more," Abe's wife had told him. "I'll have even more room to buy new decorations if you take more!"

Abe had shouted from the other room. "We'll wind up penniless, you old goat! ...But, if it makes you happy...."

Christopher had just chuckled and thanked them both. He had ridden home in good spirits and hid the ornaments in the barn until after breakfast. Over breakfast, Estella showed him the gown she had just finished sewing. He didn't know much about sewing, and even he knew that her work was beautiful. She had talked about how she might move on to some smaller projects, like making even more new clothes for Cody.

She was a clever, industrious person. He wondered why she hadn't already married someone. Any man worth half his salt should be able to see how competent she was, how smart and gentle, too. Perhaps she had had offers before and turned them all down for one reason or another?

"Chris!"

Christopher almost dropped the armful of wood he was carrying as his name was shouted from elsewhere on the ranch. He swung around and saw Jackson rushing toward him, leaping to clear the snow drifts. He was holding his hat on his head with one hand to keep it from flying off as he hurried over.

"Boss!" Jackson stumbled to a stop in front of him. He slumped over, hands on his knees. "I.... You got to come look-see!"

Christopher stared down at his foreman. "What are you doin'?"

Jackson pulled in a quick breath and straightened. His eyes were dark, darting all around in a wild display of unease, like a spooked horse. "Don't ask me no questions, Boss! You got to come to the stable right now."

Christopher found his heart in his throat. This wasn't like Jackson at all to be so flustered. "Alright. Show me."

Jackson turned around and ran back to where he had come from: the stable.

And now Christopher knew why his foreman had been so frightened.

Nippy had not improved, and she had, in fact, become worse. She had stopped eating entirely and spent more time lying down than was normal for a horse.

Asking around for a veterinarian so that he could check the cost and perhaps find the funds somewhere had proven futile. The local veterinarian had taken the train to another state to visit family for the holiday.

Jackson threw the stable door open, and Christopher followed after. He expected to hear the welcoming neighs of alert and curious horses.

What he heard instead was the worst sound any rancher, farmer, or cowboy could ever hear.

It was silence.

At just a glance, he only saw one or two horses standing. The rest of the stalls appeared empty, but all the gates were closed up tight, and Jackson would have said very clearly that the animals had escaped if that was what was wrong.

Christopher ran to the nearest stall and peered over. The horse inside, a black gelding, stood exactly the same way as Nippy had when she first came down with her strange sickness. Nose in the straw. Tail limp.

In the next stall, a brown mare was lying down but not sleeping. She was breathing low and roughly, as if each one was more difficult than the next.

"All of them?" Christopher whispered. He put his hand over his mouth and stepped back from the stall. "You don't mean to tell me that all of them...?"

"You need to see Nippy." Jackson had his hat in both hands, standing before the lead mare's stall.

Christopher moved to join his foreman, his heart heavy and black with the deepest dread. He opened the stall door and stepped inside.

The mare had died, and it had not been a kind death. The sickness had taken a very terrible turn. He could see that her hay was stirred up as if she had been kicking it. Her head was positioned, leaning back against her shoulders in a rather uncanny manner, a way no horse would choose to rest.

He could smell the sickness, too, see that her body had lost all control in her final moments. Her eyes, mouth, and nose all had a thick crust around them.

He could look no more. Christopher turned away from his lead mare, his eyes stinging with the sight. He had seen death. He had butchered chickens and other animals for food. But this? It was a waste. There was no point in this death.

"We need to get her out of here," Christopher said, his voice weak. "We need to burn her body."

"I'll get some ropes." Jackson strode away and returned shortly with the ropes.

It was a long and terrible process to move the body of an animal that weighed as much as several men. By tying ropes around her, they shifted her onto some planks of wood, which they could then slide more easily across the snow, like a sled.

They took her to a spot some distance from the ranch, in the middle of an open field of snow, and gathered kindling to light her. When the fire was strong enough, they added firewood logs. It was not lost upon Christopher that he was using the wood he had just cut to burn the body of one of his favorite animals. There was a terrible irony in it, that what should have been used to keep his house warm was now being used to destroy.

It was as if he couldn't escape fire, as if he was forever doomed to have flames ruin the good things in his life.

Jackson stood next to Christopher as Nippy burned. The smell of scorched hair was terrible. Plumes of black smoke drifted up into the sky, staining the clouds like ink in water.

"What a waste," Jackson said, his voice disgusted. "Can't even use her for meat."

Christopher gave a slow nod, his hands in his pockets. He knew what he thought was happening, and that made Nippy's meat tainted. She had to be burned, and then her remains buried so she would not taint the land he walked upon every day.

"How many of the others are like her, Jackson?" he asked.

"All except three. Most of them look just like she did before. Do you think she spread it, Boss?"

"No." Christopher shook his head. "I think this is poison."

"Poison?" Jackson exclaimed. "But how?"

"If it's affectin' all of them, it must be somethin' they all share." Christopher's jaw was tight. He knew he would have a headache soon. "It's got to be their feed, the bedding, maybe something in their stalls. With the weather like this, could be something got wet and rotted. We need to go in there and move the healthy horses to the small barn, and then we got to look through the feed bags and the hay bales, see if there's any fungus or mold on anythin'. We clean out the stalls until they look newly-built."

Jackson muttered a swear and kicked at the snow. "How're we goin' to keep this burnin' and do all that cleanin'?"

Christopher knew that a normal fire was not enough to reduce such substantial materials to ash. "We throw some kerosene on, and we take shifts to come back and look at it, keep it from gettin' out of hand. Oh, and we can throw out the old feed and bedding to be burned here, too."

"Alright. I think I'll go start movin' the horses." Jackson put a hand on Christopher's shoulder and squeezed. "You join me when you're ready."

Christopher knocked his friend's hand away and put his back to his prized mare. "I ain't never goin' to be ready. Let's go."

They walked to the barn together to get to work and hopefully get to the bottom of this before it was too late for the rest of the herd.

Chapter Seventeen

Estella withdrew the bread wreath from the oven, smiling widely at the results of her labor. The crust was crisp and deeply golden, with notches sliced into the top to show the inside filling of chicken, cheese, tomatoes, onions, and mixed greens. She immediately brought it to the table and placed it on a large platter, where it was the centerpiece of the rest of the meal she had prepared. The fried potatoes were steaming, the peas sitting in a pool of melting butter. The coffee was hot, ready to be poured.

Now, all that she was waiting on was Christopher.

Estella went to the window to look outside, as she had been doing since much earlier in the day. She wanted to know what all the smoke out there was about. She kept seeing Christopher and Jackson taking things off into the field where the smoke was coming from. She wondered what they were burning. Had some hay gone moldy and needed to be thrown out? But the men looked too busy for her to want to interrupt them and ask.

She hadn't seen them for a little while, though, which she hoped meant that they were finishing up. If Jackson stayed for dinner, she would ask him how Clementine was doing. And she would have him take a message to her and Vera, letting them know that she had finally finished the gown.

In fact, she was wearing it.

She moved away from the window and twirled a little, watching the ruffled skirt flare out around her. Dizzy, laughing a little, she stumbled against the counter and grabbed onto it to keep herself upright. Looking back at herself in the window glass, she admired her reflection. The beige and darker brown accents were fashionable, complimented by some lacy white ribbons she had found. Really, it was much too nice to be wearing while staying home and baking, although she had been extremely careful to protect it with an apron over top.

If only she had a reason to go to a party, then she could wear it, and it would be just perfect.

Cody made fussing sounds from the bedroom. Estella went to fetch him and lifted him into her arms. "Are you feelin' peckish, dear?" She leaned down and pressed a kiss to his forehead. "I can feed you before Christopher comes home."

Cody blinked up at her, and he smiled.

Estella smiled back at him, then gasped a moment later as she realized what had just happened. He had only given reflexive smiles and grimaces that resembled smiles up until then. This was different. This was a real smile, one that creased the apples of his cheeks and scrunched up the corners of his eyes.

All the hard work and worry of the past weeks suddenly was very much worth it as she was rewarded with a smile by this cherub in her arms.

She held Cody close and pressed her cheek to his. "Oh, my Cody," she whispered to him. "I love you. I'll do anythin' for you. You know that."

Cody made a little burbling sound and nuzzled against her.

Estella fetched him a bottle, fed him, burped him, and then put him back in his cradle. As she was straightening, she heard Christopher coming into the house. Might he like to know that she had received Cody's first real smile? No, perhaps she shouldn't say so. She wanted to cherish the moment for a little longer before she talked about it, anyway.

151

Estella fetched the pot of coffee from the kitchen and ducked into the dining room. Christopher sat at his place, staring dully down at his plate. He didn't look up as Estella poured coffee into his mug.

"You must be tuckered out," she said. "I saw how hard you and Jackson were workin' out there. You're a little late, too. Is Jackson joinin' us?"

Several long moments passed by, almost half a minute, before Christopher stirred. He grabbed his coffee and took a long swig, then placed it down with a thump. "More," he growled.

Estella complied, adding more to his mug. She could feel herself deflating in the face of what seemed to be yet another bad mood. For the first time, she considered that all the hard work she observed outside might not have been for a good reason.

"Christopher?" she ventured, tentative. "Is Jackson goin' to join us?"

"No." He reached for the bread wreath she had spent hours on and tore off a piece, leaving a ragged hole in her hard work.

"I just figured, since it's late, that he might stay for dinner before headin' home."

"Well, he's not." Christopher stabbed his fork into the fried potatoes and shoveled them into his mouth, chewing and swallowing seemingly without tasting them.

Estella nodded slowly and went to sit at her own place at the table. She would leave him be for a little bit, let him come down from whatever was upsetting him so.

Using her knife, she cut off the ragged ends of the bread wreath from where Christopher had taken his portion and set them on her plate. The neater edges on the wreath made her feel better, like her hard work was being respected.

I suppose I can't expect a man to know all the work that goes into making food. Most of them seem to think we have it easy, keeping the home while they go out.

She ate, and the food was good. Her mood affected the taste, giving the bread and chicken a bitterness, like the taste of tears. She drank from her cup of water after almost every bite to wash the taste out, or else it would accumulate and ruin the experience further.

Christopher finished his first helpings and reached across to the wreath again.

"Let me serve you a piece," Estella said quickly, putting her fork down and reaching for the serrated knife.

He sat back, saying nothing as she cut him a large piece and put it on his plate. Keeping a watch on him out of the corner of her eye, she thought he seemed to be eating slower that time, chewing for longer.

She knew, *knew,* that she should probably leave him alone to work through whatever was causing this mood. She just couldn't actually stop herself. She wanted him to stop and look at her and decide that he could trust her with at least some of his burden.

"I wanted to thank you properly for lettin' me decorate," Estella said. Her words fell into the silent spaces between chewing and fork scraping. "And for the rattle for Cody. It's kind of you."

No response came. Christopher didn't even appear to have heard her. Surely, he had, but he gave her no acknowledgment of it, and why should that be fair? Why did she need to answer him but not the other way around?

She put down her fork and straightened. "Did somethin' happen that I should be made aware of?"

Christopher thumped the palm of his hand down on the table, and she flinched. He pushed back in his chair and stood. "Can't a man get some peace and quiet?" he growled.

"I'm sorry. I was just concerned." She was standing, too, not having realized she had gotten up.

He waved his hand and stomped out of the dining room. Estella looked at his receding back, then at the dinner she had worked so hard to prepare for him. They could have the wreath for leftovers another day, where it wouldn't be nearly as good as it was right then. The chance for him to really appreciate it was rapidly disappearing, a gap in a closing door.

Estella grasped at that closing door, aware of the possibility of getting her fingers smashed and not caring.

She followed Christopher's stomping walk to one of the rooms she had never entered, his office. The door was ajar. She extended her hand, placed her fingertips on the wood, and pushed inward.

The door creaked softly open.

Inside the office, the air seemed to be colder than the rest of the house. There was a bookshelf next to a window looking out onto the ranch; the edge of the shelf slightly overlapped the window glass, something a woman would never have allowed if she had been the one to decorate the house. But a man wouldn't notice such things.

In front of the window was a heavy wooden desk, and Christopher sat before it in an equally large and heavy wood chair, his back bent as he leaned over an open book. One thick finger trailed the pages—searching for something by the light of the kerosene lamp. He muttered to himself, low under his breath.

Estella crept into the room, holding her arms tightly around herself. She was like a soldier who had crossed the border into enemy territory, acutely aware that this was not her space and she did not belong there.

It wasn't exactly an unfamiliar space for someone who had run their own business before, though.

Christopher reached over to the shelf and grabbed a second book, slapping it open on the desk next to the first. Leaning around him and squinting, Estella saw they were ledgers, filled with numbers representing purchases made and loans taken out, horses sold and debts repaid.

Whatever had been going on outside had made him worry about money.

"Do you need help?" Estella ventured. "I did bookkeepin' at the tailor shop. I'm good with numbers."

Christopher turned around and frowned at her, his broad shoulders squared. "I don't need no help," he growled. "It's none of your business. Leave me be, Estella."

She hesitated, standing her ground. Why couldn't he see by now that she wanted to help him? If only he would let her in, she could make both their lives easier.

"Did somethin' happen outside?" she asked.

"Estella." His growl deepened. Had he been an animal, it was a sign that he was on the verge of attack.

155

Estella backed away until she was outside the office. Christopher stared at her the whole time until she shut the door, and then she heard him shuffling, turning back to stare at his books again.

She leaned her head forward, resting it on the door. Why did that growl of his no longer frighten her? She felt that his aggression was more of a warning, that he felt he would have no choice but to lash out, like an animal cornered with its back to the wall. He was angry because he was afraid, because he didn't know what else to do.

And what could she do except back away and give him space to run off and tend to his wounds in private? Her pity for him was useless when she could not help.

If not her, then who would? Or, like the injured wolf who runs off to lick his wounds, was he destined to falter and be overcome in his weakness?

Chapter Eighteen

Christopher kicked out with his boots at the drifts of snow, clearing a path ahead of him. It was difficult, and he was tired, cold, and out of sorts. He would have rather been doing anything else.

I can do something else when I find out what's hurting my animals.

Jackson walked beside him a short stretch away, kicking his own path through the snow. Underneath his hood, the foreman's expression was grim. He looked every bit how Christopher felt.

A deep clean of the stable had revealed no probable cause for the mystery illness taking his horses to their deaths. Still, they had done the deep clean and acquired all new feed and bedding. And still, two more animals had died, which had meant more long and grueling work, burning the bodies.

Christopher was at the end of his rope. This couldn't continue. He had to make it stop, and he could think of only one more possible culprit.

Perhaps he should have thought of it sooner.

"Any sign of anythin', Boss?" Jackson called to him.

"If there was, I sure as heck would have said it," Christopher growled.

He kicked the snow and almost tripped over a buried branch. He righted himself, aware of Jackson laughing at him and choosing to ignore it because he had already seen his friend take a proper tumble. They should have been wearing snowshoes, except Jackson had forgotten to bring his, and Christopher had recently misplaced his. Perhaps it was better that they couldn't move too quickly. The longer they took, the more time they had to look around and potentially see anything suspicious.

They walked near the stream that ran through Christopher's property. A portion of it curved very close to the ranch, where they acquired water for the horses. There was also a well on the property, from which Estella got water for food and drink; the well water stayed liquid even in the midst of winter because it was insulated so far underground.

Christopher wasn't sure where he had acquired this belief from—some old tale overheard one day in the past? But he thought that the horses should only drink wild water from the stream, that it was better for them than the stagnant and still water pulled up from the well.

Having eliminated all other sources of poisoning, Christopher was now faced with the potential culprit: the stream. The humans and horses' different drinking sources were the reason why he and Estella were still healthy.

It was a risk and might well be all for naught. He accepted that. These desperate times would make a man take crazy gambles.

He and Jackson had started at the curve of the stream where they got water from and had been following the water since then, moving quickly away from the ranch and into the wooded hills from whence it flowed. The top of the stream was frozen in some spots, curls and whorls of water captured in beautiful, crystalline detail. The water still ran underneath the iced-over parts.

Thus far, there had not been a sign of anything amiss in the water, no discolorations. The stream chuckled along as if nothing was wrong while squirrels leaped overhead along the bare branches. The only other sounds were heavy breathing and snow crunching.

"Hey, Boss!" Jackson was pointing at something in the snow. "Get over here and look at this."

Christopher struggled to his side to see what he was indicating. As he neared, he saw it for himself. A trail of boot prints passed a short distance ahead, two sets going toward the stream and then pacing its length...the same as they were doing.

"Those ain't ours," Jackson said.

"Well, hell, no, they ain't!" Christopher lifted his head and stared around. Snow dropped from overhead as a squirrel scampered along a branch with a nut in its mouth, the only sign of movement. "Let's follow 'em. They're fresh, you think?"

"Ayuh, I can see the boot treads." Jackson crouched down and touched the inside of one of the prints. "No ice formation yet. Whoever left these, they're near."

Christopher marched on, making sure not to disturb the path he was following. He thought he might need the evidence to show Abe when he dragged the pair of trespassers off his property and to town.

Who were these addleheaded fools? Were they hunting on his land?

Christopher froze and held one finger up in the air as he heard a voice from somewhere close by, a muttering and then a splash like the stream had been disturbed. Jackson waved his hand and pointed up the stream to where it bent outward and disappeared into a thicket of trees. That was where the trespassers were. Squinting, Christopher could see them when they moved, two bundled figures, one standing, the other crouched down.

Christopher slowly reached his hand down and removed his pistol from its holster. Jackson was doing the same. Christopher held up five fingers and nodded at the trespassers. Jackson nodded, his mouth a grim line.

Christopher ticked his fingers down, one by one. When the last one dropped, he and Jackson lurched forward, leaping to clear the snow drifts.

"Stay right there!" Christopher shouted, his pistol up and pointing at the figures of the trespassers as he pushed through the tree line, branches slapping his face and shoulders. "Put your hands in the air!"

Jackson came around from his other side, and they pinned the trespassing men against the stream. Neither man raised his hands. They looked at Christopher and Jackson as if they were the ones who shouldn't have been there.

Christopher swore and lowered his pistol as he recognized them, even layered against the cold. "Otis Ryder, why are you on my land?"

Otis looked at him with eyes such a shade of honey-brown that it was as if his obsession for gold had become part of him. "You fixin' to shoot me, Baldwin?"

"A lesser man would've already pumped you full of lead," Christopher growled.

Jackson added, "I'm a lesser man. You'd best answer, Ryder. Before this situation turns mean." He still had his pistol up, pointed in the trespassers' direction.

The man standing next to Otis, Christopher also recognized. Nate Bolger, empty-eyed and empty-souled, was a gunslinger for hire that Otis kept around like a favored pet dog. Nate had his own pistol out, aimed directly at Jackson.

"Why don't we behave like gentlemen and put our weapons away?" Otis nodded at Jackson.

"You first," Jackson said.

"Jackson." Christopher flicked a look at him. They wanted to keep this situation from getting ugly. It would be best not to start anything they didn't want to see finished.

Jackson muttered angrily and put his pistol in its holster, and Christopher did the same. He stared hard at Nate, who stared back with those eyes as devoid of human emotion as a snake's.

Otis made a gesture, and Nate lowered his pistol, though he did not put it away. Otis said, "Now we can talk. Ain't that what you wanted, Christopher?"

"What are you doin' here?" Christopher demanded.

He didn't like this, not at all. It could not have looked worse for these two that they were messing around in the stream while something in the water might be making his animals sick.

With a smile, Otis pushed his hood back and clasped his hands together before himself. His pepper-flecked black hair was a dampened tumble about his head. With that tousle of hair and almost self-conscious smile, he seemed like a schoolchild who had been caught causing a stir at the back of the classroom. He certainly didn't appear to be a forty-year-old mining emperor. To Christopher, that was the most dangerous thing about him.

"You know that my surveyor found gold out here in the past," Otis said, as if Christopher needed reminding on that. "I thought it was high time I checked for myself. Came out to do a little panning."

Otis motioned behind them to a pan and sieve left on the bank of the stream. The pan was filled with sediment and pebbles, without a sign of gold sparkling in the detritus.

"This is my land," Christopher said. "You ain't got any right to be here."

"Any gold you find in there would belong to Chris," Jackson added.

"I know that." Otis's smile grew. "But if I did find gold and show it to you, you'd never do anythin' about it. It'd just be wasted potential. But if you would agree to sell to me, I could make somethin' of this place."

"It don't matter how many times you ask. I ain't sellin'." Christopher folded his arms. Nate's eyes were firmly upon him, observing his movements. "Now, you get your things and go before I send for the sheriff."

"You sure?" Otis tipped his head, black hair tumbling over his forehead. "I know that you're in trouble with the bank. I could make all your problems go away."

"None of your business, all that. It's between me and the bank."

Though Otis knew the people from the bank and likely had them on leashes, just like he did with Nate. Christopher suspected that Otis might have something to do with why the bank was hounding him so harshly, but he couldn't speak that without proper proof.

Otis leaned closer; Jackson tensed. Dropping his voice as if anyone around them could hear, Otis said, "I know about your sick horses. Could use some extra tin to buy you some new ones, right?"

Christopher's stomach clenched. "How do you know about that?"

"You think your ranch hands don't talk about what goes on?" Otis chuckled.

Jackson spat, "Wipe your chin. Them are good men that work for us. If they tell you anythin', it's because you've bribed them."

"Nothin' wrong with payin' back a man a debt owed, right? Even if he forgot he owed it." Otis smiled, the implication clear.

Christopher swallowed back a swear. He couldn't blame his workers. No ordinary man could resist some easy cash when it came his way when all he had to do was answer a few questions to get it. He closed his eyes and wrangled himself under control so he wouldn't go over there and whack Otis one for taking advantage of simpletons.

Opening his eyes, he said, "You leave now, and I won't tell Abe about this. Just answer one thing for me. I see from your prints that you been further upstream. You see anythin' queer that you think I should know?"

Otis picked up the panning equipment and handed it to Nate. "Well, now, I don't think that I did see anythin'. Sorry."

"Just leave," Christopher said. "I catch you again, I won't be so kind."

"Come on," Otis said to Nate and set off.

The two men navigated into the trees, heading for the other side. Jackson trailed them, and Christopher waited, tense, certain he would hear an argument or, God forbid it, a gunshot.

Jackson returned a minute later. "They're headin' straight to the border, Boss. What do you think?"

"I think that I need to tell Abe about this," Christopher said. "Get this in his mind so he'll act fast if anythin' else happens. And...I think he was lyin' about not seeing anything."

"That's my thought, too." Jackson rolled his shoulders. "Let's keep goin'."

They set off, and now Christopher no longer cared about preserving the trail left by Otis and Nate; with several trails as evidence, why not make use of this one to cut down on the effort they had to exert to walk?

Something faintly foul tickled Christopher's nostrils. Ahead, the stream briefly widened into a small pool before continuing. And at the mouth of that pool, there was something in the water.

"Tarnation," Jackson exclaimed. "What do you make of *that*, Boss?"

Christopher knew what he thought it looked like. Drawing nearer, scent and sight combined to confirm his suspicions.

The smell was of rot. Laying in the pool, partially blocking the flow of water, was a dead and decaying deer. A brown cloud surrounded the deer, tendrils pulling away into the water by its flow, gradually dispersing to seem clear and wholesome.

Christopher pulled out his handkerchief and used it to cover his mouth as he approached the deer. The young buck's small antlers had been damaged when it fell and died there...or had been placed there.

"No wonder the horses have been sick. Drinkin' this water." Jackson shook his head.

Christopher silently agreed. There was no way to tell how much of the rot made its way down the stream and into the water they brought the horses, but horses were surprisingly delicate animals when it came to their health. A man could work through a sour stomach on his own. A horse would die from it.

As long as the horses drank the water, the poison would accumulate until it killed them.

"We got to move this darned thing. Give me a hand here." Christopher bent and grabbed the buck's antlers.

"Why do I got to get the rear?" Grumbling, Jackson took the deer by the hind legs.

It was a terrible and foul thing to move the animal, though the surprise discovered underneath it was yet more unpleasant. Beneath the deer, in an even worse state, was a dead coyote.

Christopher picked up a stick and used it to heave the second body from the pool. "One dead animal I can buy," he said. "But two? On top of each other? It ain't right."

"Do you think...?" Jackson's voice trailed off, stopping short of making an accusation.

Christopher said, "This wasn't done today. If it was someone who put these in the water, they did it prior."

"I guess they could have fallen naturally." Jackson rubbed his head. It was thin reasoning, and they both knew it.

What could the scenario have been? Had the coyote been so hungry as to chase after prey much larger than normal?

Or was the buck chasing the coyote away from its herd? And they had fallen and died right there in the stream?

Unlikely, yet not impossible.

Christopher crouched down by the deer and, grimacing, searched its form for bullet holes. The rot made identifying wounds versus scavenging extremely difficult, and he gave up.

He wiped off his hands on the dry, brittle reeds beside the pool and stood. "Otis's tracks go right by here. He must have seen this. Smelled it. Why not say so? Unless he did it. Or didn't want me to find out, so more of my horses would die. I don't know. I don't like it."

"At least we know what happened now," Jackson said.

We hope this is the solution, anyway.

Christopher sighed. "All the horses get well water from now on. We won't use the stream until the spring thaw. That should ensure the water's clean again."

"And we should patrol the area. To make sure this...for whatever reason...don't happen again," Jackson said. He shook his head and moved away. "Let's get away from this stink."

Christopher stared at the dead animals for another moment, wondering. Did he just want to put the blame for his misfortunes on someone else, and Otis was a convenient target? Or was there actually foul play involved?

"Chris! What are you doin'?"

Christopher moved to catch up with Jackson, somehow even more troubled to have the truth.

Chapter Nineteen

Estella knocked on the office door, a cup of coffee in one hand. With no response, she knocked again. "Christopher?" she called in. "I brought you your coffee."

A grunt came in response, though she wasn't exactly certain what it meant. She deliberated on whether she should intrude or not. He had been very moody and secretive since coming back from his walk upstream with Jackson, spending a lot of time in his office and emerging very infrequently. He had stepped out a short while ago to ask her for coffee, the only words he had directly spoken to her in hours. Naturally, she agreed to the task, and now that she was here with it, she couldn't get him to talk to her.

It was rather annoying when she thought about it too much.

Estella nudged the door open and peeked in. Christopher sat before his desk again, bent over something before him. "Christopher?" she ventured.

He slowly lifted his head and looked over his shoulder at her. There was a mist in his dark eyes that he quickly blinked away, leaving her to wonder if there had ever been anything there at all. When he spoke, his voice came out hoarse in a way she had never heard it before. "What is it?"

She stepped into the office and placed the mug down on the desk at his elbow. "I brought your coffee. Are you feelin' okay?"

Christopher snatched up a letter from the desk and waved it. He seemed to be genuinely asking her opinion for once and that already had her on edge. Whatever this was, it was different from anything else thus far. "Can you believe this, Estella?"

The letter was moving too much for her to read the contents. His hand seemed to be shaking, but she wasn't sure about that, either. "I'm sure that I could if you told me what it is."

He slapped the paper back down on the desk and said in that strange, hoarse way, "From when I checked the mail yesterday. Didn't get around to readin' it until now. Wish I'd never read it. The bank is foreclosin' on me."

She put her hand over her mouth. "Christopher...."

The mist was back in his eyes, a glaze of disbelief rather than the tears she had at first mistaken it for. All his hard work, his efforts to start a new life not haunted by the ghosts of his wife and child, and this was what came of it.

Estella remembered once when her father had thought he would lose the tailoring business due to an unpaid loan. She had been much younger, hardly old enough to understand what was causing him such pain. The issue had turned out to be nothing, quickly sorted by a trip to the bank, where the tellers realized they had sent him a notice meant for someone else. The celebration that night had been like Christmas. They had gone out to eat at the tavern, where the musicians played all her favorite songs and gave her so much candy that she was nearly sick.

Christopher wouldn't be getting such a reprieve from his worries.

"If I don't square up by Christmas, it'll be the end of this place." He rubbed his hands over his face.

Estella leaned close to him. "Can't you sell some of the horses to buy yourself some time?" she whispered. "Or...or we could both start stayin' in the guest house. You could sell off the furniture in here. We won't need it. And we won't have to tell anyone that we're in the same house. I...I trust you to be proper."

Christoper glanced up at her. "Sometimes I forget that you don't know what's goin' on, on account of you takin' care of the house all day."

You admit that I do take care of the house, then?

She kept the thought to herself.

Christopher sat back and rested his hands on his knees. "My horses are sickened, Estella. Several have died. Some strange illness that Jackson and I been workin' hard to understand."

Now she understood, and it was terrible, that knowledge. The men had been busy because the horses were sick. And if some had died from a mystery illness, then their bodies would have been burned.

She could smell the greasy burning of the kerosene lamp and put her hand to her mouth. Several times, she had thought how that smoke smelled a little bit like frying bacon.

"What's making them ill?" Estella asked. "Did you get it sorted?"

"You know Jackson and I went ridin' up the stream today," Christopher said and told her about the dead animals polluting the stream.

Her relief made her dizzy, made her feel awful at the same time because they all could have been poisoned as well if they were drinking the stream water. At least most of their water was heated or boiled before use, but if she had to think about exposing Cody to any potentially tainted substance....

She *bathed him* in their water....

But not the tainted water, she reminded herself. She couldn't go off and get upset about things that hadn't happened. There was enough to be concerned about already.

"Only time will tell if the horses can recover if we switch them over to the well water," Christopher said. "It's a good thing we went out there."

Something in the way he emphasized what he said made her think there might be more to the story. She watched him and waited.

Christopher looked back at her. "I only tell you any of this as you've shown yourself to be strong. I think most women would've felt faint hearin' about the stream."

"Vera and Clementine could have handled it," Estella pointed out.

"They're strong, too," he said. "Most ain't like you three. Bonnie would have done burst into tears at the mere suggestion I found somethin' dead outside. And there's plenty dead things outside. That's how the outside is."

Estella smiled slightly. His praise made her warm and was a long time coming, in her opinion. And she liked it when he mentioned Bonnie so casually. He must really have come to trust her if he was willing to open up his heart enough for mentions of her to slip out.

"Now, I'm goin' to tell you about somethin' that's amiss," Christopher said. He folded his hands together before himself and leaned over them, staring at her. "I feel you can handle it."

She sat up straighter and nodded.

"Jackson and I saw some trespassers on the property, one bein' a local mining magnate and the other bein' his secondhand man. Otis Ryder and Nate Bolger. You remember their names from now on," he said, "because Otis has been causin' me trouble for a long while."

She listened as he told her of Otis's background, his poor upbringing, and his climb toward wealth. That he had found gold on Christopher's land and was now trespassing did not bode well.

"The problem is that Otis is partners with the bank manager, a man named John James. They're in each other's pockets." Christopher looked at her, his dark eyes shifting and suspicious. "I don't got proof of it, but I'd reckon Otis is part of the reason the bank is bein' so harsh on me. I know some men who haven't paid their loans back for years after they were due. And I can't prove this either, but it sure is some funny business with the stream and my horses. Makes a man suspect there's a connection."

Estella thought about the terrible implications. It was a conspiracy and all very illegal...if what Christopher was saying was true. If he went off and started to accuse people unfairly, it would bring him much more trouble.

Speaking carefully, she said, "I'm sure you considered that the harsh winter maybe caused those animals to die on their own? Or...somethin' else happened?"

"That's why I said I can't prove any of it. But a man's got feelin's in his gut that tell him the truth, and my gut is speakin' to me."

Cody began to cry from Estella's room, his distinctive hungry call. She began to excuse herself, slowly rising.

Christopher moved much, much faster than her, striding out of the office. She heard him thumping down the hall, a door being opened. Cody's cries cut off abruptly.

Estella rushed to the hall. "Cody?"

Christopher backed out of the bedroom, holding the baby in his arms. He stared right down at Cody, dark eyes wide. His lips trembled slightly. "He...he smiled at me, Estella."

Estella went to his side, reaching for his shoulder. "He likes you."

Christopher continued to stare at the baby, and Cody looked back at him, expression blank. Estella had no doubts that he had smiled, though. The approach of an adult meant being fed; of course, a baby would be happy about that. No doubt Christopher knew that, though maybe he had forgotten in the past three years what it felt like to have such a small and defenseless being in his arms.

Her heart skipped a beat.

She rubbed Christopher's shoulder.

He stirred and pressed Cody into her arms. "Here, take him." His voice was rough.

"Do you want to feed him?" she asked.

He shook his head and shifted around her to go back into the office. "I shouldn't. And he shouldn't get used to me. You two should probably find someplace else to go and soon."

"What?" And now her heart was skipping beats for a different reason. "Did I do somethin' wrong?"

Christopher faced away from her, and how she wished he would look at her. Didn't he just seem to have found respect for her? Then why couldn't he face her when he was hurting her?

"This was only ever meant to be a temporary situation," Christopher said, very quietly. "When I lose the ranch, I won't have anywhere for you to live. You should start lookin' around for another position. Maybe the church will take you in for a time."

"You don't know that you'll lose the ranch!" She went to him, touched his shoulder again.

He caught her hand in his and gave it a gentle squeeze, then placed it back down by her side. "Thank you for the coffee. I need to be alone now."

Estella lowered her head, tears blurring her vision. She did as he asked, stepping out of the room. He shut the door behind her, forcing her out on her own.

And what would she do when she was forced out for good?

Cody whined and wriggled in her arms. Estella blinked her tears away and went into the kitchen to get a bottle for him. There wasn't anything she could do right now, at night. Maybe tomorrow, she would go into town and ask around, see if anyone needed another pair of hands to help out.

She didn't hold out much hope for that, but she had to try something.

Chapter Twenty

Early the next morning, a knock on the front door brought Estella out of the kitchen, where she was just beginning to prepare breakfast.

Abe stood outside, his mouth turned down at the edges. Seeing that it was her, his lips quirked faintly upwards. "Estella, how are you gettin' along out here with Chris?"

She thought quickly through everything that had been occurring between them and simply said, "Well enough, thank you, Sheriff. You came to see Christopher?"

"I did." Abe nodded. "Had Jackson come to me and tell me it was urgent that I make my way here. He inside?"

"He's out feedin' the horses but should be comin' to the house for breakfast soon." Estella edged back from the doorway. "Do you want to come inside? I've got a pot of coffee boiled."

"Wouldn't mind a cup of black water to chase away this chill." The sheriff stepped inside and stamped his boots to dislodge snow.

Estella brought him to the kitchen and poured a mug of coffee. Abe took it with a nod and breathed in the steam. His beard began to drip as ice crystals and snow caught in the gray hairs melted. He wiped away the dampness on the back of his hand and took a deep gulp of coffee. "Good stuff you've made here, Estella."

"Thank you." She checked in the oven, pulling out a tray of hot biscuits. "Will you be stayin' for breakfast?"

"No, I've got quite a day ahead of me. Wouldn't mind takin' one of those biscuits with me, though," he added.

She smiled. "After you're done talkin' to Christopher, I'll wrap one up for you."

"Could I talk you into sendin' two along with me?"

Estella laughed. "Alright, Sheriff. Might I ask you somethin'? Can I know what you're here to talk with Christopher about?"

Abe frowned and drank more of his coffee. "It don't concern you, and it ain't my place to share private information."

He struck her as the type of man who might have a hard time believing a woman could be strong and capable. Estella looked into his pale blue eyes and motioned to herself. "I'm livin' here, so it does concern me. Christopher's told me all about his problems with the bank and the loan. I saw the letter he received."

"That right?" Abe held out his mug, and she poured him more coffee. "Alright, then you know about Otis Ryder, too?"

"I do. Christopher told me some of it last night." Estella folded her arms. "Is there anythin' else that you can tell me? Is he a bad sort?"

"He's only a bad sort if you cross him. Or if you got somethin' that he wants for himself. Otherwise, he's a decent feller." Abe huffed out a humorless laugh. "He runs them mines of his like a saint. There was a collapse a year ago, killed two miners. Otis gave their widows a payout equal to six months of labor, more'n enough for them to sort out their situations. But then there was that time a few years before that when he found out someone was sneakin' in the mine after hours and takin' gold for themselves. I still don't know how he handled that, but the thief came to me *beggin'* to be put in jail. Wanted solid iron between himself and Otis."

Estella shivered. "Then, he's dangerous?"

"I'll tell you there weren't a scratch on that thief," Abe said. "I checked him myself. If he'd been beat up, I'd have had somethin' to say about it to Otis."

That didn't answer my question, Sheriff, and you know it.

Estella listened for Cody and was reassured the baby was still sleeping when she didn't hear a peep. "Do you think that Otis has somethin' to do with the horses fallin' ill?"

"It's goin' to be hard to know anythin' for sure." Abe finished his coffee and waved Estella away when she tried to serve him more. "I will say that Otis don't like not gettin' his way, and Christopher is just about the only person stubborn enough to resist this long. It's this land. It's the only thing that kept him alive after his losses, and he won't give up his sanctuary. I'm probably goin' to have to drag him out of here at the end."

Estella lowered her head. "I feel so terrible about all of this."

"It ain't none of your fault," Abe said and put his hand on her arm. "Don't you worry none about anyone's safety. There's a good chance that this poison business has ended. It might not have been foul play. Hard winters make wild animals act crazier'n usual. Could be that the deer was chasin' a coyote away, and they tripped and fell in the stream. Deer's neck breaks, it dies. Coyote's stuck underneath it, injured, and dies. Could have happened anywhere, and we would never have known, except that it happened in the water, and they tainted it."

Her throat was tight. "Or someone shot those animals and put them there."

Maybe there was a natural explanation. Maybe there wasn't and whoever had done this would do something else to hurt Christopher.

Abe held up his hands. "Also possible. I don't know anythin', Estella. But I'll do what I can to make things right."

"You're a good man," she said softly. "Thank you, Abe."

His cheeks seemed a little more flushed than they had been. "It's my job, is all. Oh, and I'm about to have my hands full soon. People in town are goin' to be upset when they find out that the Christmas Fair is canceled."

"What?" Estella frowned. "Why? When Vera told me about it, she made it seem like somethin' everyone loved."

"The mayor normally does the organizin', but he's fallen very sick, and they don't know when he'll be back on his feet. Can't organize nothin' when you're bedridden." Abe sighed. "And it's so late by now that there ain't anyone who can spare the time and responsibility to take over. A shame, but there's always the next year."

The door to the house opened as Christopher finally arrived. He walked into the kitchen and gave Estella a nod. "Abe. Let's talk. My office."

"Nice jawin' with you, Estella," Abe said and left with Christopher.

Estella kept the food warm for whenever they finished talking and wrapped up a couple of biscuits for the sheriff, as he had requested. She could hear them talking, their voices low and serious.

In the back of her mind, there was a seed of an idea planted there by something Abe had said and growing vigorously as she nurtured it with thought. There wasn't a thing she could do about the horses and Otis, and she would drive herself right crazy obsessing over those. She had to find what she knew she could help with, and she thought that she just might have something worth putting the effort into.

The men eventually left the office, and Abe headed off—of course, after taking his biscuits with him. Estella served breakfast and sat down at the table with Christopher to eat. He did not seem particularly happy, chewing mechanically while staring off at the wall. He and Abe must not have been able to reach a proper conclusion.

Estella gently called his name to see if he would look at her.

His head shifted in her direction. His eyes were slower to focus. "What?"

In this preoccupied state, he wasn't likely to listen properly. The best thing to do seemed to be to give him her idea straight instead of working her way there.

"I know a way to get the bank off your back for a time."

Christopher's head gave a small jolt as he shook himself and looked closer at her. "What are you talkin' about?"

"The town's Christmas Fair is goin' to be canceled because the mayor is sick, and no one can take over." She sat up straighter, already buzzing with excitement at the possibilities that she hadn't even spoken aloud yet. "What if I take over the organization? We can have the fair here on the ranch. There's plenty of space if we use the fields. The bank wouldn't dare to interfere with you durin' that time. It would ruin their reputation with the townsfolk if they were responsible for ruining the fair."

Christopher's mouth was slightly open as he stared at her. He put his hand to his face, fingers digging into the meat of his cheek. "How could you even—"

She interrupted him, bouncing her feet under the table like a child eager to go play. "I've organized barn dances and parties in the past. I have the experience. Vera and

178

Clementine will help me, and the mayor is sure to know others who will assist. *And* everyone will know what to do from past fairs. All I have to do is get everyone together, and it will all work out easier than you think!"

Christopher was sitting up straight in his chair, his food forgotten, even though he still held his fork in one fist. His lips were pressed tight as he thought, then spoke. "You might be onto something here. No, you *are*. A bank depends on its community. They'll have to accept this plan if they want to keep their people happy. Estella, you are the cleverest woman alive."

His praise had her heart beating faster, and she could hear her pulse throbbing in her ears. Her hands were itching like they used to when she was young and wanting to learn, to do, to be.

Christopher smiled at her from across the table, a broad grin that showed his teeth. "Clever and beautiful, too."

"Christopher...." She caught her breath, and her stomach tingled. No man except for her own father had ever called her beautiful, and of course, a father didn't mean it in the same way as someone unrelated to her.

He shoveled the rest of his breakfast into his mouth and stood up with his plate in hand. "You can call me Chris, you know. As my friends do. If you'd like. I need to get back outside to work. Why don't you spend some time today looking around the property for good places to have the fair? And tomorrow, we will go into town to talk with the mayor and then the bank."

"That would be wonderful." Her voice came out breathy from how fast her heart was beating. "Yes, the sooner we get to work on this, the better."

Christopher put his plate on the counter next to the sink basin and headed out.

Estella looked at her unfinished food and knew she wouldn't be able to eat anything else.

She began to tidy up, her stomach still tingling and her heart still galloping in her chest. The work wasn't enough to distract her from the treacherous feelings.

She was falling for this gruff man against all the odds. She knew it would only bring pain to feel such things when he could never fall for her. She just couldn't help it.

Chapter Twenty-One

A short woman with wispy white hair opened the door and peered out at Estella and Christopher on the porch. She was nearly drowning in her demure and shapeless white dress. "Can I help you?"

Estella bowed her head politely and clasped her hands together. "My name is Estella Armstrong. Christopher Baldwin and I would like to speak with the mayor, please, ma'am."

The woman squinted; she must have been nearly blind or very confused. Or both. "I'm sorry. Cyrus is too ill for visitors."

That's what I feared.

Refusing to give up so easily, Estella made her voice gentler. "Are you his wife?"

"Yes, that's me. I can't take any messages for him. He's not well enough for business." She started to shut the door.

Estella reached out and caught her by the sleeve. "Please, listen to me, then, ma'am. You know him better than anyone else. You can tell us if he would approve of an idea Christopher and I have."

The mayor's wife regarded her, then peeked past her at Christopher. "I'm sorry, I don't follow you, girl."

Estella released her sleeve and continued speaking softly. "We know the Christmas Fair is canceled due to Cyrus's illness. But everyone in town would be disappointed. This winter is so hard that they need this celebration. And I'm sure Cyrus would want the fair to still happen. Don't you?"

The woman frowned, saying nothing. She looked over her shoulder, inside the house where her ill husband must have been waiting for her to return to him.

Estella continued quickly, before she could lose her, "I want to organize the fair in Cyrus's stead. It would be held out at Christopher's ranch, as it's not too far from the town and has plenty of space for everyone. It's a much better outcome than having no fair at all, don't you think?"

"Well, I...." Sudden tears brimmed in the old woman's pale eyes. She dabbed at them with a handkerchief. "It would be wonderful if you could do that. I know that he would give you permission, if he was strong enough to see you."

"You can give us his permission, Mary." Christopher moved closer to Estella's side.

Mary took a deep, shaking breath. "I suppose I can. If it's for the good of the town.... Yes. Organize the fair. But please, don't tell anyone that I'm the one who gave you permission. Let everyone think that you were able to visit Cyrus directly."

Estella took one of Mary's hands in hers and squeezed. "Of course. Thank you, Mary."

Mary nodded and murmured a response, then faded back into the house.

Estella could not hold back a laugh of relief and joy as she leaped down from the porch with Christopher right behind her. "Now we can go to the bank!" she exclaimed. "With the mayor's permission, there's nothing they can do to stop us!"

Christopher caught up to her and put his hand on her arm. "Easy, there," he said, gently scolding. "You fall on the ice and break a leg, and you ain't in any better shape to organize than the mayor."

"I would get a walking stick and keep workin'," she said, smiling up at him.

His scowl eased, and he smiled back. "I ain't got a doubt about that. How do you reckon Cody is gettin' along with Vera and Clementine?"

They left the baby with the seamstresses shortly before going to the mayor's house at the outer edge of town. After informing them of their plans, they received much praise for their idea. Unfair as it was, Estella's having a baby would make her seem less trustworthy and garner her less support.

They walked through the town with the snow gently falling, flakes too small and delicate to accumulate. The ground was a slush of mud and ice crystals, marked over and over again with shoe and hoofprints.

"That's the bank there," Christopher said, gesturing to a two-story building very nicely constructed from wooden slats and painted green to catch the eye. The porch was very large and covered, with curvy decorative columns supporting the roof. "Think I'll do the talkin' for this one, the land bein' mine and all. How do you feel about actin' as my assistant, if anyone asks questions about you?"

"Aren't I already your assistant?" Estella asked, mounting the steps up to the porch.

Christopher paused and looked back at her, his brow lowered. "No. You're the brains of this operation. It's just that there's men in here who won't understand that."

She touched his elbow. "I know. I'm ready if you are."

He nodded and stepped inside, and she followed him in. A fire blazed brightly in the wide room they found themselves in, keeping the air almost too warm. There were counters directly ahead where common transactions took place, with halls behind that leading to private rooms where more complicated arrangements could be hashed out.

Christopher strode directly to the counters where a thin-faced man was watching them. "I need to speak with John James."

The man laughed slightly. "You think you got the right to come and ask to see the manager, Baldwin? Where's your loan payment?"

"That's enough, Butch, thank you." Another man, short of stature and rotund, looked out from one of the rooms past the counter. "Christopher and...who do you have with you?"

"My assistant," Christopher said shortly. "Got to talk with you, John."

John waved his small, pudgy hand. "Come on, then. Let's hear what you have to say."

Estella trailed Christopher to the private office. John James pushed the door shut all the way, then looked at Estella and opened it again a crack for the sake of propriety. He lit a lamp and moved to the table next to a very large and frosted window, through which only the vague moving shapes of passersby could be glimpsed.

"Sit, please."

Christopher sat across from John, and Estella took up the chair next to him. She kept a polite amount of space between her and the men, separating herself from the money dealings that were about to occur.

John stared at her for a long moment, then evidently decided to ignore her and faced Christopher. He spoke crisply, very businesslike, as if the matter of foreclosing on a ranch was as simple as opening a line of credit. "I suspect you're here to ask for more time on your loans. I wish I could grant you that, but it's not possible. You've been given as many extensions as I can allow. You should be thankful that I'm not moving up the date. That's out of the kindness of my heart."

"I ain't here to ask for an extension," Christopher said. His voice threatened to drop to a growl. He somehow managed to wrangle it back to a level almost pleasant. "I am here to say that you can't move the date. You can't take the ranch until after Christmas."

"Why is that?" John asked. He glanced at the ajar door and then back.

"Estella and I just been to speak with the mayor. We are goin' to have the Christmas Fair on my land." Christopher leaned forward, his hands folded on top of the table.

John leaned back in response. "And why would you do that?"

"Because it's what this town needs right now!" Christopher tapped his finger on the table. "It needs the festivities, the economic boon that will come from the last-minute gift-buyin' and bake sales. You want that, don't you? Your bank operates by makin' beneficial arrangements with the townspeople, and this would benefit them and, in turn, you. So, you see, I think you'll just have to back off and wait until after Christmas to kick me out."

John shifted in his chair and looked at the door again. Estella couldn't understand why he seemed to be nervous. Did he think someone was listening to them?

"Soon as we leave here, we're goin' to start spreadin' the word of the fair," Christopher told the bank manager. "I reckon it'd be in your best interest to be on our side."

John blew out a puff of air, his chubby cheeks deflating. "Don't think that I'm fooled. You're buying yourself more time. That's your whole goal with this."

"What's the matter? Afeared of what Otis will think?"

John blinked rapidly, or were his eyes twitching? He looked at the door yet another time, then straightened and frowned. "Otis is...my good friend." The way he said it, he appeared to be trying to convince himself.

"He doesn't run the town. Not the bank, either." Estella couldn't help herself. "Cyrus does. We're acting in his stead. I think he knows what's best, don't you, Mr. James?"

Sighing, the manager rocked back in his chair. He thought about it for a long while, a play of muted emotions running across his face as he was obviously trying to keep his feelings hidden from them. Most of what Estella saw seemed to be hesitation or even fear. "Fine. You can run the fair uninterrupted. You have my support. But we will be talking again after the holiday, Christopher."

"Don't I know it." Christopher stood. "We're done here, then. Come on, Estella."

Estella spared a smile and a nod of thanks to John before following Christopher out of the bank. She felt bad for him. He was obviously very intimidated by Otis and afraid to side with Christopher, and now he had no choice except to do exactly that. Hopefully, Otis wouldn't take out his anger on him.

Christopher leaped down from the porch and reached a hand up to her to help her down the steps. Her hand was in his before she thought about it. His strong fingers closed around hers, and he tugged, sweeping her off the porch and onto the ground. His other hand wrapped around her shoulder, and he was laughing aloud.

"We did it," he crowed. "This is the best idea you've ever had, Estella."

She clutched his hand, staring into his dark eyes. Her smile felt silly and oversized, and her stomach was still swirling from the unexpected jump off the porch. Really, she knew that they had not bought more time; they had only ensured that the current time wouldn't be lessened. This was not a success, only a reprieve.

Yet, with him smiling down at her, his face leaning close to hers, the reality of all that didn't matter.

She reached up and touched his cheek, feeling the wind-scraped chapped skin and saving stubble. He leaned his head into her touch, his eyelids lowering.

His lips parted. She could see the words forming.

"Is this the woman I've heard so much about? The one livin' out on your ranch, Baldwin?"

Christopher whirled toward the voice, one hand pushing Estella behind him. "Otis."

Estella leaned around Christopher's broad back to examine the infamous man and was shocked by his handsomeness. He stood tall and straight-spined, his eyes shining like pools of honey. His face was narrow, and his body was lean but not harsh or too muscular. If he had been wearing a suit, he would have come across as a banker or politician, someone who left the hard work to those with lesser minds.

Otis swept gray-streaked black hair from his face and aimed a smile at her, his thin lips forming a gentle, mischievous curve.

Estella took a step back, the bottoms of her feet suddenly tingling. It was like she had seen a curious splotch of color in the grass and, upon investigating, discovered the scaly form of a serpent. What appeared to be bright and innocent was *not*. Her instincts demanded she not touch, not even approach another step.

"I'm Otis Ryder," Otis said, his voice smooth. "You might've heard of me by now. My reputation tends to precede me. And your name?"

"Don't you talk to her," Christopher snapped, clenching his fists.

"Why wouldn't I?" Otis smiled. "I see you've just come from the bank."

"And that's none of your business." Christopher turned away and grabbed Estella's arm. "Let's go. We're busy."

"Oh, how are your horses?" Otis called. "Doin' any better?"

Christopher let out a growl that twisted into a cry of pure anger. He swung back around, his fist flying up in the air.

"No!" Estella cried, grabbing his arm. "Don't you go and act like a fool, Chris!"

He glared down at her, his body rigid, muscles tensed. Estella stared up into his eyes, willing him to be reasonable. They could not cause harm to Otis without it coming back to hurt them twice as much.

"Please," she whispered. "Let's just go."

Christopher let out his breath, his lungs rattling in his chest. He lowered his arm and jerked his head for Estella to walk ahead of him. He kept close behind her, a barrier between her and Otis. She could feel his oversweet eyes on them, considering, judging, and did not like it at all.

They may have won a reprieve from the bank's pestering, but Otis was a far more dangerous figure to contend with.

Chapter Twenty-Two

Christopher turned his face away from the wind as a fierce howler swept through, swaying the whole length of the fence and nearly knocking him onto his rump. He closed his eyes to keep flying ice crystals from spraying into them and waited until the wind had died down some before opening them and getting back to work. As had been pointed out to him by Estella that morning, after a night of ferocious gusts, many of the nails holding certain fences had come loose, causing the entire structure to sway like ripples on a pool of water, which, in turn, loosened the nails further. He needed to go along and strengthen the fence and add some extra supports before the whole goshdarned thing went blowing away to New York.

Thus was his lot as a rancher, endlessly repairing what had already been repaired before. He didn't mind it. There was a familiarity in revisiting his earlier work and a comfort in knowing his skills had improved since the last time. If he did this job well, the fence would hold for the rest of the winter unless they had a tornado or something.

With the way my luck is, I best not think on it. Might make it come true. Then, I couldn't even blame it on God.

Christopher removed a glove to select a nail from the jumble in his pocket, then put the glove back on for the hammering. The dull pounding of metal against wood was lost beneath the constant shrilling and hollering of the wind. His face felt sore, except for the tip of his nose, which he could no longer feel. Sometimes, he crossed his eyes just to make sure it wasn't turning blue.

The past two days had been good ones, though, in spite of the weather—it seemed like everything was in spite of the weather these days.

He and Estella had spent that first day in town gathering signatures from the townsfolk after getting approval from the mayor and the bank, creating a list of all those who would be attending and what they would require. Normally, the mayor handled setting up all the different stands and tables, but this time, neighbors and vendors would lend tables and bring their own stands on their wagons when they arrived. The bakers would be there, the local candymaker, the seamstresses with mittens and scarves to sell to those who had forgotten theirs from home, as well as nearly a dozen musicians. There would be toys and treats donated to hand out to well-behaved children and demonstrations on the different crafts of woodworking, carving, weaving, and more.

Almost everyone who ordinarily attended the fair would be there, and nearly every activity would be the same.

The second day, he had been busy working on the ranch, though he kept up to date with information by Estella at dinnertime. She had gone to all the neighbors and then into town, assigning tasks and gathering decorations. When she spoke of all her accomplishments, her cheeks were pink and lively, her eyes sparkling like glass ornaments hung in firelight.

And this day, he had discovered that a few of his horses were improving, including one pregnant mare nearly due to give birth, her sides bulging. Whether she would be strong enough to deliver, and whether the foal had survived the poisoning....

He turned his mind from those thoughts and just pictured Estella's brightness as he worked the hours away. She was loving the work, shining as the head of organization. He no longer had any doubt at all that she had run her father's business well before his death and probably saw even more success afterward. She was the type who wanted to go above and beyond what was asked of her.

She had put herself in danger and poverty to take care of the child entrusted to her. Not many people would do that.

Was it a wise thing for her to have done? Not at all, but it was a mark of her passion. As someone who had fallen back onto his one remaining passion in order to stay alive, he respected her choices now.

When he had finally finished with the fence repairs, he packed up his things and headed back to the house. Estella kept a pot of coffee hot and ready almost constantly, and he could use some warmth in his belly.

As he came around the sides of his building, he caught sight of her by the stack of firewood, selecting a few logs.

There was someone on a horse watching her.

Christopher's heart dropped clear to the bottom of his stomach. A cloaked figure perched on the back of a white horse was right there in the shade of the nearby trees, facing Estella. She gathered up the wood she had selected and went into the house, completely unaware of anything amiss.

Christopher let out a swear and rushed toward the trees. He dropped his tools and pulled his pistol from its holster. "What are you doin' on my land?" he shouted.

The horse startled slightly, swiveling to the side to get him in its line of sight. The figure pulled down its hood, revealing itself to be none other than Nate Bolger. The wind tore at his cloak. His curly, bright red hair wavered about like stirred flames.

Christopher stopped short ten paces from horse and rider. He flicked up his gun, pointing it right at Nate's chest.

The gunslinger regarded him with flat and unbothered eyes. He lifted his hand slightly, and Christopher saw the gun there, which must have been pointed at him long before its presence was revealed.

If it came down to a shooting match, Christopher knew he wouldn't win. He had seen Nate at the shooting galleries that sometimes popped up at festivals, where men competed for monetary prizes. Nate always won and refused the money, leaving it to be passed on to the runner-up. It wasn't about financial gain. It was about asserting himself as the best, ensuring everyone knew what he could do and that it could be done faster than the blink of an eye.

Some said the gunslinger had been born with a pistol in hand.

Some said that when he was still inside his mother's belly, she saw a man shot dead, and the horror of the event was imprinted upon the unborn child.

Whatever the story, wherever he came from, he was dangerous.

Christopher slowly eased his finger away from the trigger so Nate wouldn't get the wrong idea and pop him one. He raised his voice to be heard over the wind. "I know Otis sent you to do his spyin' for him. You can tell him that what goes on here is none of his business. He wants to talk, he can man up and come to my front door instead of sneakin' around and sendin' spies."

Nate tilted his head ever so slightly to the side.

"As for you," Christopher growled, "you ain't welcome. Not now, not ever. You take your slimy self away from here and don't come back."

Nate's usually still and immobile mouth twisted into a faint sneer.

Red pulsed in Christopher's eyes, a lightning stroke of pure, blinding anger. He lunged forward, no longer caring one bit about the gunslinger's ability and his own safety. He grabbed Nate's arm and yanked him off the back of the horse, who sidled away, whinnying. Cold metal pushed against his chest, the pistol muzzle centered right over his heart.

He didn't care.

Fisting Nate's shirt in both fists, Christopher snarled into his face, spraying flecks of spittle. "I ain't responsible for what I do next time I see you."

Nate blinked as saliva rained on him, having no other reaction.

"You think you can down me with bullets? You ever shot a galldarned bear and it just kept comin'? That's goin' to be *me* comin' for your *sorry hide* if you aren't off my land in the next ten seconds!"

Christopher released Nate, shoving him away with all his force, straining a muscle in his back.

Nate went sprawling into the snow on his back, his legs kicking up from the jolt of landing. He twisted around and got to his feet, snow and ice caking his cloak. He dusted himself off, silent, always silent. He made one of the only sounds Christopher had ever heard from him, clicking his tongue to call the horse over.

Nate swung up onto the back of the horse and stared down at Christopher. His mouth made that sneering smile again, and then he chuckled. The sound was small and might easily have been lost beneath the wind.

Christopher balled his hands into fists. His back throbbed. His entire body was aching with the urge to do something terrible. Maybe Nate would shoot him, kill him, but Christopher would leave him with a scar to remember him by.

And Estella?

He faltered.

If he died for whatever reason, the ranch would have no owner, and the bank could seize it. She and Cody would be forced out.

That powerful urge to fight ebbed just enough for him to make a decision he hoped was the right one, even though *nothing* really felt right. He just knew that, against all his better judgment, he cared for those two. He couldn't let his own foolish actions cause them pain.

Christopher raised his head and looked Nate in the eye. "Go," he said.

Nate kicked his horse and took off at a gallop into the trees. Technically, he was headed deeper into Christopher's property and would likely ride through it as long as he could, and Christopher did not care.

As long as he was away from the house.

He stood there for a long, long time, listening to the fading crash and crunch of a horse plowing through the snow until, at last, the wind obscured it from his hearing. The strength ran from his legs, and he dropped to his knees, breathing hard.

Being a target himself was one thing. But if Otis was now choosing to target Estella, he could not abide by that.

He had to keep her and Cody safe. To lose them would be like losing his family all over again.

Which means I got some real unpleasant business ahead of me, he thought wearily and lowered his head.

Chapter Twenty-Three

Estella brought Cody to the front door to see Vera as she and Clementine arrived to help out with some of the fair work. The baby was all smiles as the three women gathered around him to coo and admire his sweet features. He was quite plump, and his eyes were bright with good health. He kicked his legs when Vera tickled his belly and snagged onto any hair that came within reach of his chubby little fists.

Clementine was laughing as she untangled his fingers and gave them a kiss. "He's so very different from how he used to be, isn't he?"

"It's all thanks to Vera." Estella looked at the other woman with respect. "I don't know what I would be doin' now if it weren't for her and that goat."

Mother and daughter shared a look that was almost secretive, certainly amused. Estella watched them, smiling slightly, waiting for an explanation.

Clementine rocked Cody in her arms, gazing down upon him with such adoration it was as if he was her own child. "Mother never told you this because she enjoys taking the credit for everythin'. But when Christopher came around and asked about a goat, she didn't go get one herself. She sent me to do it. She just made the delivery."

"Now, Clem, that's not quite fair to me." Vera frowned. "I gave you the money to buy the goat, didn't I?"

"*Our* money," Clementine said, "that we make together in *our* shop."

"But I handed it to you!"

They both burst out laughing, leaning into each other. Estella smiled at their teasing. "No matter how the goat found its way to me, it's been a real boon. Though I do wonder if I should worry that Cody hasn't grown more."

Vera took the baby from Clementine and looked down at him. Cody seemed to be looking right at her as he smiled back and cooed. She dabbed at his drooling mouth with the edge of her handkerchief. "He's a mite small for his age, but he was off his feed for quite some time. Now that he's got his milk, he'll catch up."

"Even if he grows up to be a man not quite so tall, he'll be very fetching, I think," Clementine said. "Look at those eyes and that nose. So handsome already."

Estella felt dizzy, like a wind was swirling about her. She didn't even know where she and Cody would be in a few weeks. How could she even comprehend the idea of him as a man, a grown adult?

Every parent must feel like this. One day, Cody will be my age. He'll have a wife. Children. And I'll be old and gray and telling stories of these hard days to the little ones.

There was a strange comfort held within the fear of the passing of time. Time *would* pass. They would make their way through this and into the next year, and all the years after. Just because she couldn't see her way, the future being as dark as a tunnel to her eye, did not mean that she should fear the journey. That journey would happen regardless of how she felt. What should be done was to take in stride the pitfalls that she stumbled upon and continue ever onward.

"Look here, his sweet little eyes are closing." Vera's voice was hushed. "I'll go put him in his cradle and then get a pot of tea going. You girls should settle into the parlor and get to work, and I'll join in a short while."

Estella bent to give Cody a kiss on the cheek. He turned his head to hers, nuzzling at her with his lips. The automatic response seemed instead to be deliberate, a genuine expression of gratitude.

Watching Vera go off, Estella thought, *Yes, one day I'll be old and gray...and happy for having gone through this.*

Clementine took her by the arm and pulled her over to the parlor, where Estella had set up many of the supplies needed for the Christmas Fair. They sat, and Clementine combed through the boxes of scrap wood, paintbrushes, string, and bits of fabric. "What will you have us working on?"

"Yes, so...." Estella focused herself. "Since the fair won't be held in town and will be out here on the ranch, we need to make sure that people know it's still happening. Word will have gotten around since Christopher and I were asking business owners to sign up to attend, but some people will have doubts or not know all of the details. Since we can't be in town and answering questions all the time, I thought that we should make some signs."

"That's a great idea." Clementine shot her an approving smile. "You're such a clever woman for thinking about all of this, really."

Heat came to Estella's face. She tried to ignore it. Bending forward, she picked up a stack of thick paper. "I think we should make several posters to put up in the windows at some shops. We should include the location of the fair, the date, and the time. And..... What other questions could people ask?"

"They'll want to know if it's going to be the same fair as always, especially if it's in a different location," Clementine said. "We should make note of the usual activities. Shopping, free cups of hot cider and coffee, demonstrations, gifts for children."

"Perfect," Estella replied. She selected a piece of paper and smoothed it out over a board to give herself a solid writing surface. "Let's create a practice template and then we can make a few copies from that."

They worked on the template, focusing on the wording. The notices needed to be short and easy to read at a glance.

Vera walked in with the tea and served everyone a cup. She sat and observed their work. "Might I suggest a note at the bottom?"

"Of course. What sort of note?" Estella leaned to her, eager for the extra input.

Vera motioned to herself and Clementine. "As we're assisting you and live in town, we can answer the questions that other townsfolk have. Put a note on these posters to stop by the dressmakers' shop for more information."

Estella shook her head. "Are you sure? I don't want to put extra responsibility on you two."

"Go on, do it!" Clementine nudged her. "We'd love to!"

Shortly, they had the template ready to copy from.

Vera said, "I'll make another poster for our window, telling people they're in the right spot to ask their questions. I am curious as to what all the scrap wood is for, Estella."

Estella spoke as she helped set up Clementine for writing the posters, supplying her with paper and ink. "On the day of the fair, I want there to be signs pointing everyone to the right place. Many will have never been here before, and if there's snow, they'll need help finding their way. Some signs with large print and arrows pointing the way would be good to have placed in key spots, like the road out of town, the path leading to the ranch, and some in between."

"Of course, what a swell idea." Vera smiled. "It seems the simplest of our tasks so far. Not to say that you can't do more than paint a few arrows—you've accomplished much more than most—but you deserve the break. Let us take on the more complicated parts, at least for this."

Vera was only being polite by asking. She likely wouldn't take any answer except for the one she wanted. Estella agreed, and they all set to their work, painting the wood and laboriously inking words onto the paper. As they worked, they drank their tea and talked of idle womanly things, a true pleasure for Estella. Vera shared a few cooking tips, and Clementine talked of the gingerbread cookies she usually made and brought to the fair to hand out to the children.

"They do so love to nibble the little cookies that look like men. Most save the head for very last." Clementine laughed. "If I were a little gingerbread man, I would prefer my head to be eaten first."

"Should I make something?" Estella asked. "There will be plenty of food and drink already, I know. I just feel as if I should contribute."

"You'll have already contributed all your time!" Vera scolded, touching her on the wrist. "What more of yourself will you have to give? You must be careful where you allocate your energy, dear. If you try to do too much, you'll accomplish nothing at all."

Estella agreed, and they continued their work, though she couldn't stop thinking she might find the time somewhere to make a few batches of her mother's raisin-studded spiced cookies. She knew the recipe by heart. They usually required a healthy dose of rum in the dough. Christopher didn't appear to have any alcohol other than whiskey, and not much of that. She could leave the rum out, and the cookies would still be delicious. Nary a crumb ever remained on the occasions her mother presented a platter of her raisin cookies at a party.

One by one, they finished the signs and made up many posters very quickly with the template to guide them. As the sun began to drop out of the sky, Estella helped her friends gather their things and saw them to the door. They took the posters with them to hang up themselves, saving Estella from tending to the task herself. She couldn't thank them nearly enough, though she did try as she helped them into their coats.

Vera embraced her tightly, then Clementine. "Remember to count on us to help you with anything," Clementine said. "If we can't, we'll find someone else to do it!"

"I'll remember," Estella promised.

The two went to the stable to get their horses and rode off into the mounting gray of twilight, high winds whipping their clothes. Vera had to hold her hat upon her head, or else it would have blown off.

Christopher's approaching figure from the other direction caught Estella's eye. Her heart leaped with a sudden anxiety as she recalled it was nearly dinnertime. She would need to fix something quickly.

"How do you feel about ham and eggs tonight?" Estella cleared the doorway for Christopher. "We have biscuits, too."

He grunted in response, shrugged out of his coat, and threw the damp, soggy clothes aside onto the floor. "I don't care. Bring me a plate in my office."

Oh. Something's gone wrong.

She reached out to him, and he pulled away, marching off. She winced, pain stabbing her in the heart. These rejections never ceased to hurt her; each time, the pain only seemed to grow as she cared for him more and more.

"Christopher?" she called after him. "What's wrong?"

His shoulders tensed. He drew to a stop and put his hand on the wall, bracing himself there. "You and Cody got to move on. You can't stay."

Estella stepped back, her foot striking and sliding in a puddle leaking from the bundle of his discarded attire. She righted herself, breathless, her stomach still certain she was in the midst of falling. "I know that we'll need to find somewhere else soon. It's just that with the Christmas Fair comin' up, I haven't had time to work on that."

"I don't...want you around no more." His voice stiffened. "After the fair, you're gone. Hear me?"

What?

She knew what he had said, but it didn't sound right in her ears. He seemed to be saying it because he thought he should, not because there was actual belief behind the words. Why else would he say it, though? She was stunned, as if struck on the head.

She whispered, "Chris?"

His name seemed to spur him on, pushing him away from her and deeper into the house. His office door slammed shut. Cody must have awoken at the loud noise, beginning to cry.

Estella felt herself automatically beginning to go to the baby to console him. It was like watching herself act upon some strange whim in a dream, as if she was both a train and the passenger, moving and watching herself move.

She picked up Cody and rocked him as his cries softened. She held him close, feeling her heart beating rapidly.

Some part of her, a silly little girl part, had begun to hope that things might work out on the ranch. Maybe Christopher would lose it to the bank, but they could all stay together and work something out. Like the family it sometimes felt they were becoming.

Except, he had said he didn't want her around. She still didn't know why he had—if he really meant it or if something was pushing him to do this.

The result was the same either way. Their time together was coming to an end. In only a handful of days now, she would have to make herself forget about warm, comfortable beds and nourishing meals and fresh goat milk. She would be all alone again. Unwanted.

And wasn't that what she had always thought, that no man could want her? She should never have allowed any part of herself to hope and dream otherwise, not even the smallest and most foolish little part hidden deep inside.

Chapter Twenty-Four

The mare paced restlessly around the stall, often shifting her haunches and rocking back and forth on her hooves. She had no care for the feed or fresh well water in her trough. She kept laying down upon her side and panting, then rising again to pace once more.

Christopher observed all of this as he stood inside the stall with her, Jackson right nearby with a bucket of water, rags, ropes, and a few other supplies they might need for this procedure. He kept his face calm and still and measured his breathing to keep his heart slowed. He could not allow his emotions to taint the mare or influence Jackson, who kept looking at him constantly.

The truth was that he was terrified. There was this yawning pit inside him, and if he looked into it for too long, it would swallow him. Still, he could not stop coming back and looking into that hole, seeing all the darkness at the bottom.

The mare seemed healthy enough after recovering from drinking the poisoned water, but she was sure to tire easily. And she was a maiden, this being her first delivery, which meant she could take up to twice as long as an experienced horse. Would she have the strength to see this through?

If she delivered the foal, would it be alive and healthy?

Christopher had a buyer lined up for the foal. He or she would be going to a farm for normal work, so they would not bring in any special quantity of tin. But any money was better than none, and perhaps he could present the full amount to the bank after the Christmas Fair and earn a bit more time. That would only be even remotely possible if he could get the buyer to pay early, which was very unlikely. But he had to hope. He had to try.

The mare lay down on her side again, whinnying out in pain. Her flanks pulsed with a contraction. She rose to her hooves again, and Christopher checked behind her for any sign of the foal. Her tail was up, and conditions seemed right, though still, no part of the baby made an appearance.

Jackson spoke, his voice as solemn and even as if they were in a church. "You think we're goin' to have to assist her, Boss?"

"I ain't want to try that yet," Christopher said firmly. "Give her some more time before we do."

There was always the risk of harming a female animal's insides when assisting with a birth. This was a good mare, sweetly tempered, easily bred. He wanted to be able to use her again.

Minutes passed, the air cold and stiff as ice as they observed the mare in her pacing and panting. She suddenly stopped and stood rigid, her entire body quivering all over. Her flanks rippled. She squealed, stamping her back legs and tossing her head.

Even Christopher flinched.

Slowly, the contraction subsided. When it did, there was a hoof sticking out of her.

There was silence, and then Jackson said, "Well, that's bad medicine."

Christopher growled out a swear that would have made a sailor proud. Head-first was always ideal for birthing. Coming out hoof-first wasn't the worst. At least the darned thing wasn't trying to emerge sideways!

But as he looked closer, he saw the slightly elongated shape of the hoof and the anatomy of the leg. "He's comin' out in reverse, Jackson. We're goin' to have to help her after all."

"Right, Boss." Jackson brought the rope over and tied a loop in it. His hands were swift and confident, without a trace of tremor.

Christopher put a soothing hand on the mare's quivering flanks. Time was of the essence now. Whenever an animal came out backward, if the birth wasn't fast enough, it could suffocate. Not being able to see inside the mare to know what was happening, they could not know if they were already counting down the seconds toward death, so they had to act like they were, just to be safe.

Jackson handed the prepared rope to Christopher and stepped back to wet a rag.

Christopher cinched the rope around the foal's protruding leg. "You got to help me now," he said to the mare. "I pull, you push. Alright?"

He set his boots against the ground and began to pull, first gathering in the slack. The foal's leg straightened. He pulled harder, careful not to yank. What he wanted was for the mare to feel him, to sense it was time to push.

She squealed and kicked backward, a hard-as-iron hoof coming very close to Christopher's arm. Had it made contact, he'd have himself a broken wrist. That was what the rope was for, to keep his distance.

He did not flinch or falter. He pulled.

The mare's sides rolled like the undulating of stormy waters. She shrilled again, throwing her head back so far that Christopher could see her wild white eyes.

What happened next was a great and foul release, a pressured expulsion. In the midst of the terrible mess was the body of an all-black foal, scrawny and sopping wet.

Jackson kneeled by the foal with his rag and rubbed at its face, clearing the mouth and nostrils. "Not breathin' yet," he said and began to vigorously stroke its whole body to stimulate life.

Christopher held his mare by her bridle, stroking her neck as she stood there on her shaking legs, puffing and blowing.

Then, a suckling inhalation, and the foal's legs kicked. Hearing her child, the mare turned and sniffed it all over, then licked its face with her long tongue to begin the extensive process of cleaning.

But the work was not over yet. They could not rest or rejoice.

While mother and child nuzzled and bonded, Jackson and Christopher checked them both over. The mare seemed in quite perfect condition, thankfully, and the foal was entirely whole and perfect in its formation. It responded to loud sounds, blinked around, and eventually stood up.

"It's a colt," Jackson said, grinning.

"Leave it to another male horse to be causin' me trouble," Christopher said and then laughed aloud.

He wiped his face on his sleeve and laughed again, all his worries and fears slipping out of him in a few breathy exhalations. He slumped back against the wall of the stall and watched the horses.

Jackson walked over to his side and leaned against the wall with him. They still couldn't rest, not until the foal had his first meal. It could take him a little while to find his way there.

"Hey, Chris." Jackson glanced at him. "You got a terrible queer look on your face when I came and told you the mare was in labor. Seemed like you was expectin' bad news."

Christopher sighed. *Should have expected he'd hassle me about this.*

"I saw Nate Bolger on my land yesterday."

"Well, that no-good, son-of-a...." Jackson's face went abruptly still, stricken. "Weren't Clem and Vera here and visitin'?"

The way Jackson spoke Clementine's name stirred up a suspicion inside Christopher. Was there something going on between his foreman and the seamstress from town? Never mind that, though.

"Ayuh," Christopher said, "it was, though this was before they arrived. I come back from fixin' up the fence and saw him hidin' off in the trees over thataway, just watchin' Estella as she got firewood. No idea how long he could have been there and stalkin' her."

Jackson swore loudly, causing the mare to turn her head and stare with her ears twitching. The little colt was nuzzling along her side, drawn in by the milk scent.

"I chased him off." Christopher studied the layer of fresh hay covering the floor. "But I really can't stand it no more, Jackson. I can't have Estella and her baby getting all caught up in the middle of this. I told her she has to go. I said I don't want her around no more."

"You didn't say nothin' about Bolger to her?" The foreman was frowning.

"I don't want her to be afeared. I just want her safe, and she'll only be safe if she gets away from me." He grimaced at the taste of the words in his mouth, so terribly foul. Sweetness was not his to have.

"Boss, I got to ask. You getting feelin's for that woman?" A slight smile touched the corner of Jackson's mouth. "Sure seems to me like you might have."

The colt found his mother's milk and settled in for a proper first meal. The mare whickered softly and nuzzled at his back.

Christopher moved away from the wall and picked up their tools. "Got to get out of here now," he said. "Afore that mare gets too wary of us around her foal."

"Boss." Jackson sounded reproachful.

Christopher sighed and straightened with the bucket of water in hand. "Wouldn't anyone catch feelings for her?" he asked, and he was mostly asking himself, not Jackson. "She's beautiful. She's a kind, warm woman, and she deserves so much better'n this. Cody, too."

Jackson gripped his shoulder. "You know Bonnie would want to see you happy again."

Christopher shrugged his hand off and headed out of the stall, Jackson following, saying nothing more because it wasn't his place to.

Would Bonnie approve?

He asked himself that as he put the tools away and cleaned off his hands in a patch of fresh, wet snow. She had always been such a thinker, so willing to explore new situations. She might well think that it was good for Estella and Cody to be there with him even when it wasn't the proper thing. She might well encourage him.

Except if she was around to encourage him, then none of this would be happening.

His heart squeezed as if someone held it in their fist, robbing him of his breath and his will. He turned his mind from his thoughts, which seemed dangerously close to betrayal, and put himself back to the work that he knew and understood.

Chapter Twenty-Five

The head of the broom whisked back and forth over the wooden floorboards, pushing thin lines of dust into a solid pile that Estella then bent to gather up in her dustpan. She tossed the dust outside and went back in to work on the next room. A stirring against her chest interrupted her before she could continue, Cody making little disturbed movements as the outside cold touched his skin.

"Hush, dear." Estella soothed him and made sure he was tucked more securely in the sling.

Sweeping was not one of her favorite household tasks, though an important one in winter when all the windows stayed shut, and the doors were only opened when necessary. The lack of air movement allowed small amounts of dirt to settle. Soot from the fireplace, ashes from the kitchen stove, and all manner of small crumbs and minor messes accumulated into a filmy layer of grime. Getting rid of it led to feeling less stifled inside, more comfortable.

Even if she and Cody wouldn't be staying in the house for much longer, Christopher deserved to be comfortable.

She wondered when the last time was that he tidied up his room. It was the only place in the house she hadn't been yet, respecting his privacy. Now, she thought that she might as well go in. What state must it be in after three years? Perhaps even worse than the rest of the house had been? She would clean it and make his living space a good one so that he might have a refuge when she was gone and could clean nothing else.

"Let's go find out, shall we?" Estella murmured down to Cody.

She brought her broom with her to his door. Standing there before it, she had the sense she was about to do something she really shouldn't. She wasn't anything to him, just a housemate who had come along at a terrible time.

Even so....

No matter what he felt, she knew her own feelings, and she would not be happy to think of him languishing in a dirty bedroom.

Estella pushed the door open and stepped inside.

What reached her senses first was the smell, a lingering musky odor of animals and the sweat of hard work. It wasn't a terribly offensive odor, simply the smell of a room lived in. She could also detect a soapy sweetness, likely from the crisp, laundered sheets on the bed. She recognized those simple tan sheets, had washed them herself not so long ago. He had changed them on his own, then.

Estella took a closer look at the room around her and was surprised at the lack of dust and clutter. Every surface was clear, only a faint scum of dust gathered in the corners and hard-to-reach places that women noticed and men did not.

It was clear that this was a sort of sanctuary for him and equally as clear that she did not need to be in there.

She turned to leave and ran right into Christopher's chest, a solid, broad wall of muscle. She jumped back, deeper into his room than she had originally gone. She wasn't all that nervous to have been caught, just surprised. What could he do or say that would matter when she was leaving soon anyway?

Chris swiveled around her and into the room, and she edged away, back to the hall. The swap was so swift and efficient that she had to blink away a rush of dizziness.

"You don't got no business bein' in my room," Christopher said. His brow was furrowed.

"I'm sorry," she said softly, knowing he was right. "I just thought to clean. I see it wasn't needed."

He crossed his arms and stared down at her. "How would you like it if I went into your room?"

She swallowed hard, her shoulders slumping. "Well...I suppose that you'd have the right, this bein' your house."

Christopher sighed and dropped his arms from his chest. "Why you got to be makin' sense? I wanted to argue with you."

She laughed slightly. "We'll argue plenty more, I'm sure."

He wasn't laughing or smiling. The line of his mouth was a grim slash, a ravine that cleaved the earth in two. "I know you're upset with me. I'm sorry, Estella."

Her laughter dropped away, and she put her hand on his arm, feeling his warm skin. "What are you sorry for? What's this about?"

"I just...." He looked away and pushed at his sandy-brown hair. "I can't protect you and Cody. Like I couldn't protect my family before. I don't deserve nothin' good in this life."

Her heart went out to him, and she held his arm in both of her hands, looking up at him. She swallowed hard and spoke his name, calling to him, wishing she could reach him before he fell completely away into the darkness that haunted his mind.

"Chris, you didn't know there was anythin' to protect them against. You *must* forgive yourself. Please. There was nothin' you could have done. You couldn't have known."

How he must have laid awake so many times, even now, running over the events of that day that were permanently burned into his mind, examining each action like a boy lifting up rocks to find the pale insects hiding beneath. He was desperate to punish himself in the aftermath of the tragedy, to find some meaning in the meaninglessness of it all. Had there been anything amiss with the stove in the days prior? Had the fireplace needed cleaning but was neglected? Were there any lamps with cracked glass, candles positioned too close to the edges of their surfaces, from which they could easily be knocked?

She knew that he had never found a real reason to blame himself. Because she had done the same with her parents' death and then much more recently with Ada's death. Had her cousin shown any specific signs of illness or weakness that could have necessitated an extra visit to the doctor? If Estella had made her lie down sooner or had her push sooner....

But there was nothing she or Christopher could ever have done. These events happened all the time, the lightning strikes of life that came and went and left everyone stumbling and blind in the aftermath.

"I can't forgive myself," Christopher choked out. His dark eyes glistened with tears, gallons of them unshed.

Estella gently lifted her hands from his arm to his shoulders, then held his face. His chin was between her palms, her fingers upon his cheeks. His wet, wet eyes fell on hers. He was not blinking, afraid that would make the tears come falling.

This is the moment that will make all the difference.

Estella looked into his eyes and opened herself to him, letting him see that she was telling the truth to him. "You

215

deserve happiness. I believe that Cody and I could make you happy, if you would let us be with you. You're a good man. You would be a good father to him. A good companion to me. I know it."

He blinked, and two tears tracked down his cheeks, reaching her hand and running between them. He choked out a wordless breath.

She smiled at him and tilted her head. Waiting, giving him all the time that he needed. It didn't matter what he said. She had already accepted it. She had made her peace. Her heart was there for him. He could take it or leave it, whatever he so desired.

From Estella's bedroom, Cody let out such a scream, a caterwaul rivaling a mountain lion's furious call. Immediately following the cry was a crash, the musical shattering of glass.

Christopher grabbed Estella's wrists tight, squeezing until her bones groaned. "Where is he?" he shouted.

"In my room!"

He lunged past her, and he clearly must have expected her to stay where she was. She leaped after him, her heart pounding so hard her whole body throbbed with it.

Christopher jerked open the door to her room. He stopped and stood there, staring.

Estella ran into him and cried out, then shoved past his solid body to see inside, to see what had happened to Cody.

Chapter Twenty-Six

Christopher stared into Estella's room. He knew it would naturally be a neat and tidy space, though he had not been there since she arrived.

What he saw was neither neat nor tidy.

It was a sight burned into his mind forever, a brand of memory, not because it was so outwardly terrible but because it was a sign of something even more awful that had almost occurred.

Cody lay on his back in the middle of the room, some distance from his cradle. He was screaming, surrounded by the glittering, shattered remnants of a broken vase.

The window in the room was wide open, gusts of wind like knives pouring in. Snowflakes blew in on the jabs of wind, landing on the baby's delicate skin.

Estella shoved ahead of Christopher and ran to Cody, crunching through the shattered glass of the vase. She seemed to care nothing for the danger, dropping to her knees to snatch up the baby. Christopher rushed to her side as she examined Cody all over.

"He's okay," she gasped out, then buried her face against the baby and sobbed.

Christopher hurried to the window and stared out into the swirling snow, his face stinging. There was no sign of anyone, though the deepening shadows as the sun sank down and the snow made deciphering any details a near impossibility.

His eyes wandered downward. A trail of bootprints marked the snow just below the window and went off into the distance.

He swore aloud, not caring there was a woman in his presence to overhear him say such things. Turning back, he went to Estella and grabbed her arm. She lifted her head, her face streaked with tears.

"Was it an animal?" she whispered.

"You *know* this weren't no animal! The window's open, not broken!" He was shaking all over. "This is why you got to leave. I should never have agreed to the fair, to anythin'. Otis Ryder is doin' his dirty tricks. He's after you and Cody, to hurt me, make me give up to him. I can't have you in danger because of me."

Estella sobbed and rocked Cody against her. "I'm so sorry."

"Hellfire! It ain't your fault! It's mine!" He was breathing hard, his chest burning. "I should have known better! You were talkin' about things that I couldn't have helped, but I can help this. You got to get out of here, you and Cody. Immediately. You got to get out of harm's way."

Estella nodded rapidly, strands of hair coming loose and shaking around her face. "Dawn tomorrow, I'll look for another place to stay. I'm.... Christopher, I.... Everythin' I said.... This doesn't change my feelin's. I still mean it all."

He looked down at her, so pretty and kind, her eyes so large and blue. His heart quivered. He nearly wept. Somehow, he kept from fully breaking down, perhaps by the grace of the need to move.

"You go up into the attic," he said. "Bar the door. You don't come down until you hear me again." He paused, then added, "Only open up the door if you hear me say a certain word. Candle."

Estella nodded rapidly, picking up on what he was saying, thankfully. "What if...what if there's danger, an' you need to warn me without givin' it away?"

You are much too clever, Estella.

"If there's danger...I'll ask for you to come down with Matthew." He smiled slightly. He doubted that Otis or Nate had bothered to learn the name of the baby.

Estella nodded again and reached for his hand, squeezing to show her understanding. If she heard him call out for her and Matthew instead of saying the other word that meant they were safe, she would understand there was danger and do what she could to get away. There was a window in the attic that she might be able to escape from. Otherwise, she would have to hide.

Christopher grabbed her and pulled her in against him, squeezing her tight. He felt her small, soft body against his and smelled the sweetness of her hair. He could have stayed like that forever.

But there was no time.

He pushed away from her and went to grab his coat, a lantern, and his gun. Not the pistol, but his shotgun.

He left the house and went straight to the stable to grab one of the horses in good condition, then rode back to the side of the house Estella's bedroom window opened to. Holding the lantern up high, with the shotgun across his lap, he followed the footprints away from the house and in the direction of the road.

The trail of bootprints quickly became hoofprints, and the prospective thief got back on his horse. Those were more difficult to follow, and then he lost sight of them entirely, the ground too disturbed by his own people and animals to pick out a single set.

"Guess we got to do this the difficult way, ain't we?" he muttered.

He pressed into the horse's flanks with his knees, urging them up to a gallop. At the road, he turned toward town, racing through the whiteness, the dark of nightfall to either side. In the distance, amidst the snow and shadows, small amber lights burned, the only signs of life amidst the harsh winter stillness.

Reaching town, he hardly slowed, cutting across the street and urging his horse through an alleyway she barely fit into, scraping his knees on the building walls on either side. They burst out on the other side, and the sheriff's office was right ahead, with the jailhouse attached to the side like a needy child.

Christopher threw himself to the ground and rushed into the office, slamming the door open with his shoulder.

Abe was on his feet in an instant, jumping up from his desk with his pistol in hand. He swore upon seeing Christopher. "What in the heck are you doin'? Bustin' in here like that? I could've sworn I was about to be attacked by a bear!"

Christopher strode toward the sheriff, who looked at his shotgun and then up at his face.

"You ain't goin' to do somethin' you'll regret, are you, Chris?"

"I might unless you come with me," Christopher growled.

"And where are you thinkin' about headin'?"

"To give Ryder a visit."

Abe's eyes grew wide with alarm, and he reached out. "Now, you hold on. You're meant to let me take care of all this business with Otis Ryder. What are you headed there for?"

"I just had someone break into my house and try to steal Estella's baby!" Christopher shouted. "There's only one person I can think of who would stoop so low, who has reason to do somethin' like that!"

Abe's brows lowered, his eyes going dark. "Alright. I see how serious this is. You can come along with me, but Chris, I swear, you best keep your head and don't do anythin' that you will regret. My job is to keep the peace, and that includes makin' sure my friends are followin' the law."

Christopher nodded, although he really didn't know if it was going to be possible for him to hold back once he saw Otis's smug face. This was just all too much, and it had gone on far too long and reached a place it never should have.

He just wanted this to be over.

Chapter Twenty-Seven

Night had well and truly arrived by the time they reached Otis's large house, located out a mile from town and nestled back in some hills. The moon was up, bright and near to fullness, casting long and jagged shadows over the silver expanses of snow.

Abe rode ahead on his huge black stallion, his back straight and tall. Christopher kept as close behind him as he could, his rifle across his lap. His teeth were clenched so hard that his jaw was aching. Every muscle he had was so stiff that he was going to be sore for days after this. The pain would be worth it if they could solve this right here and now.

Amber light glowed from the many windows in Otis's house, as if burning from inside there.

Abe slowed a short distance from the house and spoke, his voice snatched at by the teasing, taunting wind. "You'll listen to what I say now, or I'll send you on back home like a disobedient child. You understand me, Chris?"

Christopher grunted his acknowledgment.

Abe twisted around in the saddle and glared at him. The bright lights from behind cast his face in a blanket of shadow. Only the harsh twinkling of his eyes, like diamonds in the rough, was truly visible.

"You will let me do all the talkin'. And you will leave that gun out here with your horse."

"Abe—"

Abe snapped his fingers, and Christopher fell begrudgingly silent. "I can't take the risk of you decidin' you'll take justice into your own hands. You don't want to end this night by bein' thrown into the hoosegow. So, you'll leave that shotgun outside and let me talk."

"Fine," Christopher spat. "Let's just get this done."

Abe nodded and dismounted, and Christopher did as well. They tied up their horses close to the house where the huge walls could provide some shelter.

Christopher propped his shotgun up against the wall. He stared at it there, like it was a sign of abandonment. But if this was what he had to do, he was abandoning nothing. He was instead doing his best to see his goal through to the end.

Abe led the way up to the huge front porch, which wrapped around the front and one side of the place. He motioned for Christopher to stand back, then slammed his fist on the heavy, solid oak door.

"It's Sheriff Hudson," he yelled and pounded the door again. "Open up."

The knocking seemed to echo deeply into the house, showing just how truly large it was. Christopher crossed his arms over his chest as they waited, shifting from one foot to the other to combat the cold. It seemed very wrong to him that a single man could have the wealth to build such a place, a mansion fit for one of those British lords, while the sheriff had to do with a small, cramped office. Shouldn't Otis's money be put to a better use than buying tons of land and expensive items?

Abe lifted his fist to pound the door again.

It opened just before he could.

A thin, well-dressed boy blinked up at them, his hair slicked with grease. "Hello," he said, and his accent was decidedly not from the area. "What have you come visiting for?"

Abe stared down at the waif of a boy pretending to be a man. "I'm the sheriff. I need to see Otis Ryder."

"Mr. Ryder isn't currently seeing visitors at such a late hour," the boy said. "You'll have to come back tomorrow."

From some unseen room in the house came a burst of laughter.

Abe stared past the boy, his mustache twitching. "No visitors, huh? Might need to go and see about that for myself."

"Sir...."

Otis's smooth voice came from a side room. "It's alright, Jacque. I'll see them."

The boy bowed and backed away.

Otis stepped out into the large entrance hallway that Christopher hadn't even been paying any attention to until right then. Its large size, height, and abundance of mirrors all felt very pointless to him. And how could the carpet look so full and thick, as if hardly walked upon? Was it newly installed?

Only an extremely rich man would bother with replacing his carpets.

"I apologize for the boy," Otis said with a lazy chuckle that made Christopher want to grab his throat and throttle him. "Impudent, ain't he? He's from Europe, and they raise them different over there."

"I don't care where you get your servants from," Abe grunted. He stepped up to the door. "I'd like to come inside and talk with you about somethin' very important, Otis."

Otis held out his arm, barring Abe from entering. He spoke low, flicking his eyes from Abe to Christopher. "I apologize, but I don't think that I'll be allowin' that to happen. Not while you have Baldwin here. He'll only cause me trouble, and it's much too late for that. I only deal with troublemakers when the sun is up."

He's keepin' us out here in the cold because he can. He knows that Abe can't force his way in without repercussions.

Christopher tried to prevent himself from shivering, showing even any bit of weakness in front of this criminal.

"Are you going to tell me why you're here, Sheriff?" Otis prompted.

Abe let out a low growl. "Alright. Have it your way. But don't think I won't remember that you left your poor old sheriff out in the cold when he done come all this way."

Otis just smiled and clasped his hands in front of himself.

"You got an alibi for where you done been today?" Abe asked.

Otis raised his eyebrows. "I've been home all day. Didn't even visit any of my mines. Been havin' a party today, you see. So, yes, I have an alibi. There have been dozens of people who have come to my house today and seen me here. Why are you askin'?"

Abe gestured to Christopher. "He has been havin' intruders on his land. Just tonight, he had someone break into his house and try to take away somethin' valuable. The window

225

in the room was left open, so don't try to say it were an animal."

Otis made his eyes wide with a false, glassy sympathy. "And what was the item of value? How can you tell someone tried to take it?"

Christopher jabbed his finger at Otis. "You *know* I got Estella and her baby stayin' out at my place. Someone came in and grabbed the baby! They would have done got away with it if the baby hadn't screamed. Guess he didn't like the ugly face of whoever grabbed him."

"Maybe you shouldn't have an unmarried woman and her child on your property," Otis said, his voice a smooth hiss. "It isn't a good thing to have other people livin' there when you're so close to havin' the bank take it away."

Christopher's vision glazed over with red. He couldn't breathe, he was so filled with pure fire. If he had been able to speak, he had the strongest of words lined up for Otis, never mind that the sheriff was shooting a glare his way for having spoken when he wasn't supposed to say anything.

Abe turned back to Otis. "You don't mind givin' me the names of some of the people who have visited with you today? And what about Nate Bolger? Where's he been at?"

As if speaking his name was a summons, Nate strode into view some distance down the hallway from the direction of all the laughter and happy, celebratory voices. He walked up behind Otis, hands in his pockets. He had a gun holster on his belt in spite of supposedly partaking in the light, party atmosphere.

Nate looked at Christopher, and his lips moved to form the slightest, most smug, and self-assured grin any man had ever worn.

Christopher's control snapped, the tenuous, worn threads coming all apart. He ran past Abe and grabbed Nate.

Nate knocked his hand away and stepped back, his pistol snapping up in the air between them.

"Stop!" Abe shouted and put himself between them. "Bolger! Chris! Both of you, take a pace back."

Breathing hard and shaking, Christopher couldn't move. If he did, he knew he would be jumping forward at Nate again.

Nate also didn't move, his gun hand as steady as stone.

Abe spat on the ground. "Otis, where has Nate been all day?"

"Right here with me." Otis suddenly laughed. "He's my pet dog. Isn't that what people say about him? I keep him close. There isn't any way that he could have done what you're clearly accusin' him of. There's dozens who have seen him around all day, too."

Otis made a gesture, and Nate lowered his pistol and walked away. Christopher took a step forward, aching to jump at him.

Abe grabbed his arm and gave him such a harsh glare that he knew he had pushed his luck as far as it would stretch. "Thank you for lettin' us talk with you," Abe said, his voice tight. "I hope I don't have to make any further visits to you. Enjoy your party."

Otis nodded. "I hope not to see you here again, too. As for you, Baldwin...." Otis thumped his fist into his open palm. "You are not allowed on my property again. And I best not see you at *any* of my properties or near my mines. You even set a foot on my land, and you'll regret it."

"Same goes for you and your dog," Christopher snarled, feeling much like a rabid dog himself.

Otis shut the door, putting an end to the talk.

Abe tugged on Christopher's arm, and they went back to their horses. When they were mounted, Abe moved his stallion in close and whacked Christopher upside the back of his head. "You and your temper! If Bolger charges you with assault, I'm goin' to have to side with him."

"Bolger don't talk," Christopher said.

"Otis would do it for him, and I'd still have to take it seriously." Abe flicked his reins and rode off back toward town.

Christopher did the same, quickly catching up to Abe. "You understand why I'm all upset?" he demanded to know. "I keep comin' to you for help, and you ain't helpin'!"

"Chris, there ain't any proof!" Abe yelled. His horse sidled sideways, unsettled by all the arguing. Abe got him back on track after a moment. "You just need to shut up and wait. I've got my eye on this. I'll nail Otis and Bolger as soon as one of them slips up. I just have to catch them in the act. Understand? If I arrested every person that was ever accused of a wrongdoing without proof, I'd have the whole darned town in my jail."

"It's just that time is gettin' real short," Christopher said.

"It will happen," Abe reassured him. "You just got to wait."

Christopher sat back in the saddle and watched the sheriff riding ahead of him. He really was beginning to think that they would never properly catch Otis. Time was going to run out...for Christopher.

Chapter Twenty-Eight

Estella stood at the window, watching ranch hands crawling all over the snowy land out there like ants on a pile of sugar. Many of them were not doing any actual work. Christopher hadn't told her exactly what they were doing, but she was pretty sure they were on patrol, keeping an eye out for any sign of trespassers.

She was meant to have gone to town to see about finding a new place to stay. However, after she had already gotten dressed and was ready to head out, Christopher had come to her and suddenly forbade it, telling her that she would not be going anywhere without his supervision...and that he could not accompany her that day, being too busy. He had seemed as upset about it as she had, but there was no way around it.

Estella turned away from the window before any of those men out there could catch her staring and potentially get the wrong idea. She went into the kitchen and looked around for the ingredients to make up a big batch of biscuits. Everyone out there was going to get hungry, and she wanted to be able to feed them all. No one had asked her to do that, but no one needed to ask her.

As she was mixing flour, salt, and butter all together in a bowl, using her fingers to integrate the pieces of butter with the dry ingredients, she heard someone knocking on the door.

Expecting it was probably a ranch hand needing a drink of water or coffee, she grabbed a towel and wiped at her floury hands while going to the door.

"Yes?" she asked, opening it.

Of all the people she expected to see, Clementine had not been one of them.

Clementine threw her arms around Estella and hugged her tightly. She drew back, still holding onto Estella's shoulders. "Mother and I thought we would be seeing you today for some final preparations, considering that the fair is tomorrow. I came to check on you and see if I could help with anythin'."

Estella looked at her friend's kind face and felt all of her worries and concerns come crashing to the surface, pushing her right to her limit and then overtaking her. The intruder. Almost losing Cody. The fair and all the last-minute preparations she still needed to make.

It was all too much.

Estella leaned into her friend and began to sob, choking on her breaths as tears slid hot down her face. "Oh, Clem," she cried. "I'm tryin' so hard, and nothin' is right."

Clementine made a surprised sound and hugged her tighter. "What is it?" she asked softly. "What's gone wrong?"

Estella shook her head, unable to speak anything more than she already had. There was nothing else that she could say, and she didn't feel like going over everything out loud. Talking of it wouldn't help, and she was tired of trying, tired of everything.

"Come over here with me." Clementine pulled at her, and Estella followed her, dragging her tired feet on the floor. They sat on a couch in the parlor, and Clementine put an arm over her shoulders. Estella leaned on her again and covered her face with the floury towel, her tears soaking into it.

Clementine stroked her arm and smoothed her hair, petting her like she was a frightened horse. "It's alright, Estella. Really, it will all be alright."

"It won't," Estella sobbed, muffled, into the towel. "I feel like I'm goin' to fall apart."

Clementine laughed softly, surprising her. "You're a *tailor*. You know that when things fall apart, we can stitch 'em back together."

Estella dabbed at her burning eyes. "Some things can't be fixed like that."

"Then we take the scraps and make somethin' new of it." Clementine kept petting her hair. "Why don't you tell me what's got you so out of sorts, and we'll see what we can make of it?"

Estella wiped her eyes again, the rough towel abrading the sensitive skin of her lids. She leaned her head back against Clementine's arm. "There was an intruder. Christopher and I were talkin', and we heard a crash. Someone came into the house and almost stole Cody!" Her voice rose, her breath hiccupping. "They would have gotten away with him if they hadn't broken a vase and fled the scene. I-I can't even spend another second thinkin' about it, or I'll be sick."

"My goodness!" Clementine gripped her arm, her strong seamstress fingers digging in painfully. Her face paled.

Estella twisted the towel up in her fingers. "But I can't stop thinkin' about it. All I see when I close my eyes is that baby on the floor."

"Where is he now?"

"In his cradle. We moved it to the hallway where there aren't any windows directly nearby."

"You poor dear. I can't imagine you've been restin' well after that," Clementine said.

"I haven't. And with the fair comin' up tomorrow and there bein' so much still to do...." She had the towel in a knot by this point. "I can feel it all comin' apart, and I can't hold it together. What am I supposed to do, Clem?"

Clementine was quiet, and in the silence, Estella's heart was sinking. There wasn't anything that could be done, and it was terrible of her to put any responsibility of thinking up a solution onto her friend.

"I'm sorry." Estella started to stand. She'd send Clementine back to town where she wouldn't have to be around all this sadness and confusion.

Clementine grabbed her wrist and hauled her back down. Estella let out a yelp as her rump hit the seat, and she twisted to give Clementine a puzzled look. She didn't understand why or how her friend was smiling at her right then.

"You at least should listen to my idea. It's only polite." Clementine continued to smile. "Why don't you come and stay with me and Mother? You would be safer, wouldn't you? With all of us in the middle of town and watchin' Cody, there's no way that any intruder would ever get to him."

Estella couldn't even speak for a moment, too many protests slamming their way up her throat. "I couldn't!" she managed, one weak little objection making its way through. "I couldn't impose on you."

Clementine gave her a look and kept speaking. "My mother, you know she's a busybody. Not only does she know everyone in Ranger's Peak, but she also knows everyone in all the nearby towns. She's got a friend, a very talented baker, who lives over in Bulltooth. They exchange letters. Last Mother heard, there's a job opening for a woman with sewing talents. They've got an orphanage there and some mines, and we know how rough men and children are with their clothes. There'd be lodging provided."

"I.... How far away is Bulltooth?" Estella bit the inside of her cheek.

"About a day's ride."

Estella sighed. Clementine looked so hopeful. She would hate to crush her spirits with protests, except this wasn't something she could just blindly agree to go along with. "How long ago did Vera get that letter? It sounds like a good job. Surely, it must already be taken."

Clementine held up her hand to stop her, and Estella paused, eyebrows raised. "Bulltooth doesn't even have a local tailor, last I heard. They've got lots of mining men and destitute folks, and not much of anyone with real skills like yours. I can ask Mother to write her friend and ask after that job. If it's still available, you should take it. It would be a lot of work, but steady work. And with lodging provided? You know you can't turn away from this chance."

Estella continued to bite at the inside of her cheek until pain and the tang of blood made her stop.

"You could establish yourself there, start up a tailoring business. And with no competition?" Clementine's eyes shone. "I meant to tell you about all this after the Christmas Fair so you wouldn't feel overwhelmed, but it's all out in the open now. I think you have to try at this. What other choice is there?"

"I don't want to get my hopes up if the job is already gone...." Estella frowned. And if the job was still available? She'd be a fool not to take it. She needed work and a place to live, and this opportunity was right here in front of her. It would be like having a prayer answered...if things turned out alright, which they often did not.

"So, I'll have Mother write her friend, and we'll get word soon. And you and Cody will come stay with us in the meantime." Clementine said this as if it had already been agreed upon, and at this point, Estella was too tired to argue with it, even if she didn't agree. Any arguing would have to wait until after the Christmas Fair when her mind was less full.

"I'm sure Mother wouldn't mind comin' to pick you up with our wagon, even," Clementine continued. "So you wouldn't have to ride or walk to town with your belongings and a baby."

Everything you say just adds to how much I'm going to be inconveniencing you.

Clementine stood, and Estella looked up at her. "I know this is a lot, and it's too much, so we won't talk about it any longer. At least I know now why you haven't come to town. Why don't you give me anything you still need to take care of in town, and Mother and I will get it done for you? Then you can focus on everythin' here."

Guilt at having to depend so much on her friend and pure, sweet relief at having her responsibilities lessened mingled uneasily in Estella's chest. It felt like a cat chasing a dog, neither happy with the presence of the other.

"We're goin' to do it anyway. I'm just bein' polite by askin' about it first." Clementine's lips curved in that bright smile she was famous for—the smile that Jackson must have started falling for.

Estella gave in and went along with it, knowing her cooperation would make things easier for the seamstresses. She gave Clementine a list of the last-minute things to do in town, as well as the signs that would need to be put up early the next morning.

Having gotten her way, Clementine took everything to the front door and prepared to leave. Estella hugged her arms around herself, her heart thumping unsteadily in her chest.

Clementine turned to her and held out her arms, and Estella went to her. They embraced, and Clementine brushed something from Estella's cheek with her thumb, perhaps a smidge of flour.

"I'll see you tomorrow," Clementine said and kissed her on her now-clean cheek. "I better see you enjoyin' yourself, or I'll make it my responsibility to cheer you up."

Estella returned the cheek kiss. She almost didn't dare to say the one last thought about all of this that was in her head. She forced the words out, feeling them rip from her like fabric catching on thorns. "You know that if I accept this job in Bulltooth, we won't see each other much."

Clementine nodded. She swallowed and looked off to the side, blinking rapidly. "We can write letters and make visits. I'll be fine as long as you're happy."

"Oh, Clem," Estella whispered.

Again, she experienced relief, and this time, it was without any guilt accompanying it. What a true and selfless friend Clementine was, thinking of her and not herself. She would do the best she could and make her proud of her.

She gave Clementine another hug, longer and tighter than the one prior. "You are so very special."

"As are you." Clementine drew back, a shimmer of tears in her eyes in spite of all her blinking. "See you tomorrow."

Estella opened the door and helped her out. She didn't stay to see her go off, withdrawing into the house again to avoid the prying eyes of the patrolling ranch hands. Turning to lean back against the closed door, feeling the cold clawing at the wood, she closed her sore and tired eyes. More tears leaked out, trickling down her cheeks.

She could no longer imagine why she had been so excited about all this. She didn't even care about Christmas.

She just wanted this to be over.

Chapter Twenty-Nine

Estella stood outside, looking up at the pale gray sky. Pink still stained the very farthest edges of the clouds, a reminder of the dawn so recently passed. She could hardly believe the day was still so new when she had been up for so long and done so much already.

She could hardly believe she had reached a point like this where there wasn't anything for her to do, a temporary reprieve from all the bustle and chaos that had consumed her for hours prior.

She had arisen in the dark to fashion a quick, cold breakfast for herself and Christopher, leftover oats from the previous day and biscuits with cheese and apple slices. She had made herself eat every bite, even though she was too nervous to want any of it, knowing she would need the strength.

When breakfast ended, Christopher left wordlessly to tend to all the chores, and Estella busied herself with making several batches of coffee, storing the liquid in different containers to be reheated as needed. She also threw together some of her mother's spiced raisin cookies and had only started to bake the first tray when she heard wagons coming, wheels crunching through snow.

The wagons brought the first vendors, and she directed them to the chosen field to set up their stall. She had mapped out approximately how the stalls should be arranged to leave plenty of room for the crowds to move around.

More wagons had come swiftly after that, and she was so busy showing them around that she nearly burned the cookies. Another batch of cookies went in to bake, and she was back outside, sticky dough and cinnamon freezing to her apron as she continued to help everyone get in place.

There were expected disturbances during the setting up, broken stalls and forgotten supplies. She had thought of and prepared for as many of those eventualities as she could, and what she could not provide, the other vendors assisted with. There was a sense of community filling the ranch that had not been there before during the whole of Estella's stay, everyone working together, lending their neighbors a helping hand and trading stories all the while. Shouts and laughter rang out under the dark sky.

Then, as dawn broke, the first of the guests had arrived. Now, the ranch was filled to bursting with townspeople, clusters of folks she barely knew gathered around the different stalls with droves of children running all through the gaps. With the stalls all set up—except for some stragglers that she had been reassured were always late—and the guests able to see where to go, she could just stand there and breathe for a bit.

Through it all, Cody had been with her, snug in a blanket inside his sling. The constant pressure of his little body against hers, his gentle warmth, was a blessed and much-needed reminder of why she was doing all of this. Everything was for him. If she hadn't managed to get this Christmas Fair going, the bank would almost certainly have found a way to kick Christopher off the land prematurely, and then none of them would have a place to stay. Instead of standing at the edge of celebration, they would be freezing on the roadside, starving, begging.

Estella heard a horse approaching from behind her, the distinctive rumbling breaths. She turned and saw that it was not a horse at all. Almost, but the face was strangely shaped, the ears much larger.

A mule.

The mule was dappled gray all over and had a rounder stomach than she would have expected a working animal to have. Her eyes wandered up to the rider, curious.

The rider pushed his hood back, and she saw John James, the bank manager, peering down at her, his chubby cheeks and the tip of his nose nipped red by the cold. He regarded her with his small eyes, his mouth pressed thin.

"Christopher's assistant," he said. "Or rather, the true organizer of all this, isn't that right?"

Estella regarded the small, round man and tilted her head. She was not afraid of him. Really, what she felt was bordering upon pity. He was so bound to Otis that he likely did not have much in the way of free will. That he was here at all might have been strange if it wasn't obvious that he was there to spy.

"Mr. James," Estella said. "I didn't expect to be seein' you here."

"I grew curious, is all." He looked off at the crowd, and the thin line of his mouth eased somewhat. "You have made more of this than I ever expected. So many folks from town are here already, and still so many to come, I'm sure."

"It's a success," Estella replied and felt pride in herself stirring.

"I didn't expect it would be. But...you are right." John looked down at her, and she wondered if he was smiling. She couldn't quite tell *what* that strange expression on his face was. "It's good weather for it, too."

She nodded her agreement. The only snow in the air was what blew on the winds. The drifts and mounds covering the ground were being trampled to slush, the passing of many people and horses creating trails small and large.

"I suppose I'll leave you to it," John said and picked up his reins.

"Wait." Estella didn't want him to go, not yet. Even stuffy bankers deserved to enjoy the holiday. "You should stay awhile. There's coffee and cookies in the house. Some other treats, too. Since you came all this way, shouldn't you make it worthwhile?"

John gave a brief chuckle, no more than a single gust of breath. "It's worthwhile enough to know that everything is going well. But...do you make a strong cup of coffee?"

Estella smiled. "I do. And there's plenty. Just heat it up a minute or two on the stove."

He nodded and turned his mule toward the house. "Thank you. Take care."

Estella patted Cody through the sling as she watched the banker ride off to the house. He didn't strike her as a bad man, not really. Maybe it was Otis's influence over him that had turned him sour.

She decided it was time to go into the crowd and see how things were progressing. She waded in amongst all the other people and went to each stall to check on the sellers. The bakers and chestnut roasters had very long lines before them, and a group of women and children stood around a carver as he used quick flicks of his knife to fashion toys from blocks of wood. Estella paused to watch for a short time as he finished carving a small rabbit. He handed it off to a little girl and half of the children clustered around her to admire it while the rest pressed in on the man and made requests for what he should make next.

The carver glanced up and caught Estella's eye. He smiled. "Like bein' surrounded by a pack of ki-yotes."

She laughed. "Do they bother you?"

Overhearing the conversation, the children looked at the man, eyes wide and anxious as they awaited his answer. And he just laughed, picked up another block of wood, and began to carve again. "No, ma'am. It's my favorite time of year."

"Estella!"

Estella whirled as a blur of red fabric and blonde hair swept in her direction. Clementine hugged her tightly.

"Clem!" Estella hugged her back and noticed Jackson lingering a short distance away, very obviously pretending not to be watching them. She leaned back and looked in her friend's clear blue eyes. "I know we saw each other earlier when you first arrived, but it feels like years ago. How's the stall?"

Clementine laughed. "You wouldn't believe how many scarves and gloves we've sold. But that doesn't matter to me. This fair that you've put together, it's wonderful. Everyone keeps saying so."

"Do they really?" Estella asked, smiling.

She looked around and saw all the smiling faces as families went about shopping, almost everyone with a cookie or piece of fudge in hand and a steaming drink, if not holding food. Every stall had pine branches attached, with little ornaments and fabric bows dangling from between the needles. Children kept reaching up to touch the shiny ornaments with their small, curious fingers.

"Yes," Estella said after a moment. "It *is* wonderful, isn't it?"

Clementine bounced on her toes and laughed again. "Yes. Take all of the credit for it! It was your idea, and you're the one who executed it. I've been telling everyone that that's the truth if I hear them give Christopher any glory for it. I ask them if they have even seen him yet, and the answer is always no. But who do they see? You!"

"But it's his ranch. It couldn't be done without his generosity. He deserves some acknowledgment," Estella insisted.

A tug on her arm made her turn toward the sheriff. His cheeks were pink, and not just from snow. She could smell the alcohol-laced cider on his breath as he leaned in. "I don't know how you managed to do all of this on your own."

"I had help," she said. "And everyone worked together to make it happen. I think people want their Christmas to feel normal. It didn't have much to do with me. I just got it started."

Abe snorted. "Gettin' started is the hardest part. Glad to have you around. This town could use more folks like you."

Estella blinked away tears as her heart cracked like a dropped vase. Oh, if only she could stay. If only things were meant to turn out that way.

"I should get back to Mother," Clementine said, squeezing Estella's hand. "I only snuck away to talk with you a moment. You must stop by in a little while."

Estella promised that she would, and Clementine walked away, where Jackson met her and hooked his arm through hers. Their heads were close together as they moved into the crowd and were swallowed by it.

If only that could be me and Chris.

If only. She kept thinking that, and every time, the shattered pieces of her heart rubbed together and made the pain even worse. She couldn't risk getting caught up in sadness when she might be needed at any moment to solve a problem. Gathering up her broken bits, she forced them to hold together just a little longer while she continued to tend to her responsibilities. That was always the most effective way for her to work through her feelings: to stay busy.

Estella lifted her head, shook her head, and went to the table where an old retired lady was passing out cups of cider and liberally dosing the contents with alcohol upon request. Estella seemed to remember her name, Sara.

"Any budge in yours, honey?" the old lady asked when Estella picked up a cup for herself.

Estella hesitated. "I'm not much for drinkin', really."

"Oh, but Christmas is a time for doin' what we ain't normally do." Sara smiled and held out a bottle. "You been workin' so hard. Just a splash will keep you warm an' help you relax. You deserve that."

Estella didn't want to offend her and allowed what seemed to be much more than a splash to enter her cup. She sipped the hot liquid, the tang of apples mixing with cinnamon and clove spices. "Do you make this cider yourself?"

"I do, I do. But once per year. Oh, but I'm old now. My hands ain't work quite like they once did." Sara lifted hands as knobby and crooked as oak branches. "I always ask for help with preparin' the apples. Only ask people I trust with my recipe. Might be I'll ask you next year, dear, if you stick around."

Little did old Sara know she had picked up the shattered pieces of Estella's heart in her crooked hands and thrown them back onto the floor to break even further.

Estella turned away, clasping the hot cup of cider tightly. "I'm...I'm sure I would like that."

She moved on before she could hear anything else painful like that.

She was not successful.

As she moved through the crowd and spoke with everyone, from the sellers to the guests, it seemed they had all unanimously decided to echo the same sentiment to her. They were so glad she had made the Christmas Fair possible. They hoped she would stay in town and help to organize their Easter Fair come springtime.

One of the bakers gave her a gingerbread cookie decorated to look just like her, and the post office manager insisted upon sharing some of his freshly roasted chestnuts with her. The starchy burn of the hot nuts on her tongue meant she drank a lot from her cider. Without being able to taste the alcohol, she could still feel the warmth of it in her stomach.

The musicians were some of the last to arrive at the ranch, coming at almost noon. They brought with them bread, dried meats, cheese, and apples to feed anyone who hungered for something more substantial than cookies and fudge, so no one much cared about their lateness except for the old-timers. Those same old-timers were the first to gather around the improvised stage of hay bales and wooden planks, clapping and singing along as the guitars twanged and the horns made their brassy calls. Someone started to dance, an old gray midwife whose steely face cracked like an egg to reveal a smile as bright and timeless as the sun. Others joined her, couples twirling about in each other's arms.

The whole time, as the hours passed and the sun crossed the sky, Estella caught only infrequent glimpses of Christopher as he kept a watchful eye on the goings-on. She eventually figured out that he had others also patrolling, though they were getting drunk off whiskey and not taking their job nearly as seriously as he was. Every time she thought about going to him and asking him to relax for just a little while, he would disappear from her sight again.

Slowly, the children grew tired, at last running out of energy. The youngest ones went right to sleep where they stood, to be picked up and carried to their families' wagons to head home. Shouts of farewell suddenly mixed with the general chatter. Friends and family hugged before departing.

With the crowd depleting and sundown only an hour away, the vendors packed up their stalls to head home as well. Estella helped as much as she could. Most rejected her offers to assist, telling her to sit down and rest for once. Even Vera and Clementine wouldn't allow her to touch anything as they packed away the few items they hadn't managed to sell.

For all their lateness, the musicians seemed determined to say, continuing to play their instruments for the last determined dancers.

"Hey." Christopher strode over, hands on his hips. The line of his mouth wasn't stretched as severely as it had been while he was patrolling, and his jaw wasn't quite so clenched tight.

Estella smiled at him, glad he had come over to her at last, even if it was a little late. "Don't you think the day went wonderfully?" she prompted.

He nodded and dropped his arms down by his sides. "Yes, I do. I'm glad there weren't any incidents."

"So am I." Cody moved inside the sling, and Estella stroked him to soothe him. She would be glad to get him into his cradle and herself to bed soon. "I wish that you could have enjoyed it."

"There's still time." Vera moved to their side and held out her arms. "Why don't you two have yourselves a dance? I'll take Cody."

"Oh, no, I don't want to delay you gettin' home," Estella protested.

"Actually," Christopher interrupted, "I think it's a good idea. Estella, would you have a dance with me? Just one?"

She blinked in surprise that he was agreeing. Was he only doing it because he thought it would make her happy? Or did he really want to dance with her?

Vera made grabbing motions. "Let me cuddle that baby."

Estella wasn't sure what Christopher wanted, but she knew what she wanted for herself. She gently removed Cody from the sling and passed him over to Vera. Before the baby could even begin to fuss at the shock of cold on his delicate skin, Vera had him swaddled inside her coats to keep him warm.

Christopher held out his hand.

Estella swallowed hard and placed her hand in his. His fingers held her tightly, securely, as they walked over to where other couples were dancing.

He turned to face her and put his big hands on her shoulders. His dark eyes glistened. He didn't move.

Letting her take the lead.

She put her hands on his broad shoulders, feeling the muscles shuddering. He was afraid of what they were doing, and so was she because they shouldn't have been doing it. She couldn't stop herself now, her body moving on its own, taking a step to the side that he mimicked. Another step, and he moved with her, and she fell into the rhythm just like riding on a horse.

It was somehow natural to sway with his body so big and warm against hers. Surely, there had to be people looking at them: the widower and the out-of-towner, the man who had lost his family, and the woman with a baby not of her own blood. There had to be judgments, scorn, and perhaps even just plain confusion.

She wasn't feeling any of it, as if his body was shielding hers. Or it was more like they were making something together that shielded both of them.

She leaned into him, and he held her upright so easily, his form so strong and steady. Her eyes closed. Her shoes crunched in the snow slush as she turned so slowly in his arms, spiraling toward something they could never have.

She could never be his.

They could not be together. The situation was all wrong, and he could not accept her into his life when he was unable to forgive himself, anyway. And he did not know of the scars on her body, though he was so close to touching them. Surely, if he discovered that she was damaged, he wouldn't choose her anyway.

It was all for naught. It was all a dream on the verge of dissipating, breaking apart as all dreams did upon waking.

That didn't mean this was pointless, though. Even if he couldn't forgive himself now, maybe she had shown him a glimpse of what things could be like if he did. He might find another woman someday, a whole and beautiful and kind woman who would capture his heart and give him all he needed.

She hoped for that.

Christopher stopped dancing.

The interruption in their rhythm made her stumble. His body against hers prevented her from falling. She lifted her face to ask him what was wrong and saw him looking down at her, his eyes wide and so very soft, full of things she was afraid to recognize.

"Chris?" she whispered.

His head tipped slowly toward hers, his wide eyes beginning to close. She saw where his lips were aiming as he neared her, and even though she had just had all those thoughts about how they couldn't be together, her own eyes were closing, her face tilting up to meet his.

Just one kiss. She could take that. She would remember it forever, carry it with her always, this moment of bliss where she was on the cusp of believing a man could...love her.

Someone shouted out. Estella barely heard it, lost in the sensation of delicate warmth as Christopher's lips came so very close to hers. Then, there was a crash, and she leaped out of his arms with her heart pounding in her chest.

"What was that?" she cried.

Christopher reared up like a furious bear, lumbering in the direction of the crash and the shouts. Estella raced after him, clasping onto his hand.

What had happened now? she asked herself.

Why couldn't they even have a single moment to themselves without being interrupted by terrible events?

She had no proof that it was a terrible event yet, but her heart, her soul, knew the truth. No one would be shouting like this if a stall had just been knocked over by the wind.

Chapter Thirty

The last folks remaining at the fair fled the scene, grabbing at their loved ones as they went. A blur passed Christopher on his right, one of the musicians running faster than he had imagined a person could move, especially while toting a guitar case upon his back and holding the instrument itself against his chest.

Christopher's heart hammered in his broad chest, blood rushing in his head. He realized Estella was still holding his hand. He stopped and motioned for her to get back. She hesitated, staring into his eyes.

"Go!" His voice was a low growl, roughened by what she recognized as fear for her safety.

Her throat bobbed as she swallowed hard. Her fingers trailed away from his, and she ran back to where Vera and Clementine were just finishing with their packing. She nearly snatched the baby from Vera, pulling him in tight against her chest as if she couldn't bear to be apart from him for another second. Jackson was nearby, his hand on Clementine's shoulder.

Vera and Jackson will keep her safe.

Turning away, Christopher continued in the direction of the initial crashing and screaming. He rounded the corner of his barn and saw a mess in the snow. Two of the friendliest sellers were staring at the smashed remains of their stall. Broken pieces of wood were strewn all about in the snow. A box of leftover candied apples had been spilled, and the colorful treats were now covered in a mixture of wood splinters and mud.

Christopher grabbed the male vendor by the shoulder. "What happened here?" he demanded. He was shouting, making the other man flinch and blink rapidly. This was clearly no ordinary accident where the stall had been dropped while it was moved. It had been smashed into bits.

"We were attacked!" the other man managed. He wriggled out of Christopher's grasp and went to his wife, holding his arm around her as she wept in shock.

"Attacked by who?" Christopher demanded.

"What's goin' on here?" Abe's voice boomed as he approached the scene. His face was red, his breath reeking of alcohol. His eyes were clear, though, his manner stern and unable to be denied.

"Someone attacked us," the vendor repeated. "While we were headin' to our wagon to load up and go home."

"Who did it?" Christopher demanded again.

Abe stared at him. "You let me handle this now, Chris."

"It's my ranch," Christopher snapped back.

"I don't care who handles it!" the vendor exclaimed. "It was three men. I didn't see where they come from. Just they was suddenly here, knockin' everythin' onto the snow and smashin' it all. Then they was gone again."

Nearly a dozen wagons were exiting the ranch at the same time, as well as several riders on horseback, all jamming together on the path as everyone attempted to get out first. The ranch was all at once very quiet, with only a few stragglers lingering, namely Vera, Clementine, and Jackson, a short distance back. The silence in the aftermath of any event, accident or tragedy, was always the worst part, when the worst was over and treacherous thoughts entered the mind.

"I need you to take a deep breath here," Abe instructed, hands on his hips. "And tell me everythin' you can recall about these three who done attacked you."

"We didn't see them," the wife wept.

Her husband held her tight and stroked her arm. "Unfortunately, she's right. They came on so fast, and they was all in their winter layers, with hoods up. I could only tell they was menfolk, and that's all. Well, one of them was real tall, a head over the others."

"There really ain't nothin' else you can tell me?" Abe demanded. "Which way did they come from? Which way was they goin' when they left?"

The vendor said, "They came from behind this barn here, I think. Where they went, I don't know. They could have gone and blended with the crowd. Could be long gone by now."

Abe muttered a swear, which made the already upset woman gasp. He held up his hand. "Sorry for my words. I'm just wishin' I knew more. You folks should go on home. I'll get this cleaned up. Unless you want to save the apples?"

The wife looked at all the bright red apples in the dingy snow, like large droplets of blood, and wept harder. "They're all dirty and ruined! We can't bring them to town to hand out for free tomorrow like we always do."

"Hush, my girl." Her husband ushered her away with a final glance over his shoulder at the sheriff.

Abe kicked at the shatters of wood in the snow and swore again, softer, so the vendor's wife wouldn't overhear. "What a terrible way to end such a good day. I hope this ain't goin' to sour everyone's opinions. It was still a goshdarned good fair."

"Yes, it was." Christopher clenched his hands into fists. "You and I both know this was Otis Ryder's work. He sent his men to do this. I would bet you my newborn foal that the tall man was Nate. He can't be too far gone by now. We should saddle up, try to find him."

"He could be anywhere by now," Abe said. "If it was even him. We got to accuse one tall man, we got to accuse them all because we don't have any proof. And those other men? Who were they?"

Christopher thumped his fist into his palm. "We can beat the truth out of Otis."

"And be no better than him." Abe shook his head and spat in the snow. "Chris, I know what you feel. That this is all happenin' while I'm supposed to protect everyone makes me feel so sick. I'm off my feed. Can't keep nothin' down these last few days."

"You can't be feelin' that sick if you were drinkin'." Christopher could feel the fight draining from him as they stood there with the minutes passing by, the immediate danger becoming further away.

"No, a little nose paint is all that makes me feel better." Abe motioned to the ground. "I'll help you clean all this up. Shame about the apples."

Clementine, Vera, and Jackson rushed past without so much as a farewell. Estella arrived a moment after, walking up to the men as they stood around the broken mess of wood and candied fruit. "I'll help," she said.

"Ain't no way." Christopher pointed at the house. "You get in there and start cleanin' up."

He really only wanted her somewhere he could easily protect her. The glare she gave him said that she understood, but she also didn't appreciate the insinuation that she was only useful for cleaning his house. She turned away and went to the house, slamming the door shut behind her. Her reaction didn't worry him much; she must have known he was just trying to keep her safe and would soon soften. Her emotions were high right now; that was all.

"Chris," Abe started to say.

"I don't want to hear nothin' else." He bent and righted the apple crate. At least that hadn't broken. "There's a wheelbarrow in the barn. Fetch it."

Abe brought the wheelbarrow over, and they piled the pieces of wood and apples onto it to be taken out to the fields and dumped. By the time the work was done, all the wagons had gone. The only signs remaining of how many people had been there only a short while ago were the churned snow and scraps of dropped food.

The wheelbarrow was returned to the barn. Abe turned to Christopher. "You should get back inside. Have yourself some dinner. I'll go into town, see what I can learn about all this. Alright?"

"Fine." Christopher waved him away. "Just don't fall off your horse. Can't have you breakin' your neck. Who'd be sheriff then?"

"Might be we don't want that question answered." Abe's mustache twitched as he moved away to the stable to grab his horse.

Christopher went into the house. Clattering sounds drew him to the kitchen where Estella was cleaning up, rinsing out the containers used to store coffee.

"Before you say anythin'," she said, her back still to him, "I'm packin' up my bags tonight. I'll leave in the mornin'. I asked Clementine to fetch me in her wagon."

His mouth fell open. He immediately snatched it shut, clenching his jaw. They knew they were going to have to part ways, yet they kept putting it off, and some little niggling bit of hope inside himself had been wondering if it would ever actually happen. Now, he was getting his answer.

"Where are you goin' to go?" His voice was weak and shaking.

She set aside a bowl to dry out and turned to face him. Cody was in the sling on her chest; the barest glimpse of the baby in there, all snuggled up and safe, made his heart squeeze terribly.

"In Bulltooth, there's a job openin' for someone with seamstress or tailor skills. I heard about it from Clem." She lowered her eyes. "Vera is goin' to send a letter to ask if the job is still available, and if it is, I'm takin' it. Until then, or until *somethin'*, I will be stayin' with them in town."

"Bulltooth...." Sharp fear jabbed him in the stomach, as if she had taken one of her sewing needles and stabbed him. "That's not a good town for a single woman with a nipper. And I don't ever get out that way."

Estella's shoulders slumped. "Maybe it's for the best. Christopher...this is the end, right? We both knew it was comin'. It's here now. We have to accept it." She sounded tearful.

He didn't know what to say. She was right. Of course, she was right. He wished that he could beg them to stay, think of something that would make this all turn out the way he would rather have it. But there was nothing. He couldn't protect her and Cody. He didn't deserve them.

Estella took in a shuddering breath. "Chris...you *have* to forgive yourself. You need to open yourself up to love. It's the only way you can be happy. When I'm gone, wherever I go...I want to think that you're happy."

His eyes burned. He put a hand to his face. "This time we've had.... Sometimes, I was happy."

"Me, too." She touched his wrist with her callused fingertips. "Me, too. Chris?"

"Yes?" He fought to keep his voice steady.

Estella chewed on her lower lip and leaned her head forward, hiding her face from him. "There's something I've never told anyone. It's my secret. Only some people back home knew."

He didn't know what she was talking about, couldn't even begin to guess what she might be hinting at. He just looked at her and waited to hear.

Estella wrapped her arms around herself, still avoiding his eyes as she prepared to tell him whatever this secret of hers was. He ached to hold her, sensed that it would be the wrong thing to do right then.

She said, "Chris, even if I could stay, I would never be a good wife for you. I have these...these...this disfigurement."

Christopher looked at her and didn't understand. Every inch of her that he had seen—her face, her arms and hands—was whole and perfectly formed. She had never shown signs of weakness or a limp.

"When I was only a little girl, I pulled a pot of boiling water off the stove. The doctors didn't think I was goin' to survive. I did survive, but now I've got these scars, all on my side." She waved at herself, her face pinched tight. "You wouldn't want a wife like that. You need to open yourself up so you can find yourself another beautiful, wonderful woman to love."

He stared at her, at once moved that she would tell him such a secret while also wondering why it mattered. Then, he understood. "You're tryin' to chase me away? You think I'm addleheaded enough to care about that? Everyone's got scars! It don't make *you* any less beautiful or wonderful."

She let out a small sob and turned away from him. "It would be easier if you thought different."

"I know." His lips trembled. He was close to weeping himself. "If you were my wife, I'd.... I wouldn't even see those scars. All I would see is you."

She sobbed again and gripped the counter. Cody was beginning to fuss as well, no doubt picking up on his caretaker's distress. "Leave me, Christopher. I need to clean. And then pack up. I.... Just leave me for a while, please."

He bit his tongue to restrain a cry, knowing she hadn't believed him. He backed away until he ran into the wall. Hot all over and shaking, he ran out of the kitchen and outside into the cold. Snowflakes blew into his face, larger and thicker than what the wind had been scraping up from the ground. It was fresh stuff, blowing in from the west to blanket the disturbed world in a new layer of white.

Christopher breathed in deep lungfuls of the cold, his face burning and tight.

I am always going to be alone.

He put his hand to his stomach, where the pain was still jabbing him. After all this time, that pain he felt from losing his family had transformed into something worse. He didn't know how he was going to handle it this time.

Chapter Thirty-One

Two small bags sat next to the front door, one with Estella's belongings and the other with Cody's. Estella stood by the window, looking out at the snow that had begun falling thicker and faster throughout the night. She hardly recognized any of the vague shapes out there, even though she had come to know this ranch like the back of her own hand. She was reminded of when she rode the train into town for the first time, how she had not been able to see anything at all. Only when the lantern lights burning in all the windows were visible had she known they were arriving.

She would be heading back into that same town in the same conditions. There would be lanterns, glows of orange spilling out of the homes and businesses. Yet she knew she wouldn't feel as though she was being guided by those lights. She didn't really know where she was going. Ranger's Peak was only a temporary stay; then, hopefully, she would be on her way to Bulltooth...if the job was still available. And if not, she would hurry and find something else to prevent herself from burdening her beloved friends. But what she was supposed to find, she didn't know. The future was as white and blank to her as the wall of snow outside.

Hugging her arms around herself, she wished she had thought to bake something to bring to her friends, to lessen her burden even a small bit. That wouldn't have been right, though. She couldn't use Christopher's food supply to pave her way.

I should have baked for him, she thought.

She couldn't expect him to take proper care of himself when he was in such pain. If only she had made a batch of biscuits, something that could be grabbed and eaten cold.

It was too late now, though. Clementine was due any time. She had promised to come around noon, and the vague brightness of the sun through the snow and clouds was directly overhead.

Clementine's promise had come before the snow started. Estella shifted on her feet, prickles of unease going up and down her spine. Clementine could be late, having to drive the wagon through such snow.

"Maybe I can make something quickly," Estella murmured to herself.

The thought of measuring out ingredients for biscuits and spending all that time cutting the butter into the flour was tiring. Pancakes would be easier to make, though she would have to cook them only one or two at a time.

Maybe if I fill up a whole tray with the pancake batter and cook that in the oven....

A faint, gurgling laugh reached her ears. She lifted her head and turned from the window, the cold seeping through to stroke her back with iced fingers. Moving lightly on her feet, she followed the soft laughter to the hall where Cody's cradle had been kept since the attempted theft incident. She peeked around the corner.

Christopher crouched next to the cradle, his body looming large over the piece of baby furniture. He used just the barest tips of his fingers to tickle Cody's milk-round belly. Cody wriggled around on his back, his chubby legs kicking.

Estella froze and held her breath, praying she wouldn't disturb this sweet moment.

A soft smile adorned Christopher's face. In that moment, he looked less of a hulking bear and more like a friendly, gentle children's toy, all his harsh edges smoothed out. He tickled Cody again, eliciting another laugh as sweet as a bell. Reaching into the cradle, he lifted the baby out. He could hold the infant in both hands, owing to a combination of Cody's smallness and his large size. Still, tiny as Cody was, Christopher held him so carefully in his big hands, as if he was the most delicate glass ornament ever crafted.

Estella's heart ached, and so did her lungs. She wasn't able to hold her breath any longer. She let out the stale air in a gasp.

Christopher's shoulders stiffened. He stood, holding Cody with his head carefully supported. "I wish that you would take the cradle," he said. "After the trouble I went through to get it."

"I'm sorry," she said. "It's just too large to bring with me all the way to potentially another town."

Christopher looked down at the baby. "You goin' to make him sleep in a crate again?"

Dimly, she recognized that he was trying to be light and make jokes. "I imagine Vera has spare boxes lying around."

He snorted. "At least take that basket with you. The one you put him in when he ain't in the cradle or sling."

"It's your basket, Chris. I can't take it."

"What am I goin' to do with it?" He held Cody out to her and she took the baby, their fingers grazing with a soft heat. "I'll go get it. Meet you at the door."

Estella cradled the baby to her chest as she went back to the window. A quick glance outside confirmed Clementine hadn't arrived while she was away.

Christopher walked up behind her, carrying the basket. She turned and gave him a smile, though it was hard to make her mouth move correctly. "Thank you."

He set the basket down next to her and stepped back, putting a distance between them that was only going to grow wider and wider. He looked past her, outside at the thick snow. "Clementine will be able to get through this."

"Are you sure?" Estella had her doubts. "There's going to be so much fresh snow that won't support the wagon wheels. I almost don't want her to come."

Christopher gave her a plaintive look and shook his head. "Don't say things like that."

She held up her hand, her throat tight. "That's not what I meant. Please."

"Then say what you meant," he grumbled.

She frowned at him. Inside, she was going to miss the way they could argue with each other like this. It was fun to squabble over the parts of life that weren't so serious.

"What I mean is that I would hate for her to get stuck alone out there." She rubbed her eyes. "I have a feelin' she's not the best driver and will push the wagon until she's mired. And it will happen at the worst spot, where she's farthest from us *and* the town. She could freeze while walkin' to get help."

"See, I'm thinkin' that she's much too stubborn to get stuck like that." Christopher pushed at his hair. "She'd get out, dig those wheels free. Put the harness and bridle on and pull the wagon herself if she had to."

Estella laughed, imagining such a silly thing.

Christopher looked at her, his eyes softening. His jaw worked for a moment. "I'm...I'm goin' to miss you, Estella. You and Cody."

"I'll miss you, too," she whispered.

She thought about telling him to write a letter and reconsidered the idea as soon as it came. She didn't know where she would end up, and he might not be at the ranch any longer. Even if they could somehow learn each other's addresses to write a letter, that kind of continued communication would only keep their wounds open. This had to end cleanly so that he could begin to heal again, like a bone rebroken to set up right the second time.

"Well, I'll be darned." Christopher leaned around, looking past Estella. She turned and looked, too, and saw the heavy, dark shape of a wagon bumbling through the snow.

The horses pulling the wagon weren't ones she recognized. Clementine must have borrowed a strong pair from someone in town to get her through all of that snow. The seamstress herself was so bundled up in thick coats that her face wasn't visible.

This is it.

It was time to make that clean break. She could say no more, linger no longer, cause no more hurt.

Estella pulled in a deep breath and bent to pick up her bags. Christopher reached around her and opened up the door. He whispered something, his voice broken. It might have been a farewell. She didn't stop to hear it properly, plunging outside into a drift of snow that had been piling up against the door. The cold grabbed at her, stealing her breath. She fought through it, shuffling step after step. Cody started to fuss, and there was little she could do for him. The wind was too loud for him to hear her comfort, even if she had had the breath to speak to him. The best that she could do for both of them was to get inside the wagon swiftly.

She struggled past Clementine's still form on the bench, thinking it was strange how her friend made no move to assist her when she was carrying two bags, a basket, and a child. Maybe she thought that Christopher would help? That the two of them might have some final words to say?

Glancing back and squinting through the snow, Estella saw that he had already shut the door. The curtains were drawn over the windows, letting out only a thin line of light between.

And that was for the best, though it hurt so much it took her breath away even more fiercely than the wind and cold. They had said all that could be said. There wasn't anything left for them. The time had come, and they could not deny it.

Estella thrust her first bag into the back of the wagon, then the second. She hoisted herself in, the wagon creaking and shifting slightly under her weight.

Reins cracked, and the horses started off, huffing and blowing as they made a slow, wide turn to go back toward the road. Estella crouched and wrapped herself around Cody to keep him warm, shivering terribly herself. She wished that Clementine would say something to her. Anything. Even if she couldn't understand what she said because of the wind, hearing her voice would be enough.

She was so alone in the back of that wagon, headed toward a future she didn't know. Her shivering grew worse with more than just cold, fear gripping her tight. Closing her eyes, she bent her head down and prepared to wait out the long, long wagon ride to town.

Chapter Thirty-Two

Christopher peered through the gap in the curtains as the two powerful horses pulled the wagon in an agonizingly wide, slow turn.

I should have sent her off with some blankets, he thought, his throat filled with thorns. *Something to keep her warm in the back of that wagon.*

He could grab some from the linen closet, but he would have a hard time facing her again after she had only just left. They couldn't have a second farewell. Unideal as it was, this was how things had to play out.

He shivered and rubbed his hands together, the house suddenly seeming extremely cold with the absence of Estella's voice and Cody's little coos. Those people he had come to know so well were out there, and oh, how he ached to be with them. How he ached for this life to have turned out differently in *some* way so he would not have to feel this pain.

He couldn't stand it. He had to think of something else.

Casting out a mental line like a desperate fisherman, his thoughts snagged on something he hadn't even realized he had noticed. Was it really Clementine out there, driving the wagon? Admittedly, he didn't pay too much attention to her and wasn't sure of her exact height. He did think the bundled figure on the wagon bench seemed unusually tall. Maybe it was Vera? She was taller than her daughter. What did it matter, anyway? It only seemed a little strange that whoever they were hadn't gotten off the bench to help Estella with her bags and the baby.

With that long drive in this weather, maybe she doesn't feel like she can move.

He had heard of people freezing to their seats before, even. What might seem strange to him would surely have made sense if he knew the reasoning behind it.

He needed to stop thinking about it.

He turned away from the window and went outside. The wagon tracks were rapidly filling in with fresh snow. He shoved his way past them and to the barn. A series of whickers and snorts greeted his entrance. He went to the stalls and gave every horse a stroke and a handful of oats, busying his mind with checking on their health.

Almost every animal had recovered from the poisoning that he was now entirely sure was Otis's doing. One more had died in the early days after removing the blockage from the stream, and their body had had to be burned. A few still showed signs that they were not back to full health, with drooping ears and a tendency to stand at the back of the stall even when a handful of oats would ordinarily have coaxed them right to the front. Christopher hoped that they would get back to normal and *very* quickly. When the bank people came to take his ranch, they would take everything on it, including the horses. He thought he might be able to barter to keep one to ride and get some money for the others since they were not originally part of the ranch.

Technically, he could try the same tactic with his other belongings. John James would be glad enough to have him off the land that he would be willing to work with him.

There wasn't anything else that mattered as much to Christopher as his horses. The belongings he needed and wanted all fit easily into a single bag.

The newborn black foal stayed close to his mother's flank as she lipped up the heaping handful of treats offered to her. Christopher looked at that small and perfect being for a long while, his heart heavy with a sorrow that he would not get to raise it. In his mind, he had named it Blizzard. He didn't say the name out loud, nor had he been introducing the foal to the concepts of rope and halter. There wasn't a point in getting attached to it. Someone else would take it and raise it in their own way.

"Anyone in here?" The stable door opened, and Jackson stepped inside, shaking snow from his body. He guided his horse in after him and took it to a stall to wipe down.

Christopher moved over to join him, hands on his hips. "What in tarnation are you doin' here?" he snapped. He wasn't angry; it was just easier to act that way. "I didn't think I'd be seein' anyone in this weather."

Jackson briskly rubbed his hands over his horse's legs to warm them up after what had to have been an arduous ride in the snow. "I knew that Clem was goin' to be here to pick up Estella. Thought I'd come over myself to, uh, help out."

Christopher snorted. He stepped around Jackson and into the stall. There was water in the trough, covered in a layer of ice. He broke the ice with the side of his fist, the shards crackling like thin icing on a cookie. "What you wanted was for Clementine to see you and think you're some helpful type since you want her to fancy you."

Jackson rubbed his hands together. "The truth on that is I don't just want her to fancy me. I fancy her, too. More'n that. I love her, Boss."

This romance had been budding under his nose the entire time, and he hadn't seen how serious it was getting. Christopher tried to think of something to say that wouldn't come across as bitter when his own potential relationship had just broken into so many pieces like that ice in the water trough. He was definitely jealous, wishing that he could have what his foreman did, but he was not bitter about it. Jackson was a good man and deserved happiness. Christopher reasoned that it was good for *someone* to get something meaningful and lasting from all of this.

"I'm glad for you," Christopher said at last. He struggled to put the proper feeling in his voice and hoped his ranch hand would understand the lack of enthusiasm. "Unfortunately, the fat's already in the fire, Jackson. Clementine brought the wagon a short while ago."

"Oh." Jackson rubbed his hand through hair damp with snowmelt. "Then, Estella's...gone?"

Christopher said nothing, his throat tight. His eyes burned, and he thought he might begin to weep if he tried to speak. He couldn't stand to make a fool of himself like that in front of his friend.

"I hate to ask this." Jackson kicked at the hay. "You think I could grab a fresh horse? Sounds like they didn't go off too long ago. I should be able to catch up."

Christopher grunted his acquiescence. "But what do you want to do that for?"

"I just want to escort them back to town, make sure they get there okay." Jackson walked down the row of horses, eyeing them. "I can't believe that Clem was able to make it through this. And it's only gettin' worse out there. Several trees were down across the road when I was on my way here."

Christopher put his hands to his face and rubbed hard. "I feel like a fool for just lettin' them go."

"Then why don't you come and ride with me?" Jackson suggested. He chose a horse, guiding the gelding out to put a saddle and bridle on him.

"I trust you to do it right."

"Sure, you trust me, but I know that ain't enough for you." Jackson adjusted the many straps, his movements practiced and casual. "You need to see things with your own eyes. You might think you'll be satisfied if I go and do it, but you really won't be. It'll eat at you and eat at you until you're all skin an' bone."

Christopher knew that his foreman was right. He could do nothing for Estella and Cody now, but shouldn't he make sure that they got to town safely? Wasn't this one final thing he could do for them?

He went to a stall and studied the horse there to ensure she was good and ready to be ridden out into the storm. Behind him, Jackson gave a chuckle, soft and sad. "You do love her."

No, he thought, and it felt like the worst lie he had ever told.

It came over him like a wave, the truth engulfing him so he could not escape. He tried to breathe and found it filling his lungs, becoming a part of him even though he had spent so much time denying it.

He loved Estella. She had come into his life and changed him whether she meant to or not. Her soft laughter and her genuine smiles, her sewing and baking skills, her sense of humor, her kindness, all of it had left an imprint upon him, like a scar. It was a part of him.

"I love her," Christopher whispered.

When his strength left him, he leaned heavily against the stall to stay upright. He closed his eyes, and she was there. The image of her with her dark brown hair done up all pretty stood out against the abyss behind his lids as if she were right there before him. Her eyes were bright, filled with that mix of sweetness, passion, and strength that made her such a rare person.

Opening his eyes, he swung around to Jackson, startling the gelding. "I love her!" he cried, trembling all over.

Jackson grasped his shoulders. "We all knew it. It's just you're too stubborn to say it! I got a plan, Chris. You might think it's all crazy talk. I think we can make it work. Everyone can be happy if we can just do this."

Christopher stared at his friend. "What are you talkin' about?" he asked.

"Estella and Cody can go live with Clementine. Maybe Estella will go to Bulltooth a time for that job. She'll earn money while havin' a place to stay. And you can come stay with me at my place." Jackson smiled. "You'll find a job. You're too good at what you do for someone around here not to hire you. With you and Estella both makin' money, you can work to be with each other again. You could work your way back to buyin' another ranch, gettin' more horses to breed."

All of this seemed so very obvious. Why hadn't they thought of this before? Christopher voiced the question to Jackson, a little afraid of the answer.

"Because you wouldn't admit you love her!" Jackson shook him, then pushed him away to stumble to his feet. "But you've said it out loud now. Ain't it best for her to know she's loved? To know that you want her? It's because she didn't think you could love her that she's goin' off in that wagon, thinkin' she'll never see your sorry hide again! But now you've realized what the rest of us already knew...."

Christopher tore at his hair with both hands. "We need to go right now!" He couldn't bear to spend one moment longer thinking about this. He needed to act.

"Then, let's go!"

Christopher quickly prepared his horse, his hands shaking fiercely. He gave up on getting the straps just right and settled for good enough. He stepped into the stirrups and swung into the saddle. Jackson was ready and waiting on him by then.

They rode out into the snowstorm, the wind screaming like a hundred furious women, swaying all the trees and rattling the reinforced fence lines. Christopher squeezed with his knees, urging his mare to go as fast as she could. The snow was almost up to her belly in some spots. She slipped and stumbled, jerking up and down as her hooves punched through the heavy, wet layers blanketing the ground. Staying on her was a struggle. Christopher kept wanting to tense up and grip her as he was jostled from side to side and back and forth. It seemed like he had forgotten all of his training and he had to continually remind himself to loosen up, to move with the mare rather than fighting against her.

Though Jackson was only a horse's length away, he was only a ghost, the snow nearly a solid wall separating them. They wouldn't be heard if one of them shouted to the other.

I knew Clementine was stubborn as a jenny, but it's insane that she managed to get through this!

The road was entirely hidden. The tops of the trees disappeared into the snow like mountaintops touching clouds. There were no identifiable landmarks, nothing to reassure them they were heading in the right direction.

Christopher could feel it, though. His heart was pulling him toward Estella, and he was sure that Jackson's heart must be guiding him to Clementine. They knew where they were going, where they belonged, like birds migrating at the change of seasons.

He had been such a fool this entire time, refusing to admit to himself that a life with Estella could work out. He had been looking for perfection and, not seeing it, gave up much too easily. But what was perfection? His life with Bonnie hadn't been perfect. They had argued. There had been sleepless nights when Troy would not settle and fussed until dawn. That was *life*.

If Troy hadn't fussed until dawn, Christopher would never have been standing out on his porch to see that beautiful sunrise, all the stars shrinking away into pinks and purples.

For everything that was bad, there was something good to come of it.

He could take all this badness and work to make something of it with Estella. It would take time, perhaps years. But after that, the good years would far outnumber what they had gone through.

He still didn't know if it was a betrayal to love someone after losing Bonnie—if he deserved this beautiful woman he was chasing through the storm. Previously, he would have said yes.

And now?

Now he knew he would do anything to see Estella again, to hold her in his arms and kiss her because she deserved to be loved.

Chapter Thirty-Three

The whole wagon rocked as the wind ripped at it. Estella braced herself to keep from being knocked to the floor. Her heart hammered in her throat. She had never experienced weather so terrible. It was as if the world itself was trying to stop them from reaching town. She couldn't even tell if they were moving at all through the snow, couldn't hear the wheels, the horses, or anything Clementine might have tried to shout to her.

She couldn't hear Cody either. He was wailing, and she could feel it, his distress at the terribly loud noise all around him. Her heart ached, and she held him against her in the sling, knowing it would comfort him little. She could hardly feel her hands well enough to soothe him, if he would even be soothed at all.

At a point when the wagon wasn't rocking so hard, she shifted across the floor of the wagon and fumbled inside for one of the bottles she had packed. Her numb fingers struggled to identify the contents of the bag that she should have been so familiar with, having put them all in there herself. She pulled the bag more to herself and squinted at the darkness inside. Sight was no help, and she resumed her fumbling about, groping deeply inside. Her seeking touch discovered a smooth surface. She forced her stiff hand to curl around it and pulled out the bottle.

Even before she took it out, Estella could tell something was amiss. The contents did not slosh and shift when tipped. She gave the bottle a shake and confirmed the issue: The milk had frozen completely solid. She wouldn't be able to feed Cody until they were inside somewhere with access to a fire.

She shoved the bottle away and sank back into her spot on the floor, which was already as cold as if she hadn't been sitting there only seconds before.

This is how people have died, she thought.

Fear twisted her stomach.

She knew of people who had gone on journeys to new lands, only to miscalculate and be caught unprepared in the dead of winter, their frozen bodies only discovered in the spring when the next group of people was coming. It frightened her, the idea that a person alive could die just like that, even more so because she had seen it happen with Ada. It was no grand thing, death. There was no transition, no exalted shift from one to the next. There was only a stillness that crept in, so sneaky that pinpointing the exact moment was impossible. A person became a doll, eyes glassy, face pale, stiff in the limbs.

She did not want to become a doll. And she did not want Christopher to find them like that.

The wagon gave a jolt, as if the wheels had struck something buried in the snow, and stopped. Estella could feel it now, the stopping, so subtly different from the crawling forward movement.

"Clementine?" she called out. No response came, and she doubted Clementine had even been able to hear her.

Seconds ticked past, every one an agony of cold. Estella knew she couldn't stand it for much longer. She had to get out and see what was wrong. Even with as little protection as the wagon canopy provided, going outside would feel awful.

She crouched there, steeling her nerves to do exactly that when the instinct was to do as rabbits and foxes did, to burrow and hunker down and wait.

The canopy at the rear of the wagon tore open. Estella flinched and reached out to pull the flaps closed again, assuming the wind was the culprit. Then her eyes landed upon Clementine standing there, staring out at her from the depths of her hooded coat. Their gazes locked. Clementine's lips were parted, her throat flexing. She seemed to be silently begging, asking for something, though it was difficult to tell in the darkness.

There's something different about her than before, Estella thought.

She wasn't sure what the difference was and didn't think it mattered. The distress on her friend's face was clear. Somewhat was wrong, and she needed help.

Estella peeled her cold body off the wagon floor and shuffled to the opening. She stepped out and immediately sank into the snow. The whole world around her was white and shifting, the snow a chaos of swirls and whorls upon the wind. Trees creaked and groaned all about them. Craning her neck and looking around, Estella realized they had pulled off the main road into some side path or hollow where the trees almost fully encircled them. She hadn't even felt the turning, it must have been so gradual.

What were they doing, pulling off the road like this? What she could see of the road ahead—what she thought was the road ahead, at least—revealed no obstacles that might cause Clementine to want to turn back. Had something else gone wrong?

Estella turned around and looked back at Clementine.

Gray pulsed in on her vision like moths gathered to a lamp, blocking the light with their dry, papery wings. She couldn't feel her legs, any part of her body. Though not a woman given to fainting spells, she recognized she was on the verge of blacking out.

Someone stood behind Clementine, a person who must have been hiding around the side of the wagon unseen. Their arm was extended, a gloved hand holding something instantly identifiable and undeniable.

It was a gun, and the muzzle was pointed right at the back of Clementine's head.

The figure behind Clementine took a pace forward and roughly yanked down her hood, exposing her white, frightened face to the elements. The gun pressed more firmly to her head, shoving it. Clementine's mouth moved weakly. Praying? Asking for help?

As the moths gathered in her vision even more thickly, liable to take her fully into darkness, some part of Estella spoke as to the truth of what was before her. She knew now what was different between Clementine before and now. She should have realized it sooner, though what could the knowledge possibly have done for her?

Clementine's clothes were different. She was not wearing exactly the same coats as when she had driven the wagon up to the house to fetch Estella. The figure holding the gun *was* wearing those clothes.

Meaning it was never Clementine who had come to pick up Estella. It was this person with the gun who had done so. It was no wonder they hadn't climbed down to help Estella get her belongings to the wagon. She would almost certainly have noticed something was wrong at that point and could have signaled to Christopher.

The pieces were fitting together, the story beginning to make sense. Clementine must have started the journey and had been overtaken by this person, who had taken her place and her wagon to pick up Estella themselves. But why? And where had Clementine been all this time? Standing on this side path so that the bandit could come back and hold a gun to her head? Wouldn't she have run off for help?

Another person stepped out from the opposite side of the wagon. He pulled his hood back as he walked, and Estella saw his face.

That's Otis Ryder!

The moths scattered, and she could see clearly again. No longer was she surprised, though she was plenty terrified. She understood exactly what was going on now. She had every bit of it figured out.

The wind dropped for a moment. Otis spoke, raising his voice to be heard. "I'm sorry things had to come to this. I don't like harmin' women or children."

Estella's eyes ticked from his face, so handsome and normal, to the person holding a gun to Clementine's head. Now she knew who they were, too. Nate Bolger, Otis's hired gunman.

Nate and Otis must have ambushed Clementine and taken the wagon. Otis had stayed back with Clementine; he wouldn't have risked his safety by being the one to pick up Estella. They brought her back to the spot where Otis and Clementine were waiting.

"Why are you doin' this?" Estella's voice quivered from fear and cold.

Otis let out a heavy sigh. His hair blew wildly about his head. "I'm sorry that things got to be this way," he said. "I am. But I've had enough of being challenged and argued with. Christopher should have just given me what I wanted when I first asked for it. Then I'd be rich, and you.... Well...you wouldn't be caught in the crossfire."

Clementine made a small sobbing sound.

Time was short. Estella couldn't count on anyone to come and save them. She had to think quickly, act quickly.

"You don't have to do this," she said. "Have reason, Mr. Ryder!"

"Reason only gets a man so far." His eyes blazed, and his nostrils flared. His mask was slipping, the real man underneath glimpsed, a furious and indignant person. "Christopher has made a fool of me in front of this town, shown people it's fine and dandy to push back against me. I could kill him, but that would end his sufferin'. I want him to suffer. So, I'm goin' to take everything from him."

Estella felt the bite of tears in her eyes. "Have mercy on us."

"I can't. This is what must be done." Otis shook his head. He reached inside his layers and pulled out a pistol, the gleam of silver dangerous and nasty. He approached Estella, the pistol down by his side. "Really, I've tried to think of other ways, but this is what's got to be done."

Otis lifted his head, and Estella looked him right in the face. A calm came over her as she faced her death. This was not how she imagined her life would end. So be it. She was going to face this with every ounce of strength and bravery she possessed. After all she had gone through, if this was the culmination of her life, she would not let herself down by whimpering and weeping.

Her only regret would be Cody, leaving him motherless. But she would go loving him, and that had to count for something.

Somewhere in the depths of Otis's eyes, she thought she saw a weird little bit of warmth. He might truly have felt sorry for her or regretted that he had to do this to her. Maybe he even somewhat admired her for standing up to him in a way that many men in the past must not have.

She looked back at him and hoped he could see she did not care for his regret or his admiration. She wanted to die with him knowing that what he had done was wrong. That he could not be forgiven.

If only it was so easy to die like that, with pride and strength. She had so many regrets herself. She could see each one of them in the darkness of the muzzle as he lifted the pistol and pointed it at the middle of her face. How horrible it would be for Cody to be a victim in all this. Was this monster going to kill him, too? Leave him in the snow to be killed by the cold or wild animals?

Might he even do the right thing and leave the baby at an orphanage?

She would never know, and she hated that. Everything in her wanted to fight, and oh, how she wished it was possible for her to go down like that. She wouldn't be able to move a muscle before Otis or Nate Bolger put an end to her attempt. It was better to just hold Cody and stand tall, be strong and unmoving as an oak.

And how awful for Clementine to get mixed up in all this. Estella could have wept and wailed at the unfairness of her poor, innocent friend being in danger because of her. Now Clementine was a witness, and Otis would kill her, too; otherwise, Clementine would naturally do the right thing and tell everyone what she had seen.

"You might want to close them purty eyes of yours," Otis said, his voice softening until the wind threatened to swallow it. "And think of somethin' nice. It'll all be over in a moment."

Estella kept her head up and kept looking at him, defying him in the final moments she had left.

Let my face haunt you, she thought. *Let my blood on the snow stain the rest of your sick life.*

Otis's finger tightened on the trigger.

Chapter Thirty-Four

"Look at this!" Christopher shouted to Jackson, pointing down at the snow before him.

Jackson rode over, his horse struggling mightily. "What is it?" he hollered.

"Wheel tracks!" Christopher traced them with his fingertip the short distance he could see them in the snow. The twin marks were faint, rapidly filling in. "We must be about to catch up to them."

Jackson's whole body convulsed with a shiver. "'bout time. I feel like we been ridin' for a month."

Christopher silently agreed. The going was even more difficult than he had imagined. The horses were not faring well, faltering with almost every step. There was a real risk of permanent injury from being out walking in this weather.

"Let's go." He ushered his mare onward even though she gave him every sign of being at her limit, following the wagon tracks down the road.

After a short time, the tracks veered off to the side. Christopher held up his hand to stop Jackson and pointed out the sudden turn—as sudden of a turn as a wagon could make in knee-high snow, that was. Higher, even, at the peaks of drifts.

"What happened here?" Jackson asked. "We ain't at town. Why'd they veer off?"

"Clementine got lost?" Christopher suggested, half-joking. "This ain't goin' anywhere but into the trees. I don't see a path goin' out, though. They're still in there. We can catch them, ask what's goin' on."

"Boss?" Jackson's face was red from being scraped by the wind. "I don't like it. You feel it? It ain't right."

Christopher could feel it, too, in spite of his attempt at a joke. He placed humor aside and grew serious. "Then we got to go see if we can *make* it right."

They headed off into the trees, following the faint tracks. The wind was somewhat less terrible when they were screened in, and Christopher was able to think a little easier. He didn't like this detour one bit. There was something wrong about it. He couldn't think of why Clementine would have done this.

"Wait, what's that?" Christopher stopped again, peering through the trees off in the distance. They seemed to clear, and in the midst of that clearing was a large shadowy shape, a silhouette.

"That's the wagon!" Jackson exclaimed.

"It ain't movin," Christopher said.

He was about to flick the reins and ride there to see what was amiss when he saw people moving around the front of the parked wagon. It was two people. No, three. And one of them was holding a gun to the other's head.

He sucked in his breath, his mouth going dry as the fields in the middle of summer. As he watched, the three people went around to the back of the wagon. Estella climbed out. She seemed hesitant, puzzled. She had no idea what was going on around her.

Christopher did.

He recognized those people down there even before the hoods came off. It was Nate and Otis. Nate had a gun to Clementine's head while Otis was speaking with Estella.

Jackson snarled out a swear and leaped down from his horse. He had his hand inside his coats, reaching for his gun.

Christopher jumped down and grabbed his friend by the arm, pulling him down to a crouch. The subtle rise and fall of the path, in addition to the snow drifts, helped to hide them.

"You're crazy as a loon if you think walkin' in there will solve this," he hissed.

Jackson's eyes were wide, ticking around in the sockets. "Then what do we *do*?"

Christopher thought quickly. Obviously, at some point, Nate and Otis had jumped Clementine and commandeered the wagon, bringing it to this secluded spot where they could do God-knows-what to the women. They were going to do this to punish Christopher.

After having just found the bravery to declare that he loved Estella, he could not let this be the end.

A new kind of cold took hold of him. It was something past rage, the distilled essence left behind when the fire of fury had died out. It was as if he was looking at the world through one of those magnifying glasses, all his focus narrowed in on what was before him, calm and collected.

"We move fast now," Christopher said. He motioned off to their right. "I'll go this way through the trees. You go the other way. Their horses will be hidden somewhere. We see 'em, we set 'em loose. If not, it don't matter. I'll give a signal, and then we jump them. Then we fight."

If Jackson was as good a shooter as Nate, they could end this in an instant. But with the wind what it was, Christopher didn't trust a bullet not to stray and hit an unintended target.

Jackson nodded his understanding of the plan, his eyes narrowing. He seemed to have joined Christopher in that place of eerie calm. He slunk away without another word, almost crawling through the snow.

Christopher turned and began to navigate in the opposite direction, working his way gradually closer to the clearing until only the thinnest layer of snow-cloaked trees hid him from view. That same white stuff that had been plaguing him and causing so many difficulties around the ranch was finally doing some good. The fallen leaves and branches that would ordinarily have made noise were all hidden underneath it, and he didn't have to watch his step.

Otis seemed to be saying something to Estella. He had his pistol out. Then, he lifted it.

Christopher pulled in a breath.

Nate Bolger looked around. He couldn't have heard such a small sound, could he?

And then it didn't matter as a horse's sudden scream cut through the howling wind. Everyone turned to look, even Estella, even Nate, as two horses crashed out of where they had been hidden in the woods, stampeding into the clearing.

Otis pointed his pistol in the direction the horses had come from. Nate was less hasty, scanning, eyes narrowed.

Christopher groped for something, anything. His grasping hands encountered a sizable stick. He picked it up and threw it as hard as he could.

Nate twisted, his pistol going up. He fired before he was even fully in position. Wood sprayed from the slowly twirling stick, which was knocked off course by the shot and landed with a thump in the snow.

Another stick came flying, this one from where Jackson was hiding.

As Nate spun to shoot it, Christopher grabbed the next thing he could find. He stood up, exposing himself, and threw what he held. It only registered when the object was already in the air that it was a hefty frozen rock the size of a man's fist.

The rock struck Nate right on the back of his head, and he careened to the side.

Christopher burst out through the trees and rushed into the clearing. "*Otis!*" he roared.

Otis spun to face him and fired off a wild shot that sent up a puff of snow where Christopher's leg had been only a heartbeat before. He fired again as Christopher came upon him.

Christopher tripped as something struck his leg, a knock like being kicked by a horse. His shoulder knocked into Otis and they went tumbling into the snow.

Otis writhed like a wildcat, clawing out at Christopher's face. The throbbing in his leg was distant, easily forgotten as he wrestled with the other man. Somehow, Otis managed to get away and climbed to his feet.

Christopher tried to stand, too, but the pain forced him down to his knees. He grabbed at his lower leg where the pain was, and his fingers came away slick and hot. The coppery reek of his blood filled his flaring nostrils.

"Finish him off, Nate!" Otis shouted.

Christopher threw his arms up around his head in a desperate attempt to buffer an incoming shot...that never came.

"Nate!" Otis spun.

Bolger was flat on his back and flailing, the snow around his head stained pink with blood. He pummeled at Jackson, his shots weak and uncoordinated as the other man straddled him and struck him repeatedly with much fiercer punches. The gunslinger must have dropped his trusty pistol and, without it, was reduced to a fumbling child.

"Can't trust anyone," Otis spat. "I'll finish you off myself, Baldwin!"

Knowing he couldn't stand on his leg, Christopher threw himself forward across the space between them, lumbering on his hands and his good leg like a maimed bear. His shoulders struck Otis, and they both went down again, but this time, Christopher was on top. His greater weight and size were to his advantage as he clawed up Otis's body, shoving him deeper into the snow.

"This is for everythin' you put me through!"

Christopher raised his fist and brought it down. Hard. Otis let out a choked gasp. Christopher struck him again, and the gasp turned to a gurgle.

All of the frustration and pent-up rage came flowing forth, and Christopher brought his fist down again and again. Blood flew when his hand rose and splattered when he brought it down. Some of it flecked his face, hot and then rapidly cooled to red ice.

Someone shouted something. Christopher paid it no mind, bringing his hand up again.

Two hands clasped onto his. He froze, recognizing the touch in an instant. Those long fingers, with the callused pads on the tips.

"Enough."

Estella's voice came, calm and gentle. She crouched at Christopher's side, the blood from his hand soaking hers. "You're goin' to kill him, Chris. It's enough. You won."

"I *want* to kill him," Christopher whispered, the words tumbling out. He was so very tired all at once, the hard riding and the pain in his leg catching up to him now his vengeance was interrupted. "He was goin' to kill you."

It wasn't about the ranch anymore but the terrible sight of the woman he had come to love being threatened at gunpoint.

"I know." Estella squeezed his hands. "I know you're tired out, Chris. I know this man deserves it. But you're better than him. Don't be like him."

Otis lay shaking and sputtering there on the ground. Christopher couldn't look directly at him. He didn't want to see the damage he had done.

Estella was right. By killing Otis, he would reduce himself to that terrible man's level.

He pushed away, sliding back onto his rump in the snow.

Estella moved to hold his shoulders, speaking in his ear. "He'll go to jail now, be put to work in his own mines. That's the fate he deserves, not a quick death. Come now, Chris. Please? Stand?"

"I'll do anythin' for you."

He was too tired to filter what he said through a veil of propriety.

He braced his weight on his good leg and stood, grunting out in pain. Estella clutched at him from the side, doing what little she could to support him.

Nate Bolger lay in the snow in a similar manner as Otis, the back of his head caked in blood from the stone that struck him. Jackson and Clementine stood a short distance away by the wagon, their arms wrapped around each other.

"Where's the baby?" Christopher asked.

Clementine pulled down her coat to show him Cody tucked away inside, fussy, cold, and hungry but safe.

Tears ran down Christopher's face, and he sagged, almost collapsed. Estella struggled to hold him upright, trembling with the effort.

"What do we do now, Boss?" Jackson looked at him.

Leave 'em here to let the snow claim them.

He thought for a moment before he actually spoke. "Jackson, you go get our horses. We'll see if we can find somethin' to tie up these..." he remembered the women, "these, uh, criminals. We'll put 'em on the horses and go the rest of the way into town, take 'em to Abe. And we'll spend the night at the inn. The animals at the ranch got enough food and water to last."

Jackson nodded, kissed Clementine on the cheek, and trudged back through the snow to get to where they had left the horses.

Clementine looked back and forth between Christopher and Estella. Her lips trembled, and then she burst into tears. "C-can I get in the wagon and sit for a spell?"

Estella rushed to her side and put her arms around her. "Poor, poor Clem. You were so brave," she soothed. "You did so well. Yes, sit, get your breath. It's alright now."

Christopher hobbled over to the wagon with him and went through Estella's bags, knowing what he would find and where, as he had watched her packing. He pulled out several packages of thread. They were such delicate fibers on their own, but if he used a ton of strands at once, he thought even a man in good condition would have a hard time breaking out of them.

One painful step after another, and he reached Nate. Crouching down and getting back up again were extremely difficult processes, and even harder a second time when he got down beside Otis to tie up his wrists as well. Otis was only partially conscious, though it was difficult to tell his eyes were open at all with his face so swollen. His mouth moved as though he was speaking, no words emerging.

"Save it for the judge," Christopher told him hoarsely.

As he was getting to his feet another time, he turned to see Jackson approaching, leading what seemed like a whole herd of horses. Christopher raised his eyebrows, which he could feel were crusted with ice.

"It's Otis's and Bolger's horses," Jackson explained. He appeared to have found rope somewhere, perhaps in one of the saddlebags, and had tied the animals into a chain. "They were standin' near ours."

"At least they won't freeze," Christopher said. He was sorry for the animals, the true innocents in all of this.

Estella walked up to his side and held onto his arm. "Clem's resting in the back of the wagon," she said. "Are we goin' for town now?"

"Ayuh." Jackson pointed at the two tied and bloodied men in the snow. "I'll get them on the horses and ride at the head of the line. You and Christopher should get on the wagon. We'll all go toward town, straight to the sheriff's office."

It was a good idea, not in the least because it meant Christopher wouldn't be dealing with the criminals who had tried so hard to ruin his life.

They went their separate ways, Estella to the back of the wagon to share the plan with Clementine and Christopher to the bench. He hauled himself up and thumped his rump down on the bench with a grunt.

Estella climbed up almost as soon as he sat down, sliding across the bench to tuck in against his side.

He stopped reaching for the reins and turned to her, putting his arms around her and holding on tight. She hugged him around the neck, and her cold face pressed to him. She was weeping, shuddering, her tears shockingly hot trickles.

Christopher held the back of her head in his hand. "I know you was afeared," he choked out. "You were brave. I'm so proud of you for gettin' through this."

She drew back with a sob and stared with watery eyes into his. He held the side of her face in his hand, not caring about the blood on his skin and figuring she wouldn't, either.

"How did you know?" she asked. "That we were goin' to need help?"

"I didn't," he said, shaking his head. "I just.... I realized I loved you."

There was so much more to it than that, and he could tell her on the long ride into town, but that was what mattered the most right then. He needed her to hear those words.

She looked at him for so long and said nothing to the point where he thought his heart might just explode from the anticipation. Then, a slow smile unfolded on her lips, the softest and most beautiful smile he had ever seen grace the face of a woman. Surely, Bonnie must have smiled like that, but this was all about Estella right now.

"I love you, too," she told him, her voice soft and full of truth. She wasn't saying it only to make him happy. She truly felt it.

He tilted his face to hers, and she was there to meet him, their lips grazing together for only an instant, the smallest of touches for the biggest of promises.

With his lips tingling from the kiss, Christopher reached for the reins. Estella grabbed them and placed them in his hands. Thus began the long and laborious process of turning the wagon around in so much snow.

But eventually, he did get the wagon turned around and heading back in the direction of the road. He was beginning to lose sensation in his legs, which did worry him, given that he knew he was still bleeding from having been shot. He hoped it was only a minor wound and would not be too bad, though. A doctor could patch him right up as soon as they got to town—after delivering their load of bandits to the sheriff, of course.

As they got back on the road, he saw Jackson ahead with the string of horses, though not all that far ahead, given the rough conditions. He had more maneuverability with the horses, but they kept sinking into the snow and were already cold and miserable. The wagon had a slight advantage with its wheels, though its cumbersome size canceled that out. They were soon more or less even with each other and remained that way through the rest of the journey.

When they saw the first house through the fierce, blowing snow, Christopher turned his head to kiss Estella on the cheek. They had made it.

She gave him a squeeze in return and murmured something that he couldn't quite hear through the pounding in his ears. When exactly his pulse had started going up again, he wasn't sure. But he was abruptly feeling ill, the edges of his vision fogging over. His lungs felt heavy and tired. He had to gasp to breathe. Did Estella notice? He thought she kept looking at him. He tried to give her a smile to reassure her, and that only seemed to worry her further, her eyebrows scrunching over her overly bright eyes.

Women. I'll never understand them, much as I love them.

Into town they went, their procession of wagon and horses surely gathering attention from all the folks holed up in their homes. There wasn't a single person to be seen on the street, no one to brave the awful weather. At least, Christopher couldn't see any through the fog in his vision. There was more of it than before, clustering in. He seemed to be looking out at the world through a hole in a piece of gray fabric.

The sheriff's office came into sight, and at last, there were people to be seen, two recognizable figures gesturing as they talked. Abe and Vera turned as they rounded the corner. The shock on their faces was visible even through the sheets of snow in the air, eyes and mouths stretched wide.

Jackson reached them first, dismounting from his horse. Abe went to him, grabbing his arm. "What is goin' on here?" he exclaimed. "Is that.... Is that Otis Ryder? What've you done to him?"

"Less than he deserved," Jackson growled. He began to fill Abe in, talking too quickly, causing Abe to rub his face with his hands and beg him to slow down.

Meanwhile, Vera had realized Clementine was in the wagon and was rushing to her, calling out her name. Clementine sprang out, still holding onto Cody, and they embraced fiercely.

Christopher observed all of this with a curious sense of detachment. None of it seemed to be happening to him, like he was watching the events of a play unfolding before him. Everything he had been feeling, all of the joy and triumph, had all gone away.

"Chris? Christopher, hey!" The sheriff was coming over to talk to him.

"Abe, we did it. We got them." The words were like oatmeal in his mouth, all mushy. He swung down from the wagon bench.

His boots touched the snow. His legs did not support his weight. He began to collapse, and suddenly, everyone around him was shouting. Estella was at his side, holding his hand, patting it so nicely.

Christopher looked at her face and smiled even as the fog came in over his vision and took him away. If he was dying, then so be it. He had told her that he loved her. She knew she was loved, that he loved her so much he'd give his life to save her. That was all that mattered.

His eyes slipped shut, and he finally, finally rested.

Chapter Thirty-Five

One week later....

Estella pulled the ham from the oven, a thick slab of steaming meat with a sweet maple syrup glaze on top. She could feel the weight of it in her wrists as she placed it upon a platter and brought it to the table, the grand centerpiece surrounded by buttery rolls and roasted potatoes and carrots. There were a number of candles all lit, cheery and bright little flames, and glasses of warm, spiced cider ready to be sipped to chase away the clinging chill of outside when the guests finally arrived.

Between the dishes were sprigs of greenery and bright red berries, so sweet and cheerful. She had also stitched many, many stars in anticipation of this celebration and strung them from one wall to the other. When making them, she had deliberately chosen bright colors, fabrics with sparkles and shiny surfaces to catch all the light and give the illusion of a beautiful sky that they currently did not have. There had been no more snow, but the wind had remained fierce, and the skies were constantly overcast.

None of that mattered inside this perfect house full of Christmas joy.

Estella left the dining room, there being nothing else she could do there. She went to Cody's cradle in her room and lifted him out. He burbled happily and cuddled into her arms, laying his head upon her. She stroked him and kissed the top of his head.

"My handsome little one," Estella murmured. "So dashing in your Christmas finest."

"It's only the 'finest' for a short while," a man's deep voice said from the other bedroom. "Then he'll spit up on it. Or one of us will drip gravy on him."

"I didn't make any gravy," Estella called back.

"There will be gravy. Abe makes a mean gravy."

Estella smiled and held Cody as she left the room, going across the hall to the other bedroom where the voice came from.

Christopher sat on the edge of his bed, also in his Christmas finest, a blue long-sleeved shirt and tan pants Estella had tailored for him only a few days ago. He had brushed his sandy-brown hair to silky softness. She wanted to run her fingers through it.

Christopher held out his arms, and she brought Cody to him, letting him hold and coo over the baby. She watched them with her hands clasped before her, her heart full of joy. Christopher no longer seemed shy about expressing his interest in the baby, often picking him up and even taking over some of the feeding responsibilities. She never asked him. She would be going to feed Cody herself and find him already doing it.

He shouldn't have been doing anything too strenuous at all, but he insisted upon it, refusing to wait until he was stronger.

"I can smell that ham from here," Christopher said. "If everyone doesn't arrive before too long, I might get started without them."

Estella laughed. "Why don't I go take a peek outside? See if I can see them comin'?"

"You can, if you'd like. I'll just stay here with this nipper."
Christopher tickled Cody's belly, making him giggle and kick
his legs.

Estella smiled at them, then bent over and kissed the top
of Christopher's head. He looked up, and she bent a little
lower to kiss his lips.

That was something else that had changed. Christopher
had told her about the talk he'd had with Jackson before they
had come after her and had to rescue her from Otis. He had
explained the potential living arrangement suggested and
how he had realized he loved her and couldn't let her go.
There had been tears in his eyes and a shake in his voice
when he said all that to her, and she had held him tight for a
long while after.

He was such a good, kind man. She loved him, too. She
loved him more than any other man, even her own father.
There was no longer any reason for them not to show each
other affection when the desire struck, excepting what was
proper in the public eye, but what did they care for that? Very
little.

Estella left her two favorite men and went outside through
the front door. There was a wagon coming, just turning off
the road. Her heart skipped with excitement, and she eagerly
awaited the arrival of the guests.

As soon as the wagon was near enough to the house,
Clementine leaped out of the back of the wagon and ran to
meet her. She had a package tucked beneath one arm.

The two women embraced. Clementine pushed the package
into Estella's hands. "Here!" she exclaimed, eyes bright.

"Now, what's this?" Estella could smell the sweetness of
baked treats even as she asked.

Vera got down from the bench and walked over to give her a hug. "I know you said not to bring anything," she said. "But I brought a pie. And some fudge. Merry Christmas, Estella."

"Merry Christmas," Estella said, smiling at them both. "I just finished with the food. There's cider to warm you. Plenty of it. Help yourself."

Vera kissed her cheek and ducked inside, though Clementine remained out with Estella. "I should put the horse in the stable." She added, with her voice lowered, "And I want to meet Jackson."

Estella caught movement out on the road and pointed. "We won't have to wait long."

Two riders on horseback were coming their way.

Clementine clasped her hands together and bounced on her toes. "Oh, Estella, I do so fancy Jackson. And Mother has given me approval for a courtship with him."

"I'm glad for you," Estella said earnestly. "He's a good man. He'll be kind to you."

Jackson and Abe were there only a minute after, and greetings were exchanged. Abe had brought a stew, and Jackson showed off a few jars of honey and jam that would go perfectly with the rolls Estella had baked.

The two men volunteered to get all the horses settled in the stable. They were not slow with the task, quickly coming back to the house to accept drinks of spiced cider. Soon, everyone was at the table, sitting on chairs gathered from other rooms in the house. The serving dishes and platters passed from hand to hand, everyone making sure their neighbor had a portion of everything.

Estella looked around the table at all the faces of her friends, then down at the baby in the basket next to her chair, and marveled at how all of this had come to be. All the hardships they had endured were surely worth it for this wonderful Christmas with everyone, worth it to see their happy and smiling faces.

"How is your leg healing up, Christopher?" Vera asked.

Christopher made a little grimace. "Not as fast as I would like it to. And I still feel a bit balmy every so often."

"You lost heaps of blood, the doctor said," Abe pointed out, waving a fork dripping with gravy. "You're goin' to feel like an acorn calf a short while longer."

"Let's not talk about blood." Clementine's face had gone pale. She pushed the jar of bright red jelly away from her.

Estella's heart went out to her friend. Such terrible things they had seen and endured. At least the two of them, and Cody, had come out of it unharmed. Christopher had been shot in the leg. She had known that, seen it happen, and believed the bullet to have only grazed him, as he had been able to move around afterward. It wasn't until he had completely collapsed in front of the sheriff's office that she knew something worse was afoot.

While Vera had run to fetch a doctor, Estella had stayed with Christopher the entire time, holding his hand, keeping him warm with one of her own coats. The doctor had arrived, and Abe had pulled her away into the office to get her story from her as he was having a hard time understanding Jackson and Clementine's ramblings.

The bullet had wound up passing deep into Christopher's leg, glancing off the bone in the process, nicking a large vein on the way out. Luckily, the doctor had managed to fix him up. The thick bandage layers were hidden underneath

Christopher's tan pants. He would heal fully, the doctor had said, given time.

That he could have died during that fight—that he would have willingly given his life for her—had made Estella love him all the more strongly. She had felt so much guilt over it at first, until Christopher had asked her if she was the one who had shot him. She had realized he didn't blame her at all, and that had helped and solidified her resolve to care for him as best she could until he was well again.

Estella reached underneath the table, finding Christopher's hand and squeezing it. He squeezed back.

Abe sat back in his chair, his hands on his stomach. "While we're all in one place, I'd like to say what's been goin' on in town with Otis and Bolger."

Christopher's jaw squared, and his eyes darkened. "You best have some good news."

"I do," Abe said, and his mustache twitched as he smiled. "Ain't pressin' charges on you or Jackson for what you did to Otis and Nate. You acted in a self-defense way. And it turns out that when a man like Otis takes a beatin', gets a little bit of what he's given to so many others, he cracks like an egg. He done admitted to bribin' the bank, bribin' about half the town officials. He said he was responsible for poisonin' the stream."

At that, Christopher snarled out a swear that made Vera shoot him a hair-curling glare.

"He also said he sent men to wreck that stall at the Christmas Fair," Abe continued. "All that 'n more, more 'n enough to send him off to the state prison. And Bolger will be goin' off to jail. Lesser charges, as he was only doin' what he was paid to do. Otis is the one who planned it all."

"I knew it all this time," Christopher said, thumping his fist on the table and clattering silverware. His nostrils flared. "If only we could have put a stop to him sooner."

Estella took his hand, feeling the tension corded down in his wrist. She rubbed his clenched fingers and wished she could do more for him. All she could do was be there and understand him and hope it was enough.

"This will help you some," Abe said, looking at him. "I heard John James will be in touch with you. He'll want to give you an extension on your loans."

"Why now?" Christopher snapped. "He pityin' me?"

"I imagine it will be to earn favor with the town's people," Vera said. She primly broke open a roll and swiped butter on the halves with two flicks of her knife. "They'll likely be giving many people extensions. Now that everyone has heard of Otis's corruption, the bank will want to distance themselves from that type of behavior."

The mood in the dining room was souring. Estella feared there would soon be no good cheer left, and that wasn't what she wanted, needed, from this holiday. She leaned down and lifted Cody from his basket, holding him in her arms where everyone could see him. He blinked around at all of the people, his eyes huge and sparkling in the candlelight.

"We can think of the bad some other time," Estella said, speaking over whatever complaint Jackson was in the midst of. Faces turned her way. She lifted her chin and addressed them, this community she had unexpectedly found through misfortune. "But we have to take the bad with the good. All things in equal measure. Let us have this Christmas. No more talk of what we've been through. We're here. We're alive. That is enough for me."

"It's enough for me, too," Clementine said, a little too loudly. Her hands were shaking as she grabbed up her fork again.

"And me." Jackson was quick to agree, earning him a sweet smile from Clementine.

"And for me, as well." Vera reached for Cody, and Estella handed him to Clementine, who passed the baby on to her mother.

Heaving a sigh, Christopher let his shoulders drop and unclenched his jaw. "I don't want to be thinkin' of those rats anyway," he grumbled. "I want to eat more of this delicious ham."

Estella served him a thick slice, and he began to eat in a determined manner. Gradually, so, too, did everyone else. Jackson began to tell a story of one Christmas when Abe made up an enormous batch of stew to serve at the fair and how everyone hated it.

Abe joined in on the story, laughing as he spoke. "I was so plumb busy that year I didn't even notice I was illy. Then I had dinner at the tavern and couldn't taste nothin', not even onions. It turned out I put sugar instead of salt in the stew and couldn't tell!"

"You've never known such a terrible taste as sugary beef and onions." Vera burst out laughing.

Estella was laughing, too. She looked over at Christopher and caught him smiling at her. She smiled back and mouthed those three words she had once believed she would never tell anyone ever again.

The soft shine deep in his eyes returned her sentiment.

The meal went on until everyone had eaten their fill. The men went off to the sitting room to enjoy the fire while the women tidied up the kitchen, minded the baby, and prepared coffee to go along with a fine selection of desserts. Aside from the pie and fudge, Estella had baked cookies. The leftover rolls were soon eaten as well, used to sop up the sweet cinnamon juices leaking from the fruit in the pie.

On and on, the hours passed in that room in front of the fire, in the company of very good friends. More cider was drunk, and the rest of the desserts were consumed. Abe was the first to head out. His wife had been having dinner in town with her family, and he would need to go and bring her home.

Clementine and Vera were next to go, as they would be opening their shop tomorrow morning. Jackson offered to accompany them, which they were quick to accept. There were many farewells and lingering embraces before, at last, the wagon headed off, leaving Christopher, Estella, and Cody by themselves once more.

Christopher went back into the sitting room. Estella put Cody in his cradle, taking a moment to herself to admire his sleeping face.

"Estella?" Christopher called. "Can you come here a moment?"

He didn't sound upset or in great need. Still, there was some quality in his tone that had her rushing to him. Entering the sitting room, she saw him sitting on the sofa, looking very normal. He motioned to the spot on the cushion beside him, and she went to sit next to him.

"What is it?" she asked, curious. She couldn't read his expression, like he was trying to hide something from her. It was good news, whatever he was hiding. He wasn't quite able to stop the corners of his lips from twitching up.

"I had Jackson pick this up for me in town." His voice vibrated with excitement; that was what she had heard in his tone when he called her to him. He reached into his pocket and pulled out a small fabric pouch, cinched tight at the top with a drawstring.

He placed the pouch into her hand.

"Chris!" She shook her head. "If this is a present.... You don't have the money for this."

"I do," he said. "Abe put down an advance on Blizzard, that foal born just recently. I put a payment toward the loan first and thought I would use the rest in the manner I saw fit."

Her eyes and nostrils burned as his words summoned sweet tears. She mattered the most to him. No matter what happened, they would have each other. That was something they could count on now.

Estella pulled the pouch open and turned it over. A small yet heavy object tumbled into her palm. She knew what it was even before she saw it, and her heart skipped several beats. It was a thin silver ring with an intricate twist to the band, set with a blue stone gleaming in all different hues from the minuscule facets.

"It matches your eyes." Christopher plucked the ring from her hand and slid it onto her finger.

She stared down at that ring on her finger, knowing what it meant and hardly able to comprehend it. "Chris!"

He put his arms around her and rested his forehead on hers. Their eyes met, and the whole world was just them, warm before the fireplace, safe in each other's embrace.

"I love you," Christopher said, and his voice shook. Tears rose into his dark eyes and ran down his cheeks. "I want you to be my wife. No matter if I still wind up losin' the ranch, so long as you're by my side, we can survive and start over again."

Estella sobbed and stroked his arms, pressing her forehead to his. She never thought that this would ever happen to her or that a man could love her so. It felt like a dream that she might wake up from, but it kept on going, and she knew it was real. How strange that this should be how they found each other and fell in love.

Life was not a straight road from start to end, not at all. It was a maze of twists and turns and dead ends. Perhaps the purpose was to find a good person to walk with through that complicated and puzzling path, to enjoy what was all around rather than to focus on seeking the end.

"Say yes," Christopher whispered. "I need you, Estella. I know Bonnie would want me to do this. I have found the strength to live and love again, through you."

"Of course, I'll marry you!" She sobbed and laughed, and they kissed deeply. Joy was bright and warm in her veins, flowing through her whole body. She leaned into him and stroked her fingers into his soft hair. "I don't care what happens, where we live, if we're poor. We have each other, now and forever."

Christopher smiled as he kissed her again, then took hold of her hand with the ring. "Should we go tell Cody the good news? That his parents are goin' to be married?"

Estella was already halfway through rising when she realized what he had said. She dropped back onto the sofa and clutched him. "His parents?"

Does he mean what I think he means?

"Well, of course, I'm goin' to adopt him!" Christopher exclaimed. He grinned, his whole face lighting up. "Every boy needs a father!"

She threw her arms around him again and buried her face in his neck. She would have a husband, and Cody would have a father! "This is the best Christmas I've ever had. I love you!"

Christopher folded her in his arms, holding her to his strong body. "Best Christmas I've ever had, too. Until the next one. For as long as I'm with you, every Christmas is goin' to be the best one.'

The future that had once so confused and frightened her was now bright and filled with hope. Truly, she couldn't have asked for anything more.

She just had to kiss him again.

Chapter Thirty-Six

One year later....

Everyone gathered around the dinner table for the Christmas feast, and what a feast it was, with an enormous roast and all the trimmings, sourdough bread studded with nuts and dried fruits, boiled eggs, and pickled summer vegetables.

Estella sat beside her husband, Christopher, who she had married as soon as the spring thaw had come earlier that year. On her other side was Cody. Though still a little small for his age due to his struggles as a baby, his eyes were bright, and he was talkative, babbling on about nothing as he mashed at his food with a spoon.

Across the table were Clementine and Jackson, now engaged and soon to wed themselves. They were entirely inseparable now, obviously holding hands under the table. Vera was next to them, all smiles as she sipped a third glass of spiced cider. And Abe was there, too, this time with his wife by his side.

Estella looked all around the table, smiling at all of them. The winter that year had been much milder thus far, with just enough snow falling to blanket the ground and not much more. She had all the decorations out, including some that Cody had tried to assist her with. The crooked pine branches added a nice touch of charm, in her opinion. The pinecones scattered all over the floor, less so.

"Chris," Abe said, looking up from his plate, "what did you wind up doin' with that big ole nugget?"

His wife whacked his arm. "That ain't none of your business to mind, Abe!"

Christopher chuckled and shared a look with Estella. "I don't mind talkin' about it," he said.

"What nugget?" Vera asked. "A nugget of what?"

"Gold!" Abe said.

Vera put her hand over her heart. "My word. You found gold?"

Estella knew all about it. She still listened while dabbing speckles of gravy from Cody's face. She liked to hear the story, loved the happiness in Christopher's voice when he spoke of it.

"I was walkin' along the stream a few weeks back," Christopher explained. "Lookin' to see if there were any trees I might chop down. And I saw this sparkle in the water, just a big chunk of gold shinin'. Like it had been placed there."

"Where do you reckon it come from?" Abe asked.

Christopher held up his hands and shook his head. "One whole side of it was still covered in dirt and rocks. I guess years of freezin' and thawin' just finally broke it free. I took it into town, to the bank. Had it evaluated."

Even knowing what came next, Estella's heart jumped. The bank had been very lax with Christopher ever since Otis was carted away to prison. He had worked very hard to keep up with his payments in order to keep things that way. And then he had found that big piece of gold right there on his property, something that Otis had been hoping to get his hands on for all that time and never could.

"Turned out it was enough to pay off the rest of what I owe." Christopher laughed and put his arm around Estella. She leaned into him.

"And more," Christopher added. "Plenty to put away for future emergencies."

"Are you goin' to look for more?" Abe asked him, bushy eyebrows raised.

Christopher shook his head. "I never had any interest in the gold. If I stumble on any rocks, I'll take them to the bank. But I'm not goin' to dig or pan for them. I don't care about the money."

Estella knew that his feelings ran a little deeper than he was willing to say aloud. The night after he found the gold, he had told her he didn't want to wind up like Otis, only focusing on building a fortune. He had seemed afraid she might think he was a fool not to look for more gold. But, of course, she felt the same as him and supported his decision. Life, for her, had never been about finances. Life was about the people in it and the experiences they had together.

"What do I need more money for anyway?" Christopher looked at Estella, his eyes soft and filled with that love that made her so warm. "I got everythin' I could ever want already."

Clementine leaned over to Jackson. "Why don't you ever say such things to *me*?" she asked.

As everyone else was laughing and teasing them, Estella had eyes only for her husband. He deserved this good life. They both did. The gold was, in her mind, proof that they were doing the right things and being rewarded for it.

Later that night, after all the guests had gone and Cody was put to bed, Estella joined Christopher on the sofa before the fire. Her pulse thumped in her ears. Having friends over for Christmas was wonderful, but this? This was what she had been waiting for all along.

"You look like you got somethin' to say." Christopher wrapped his arm around her shoulders.

Her stomach filled up with nerves, and she felt like a bottle of milk about to overflow. She was going to spill the secret if she waited much longer, and she didn't want to do that, having thought hard about how she wanted to tell him.

"You know last year, you gave me my ring?" She lifted her hand to show him, as if he actually needed to be reminded. She polished it every month to keep its beautiful shine.

Christopher held her hand in his and cast his admiring gaze on the jewelry. "I do. You get me a ring this year, Estella?"

"Not quite." She pulled out the package she had hidden in her pocket when putting Cody to bed. She placed it on her husband's lap. A faint rattling sound came from inside.

"Well, it's a bit big for a ring...." He chuckled and tore the brown paper open. His smile twisted into a frown, and he leaned forward slightly to get a better look. Then, his eyes widened. He looked from the package contents to Estella, then back again.

"Go on." Her mouth was dry. "Take it out."

He pushed the paper wrapping onto the floor and pulled out a little baby rattle, a smooth carved handle with a flat circular top. Beads shifted around inside the top of the rattle when moved, making a gentle cascading noise.

"A rattle? Cody's a bit old for them, so...." His eyes went even wider as his initial realization seemed to assert itself more strongly. He jerked his head and stared at her. "Does this really think what I think it means?"

"I'm with child." She took his face in her hands and kissed him, looking into his eyes. There was fear, which she expected and understood. Given what tragedy had befallen the first child born of his blood....

She had been afraid, too. Even with his love, there had been times of fear and hesitation as they had navigated their new life together. When he had first seen her scars, on their wedding night, she had been petrified... until he had shown her the scar on his leg from being shot by Otis, and she had understood. Scars were stories of what a person had gone through. She and him were both scarred, both imperfect. But together, whole.

He blinked, and the fear faded away, just as hers had. He sprang to his feet and pulled her in tight to his chest. Kisses rained all over the top of her head. "When? When will they be here?"

"Early summer!" Laughing, she hugged him as tightly as she could. "Our child! Can you believe it?"

"I can!" He drew back and looked in awe at her middle. "A brother for Cody! Or a sister? I want to know now."

"As do I. I need to know if I should make little dresses or shirts!" Estella lifted her head and smiled up into Christopher's eyes.

He grinned down at her and stroked the side of her face. "Let's have another. And another. I want as many little nippers runnin' around here as we can get."

"Let's just focus on one at a time." Estella kissed him again. "Merry Christmas, my love."

"Merry Christmas, you wonderful woman." He hugged her, and she sank into him.

They stood there in the sitting room before the fire, wrapped up in each other, listening to each other's breathing and heartbeats. The next months and years were sure to bring many joys, and many hardships, too. Estella was ready to face them all with her family right by her side.

Epilogue

Three years later....

Estella rocked in the rocking chair Christopher had built for her on her birthday a year ago. It creaked and hitched when rolling forward on the rockers. His woodworking skills had improved greatly since then. She loved the chair all the same, seeing it as one out of hundreds of pieces of proof of his feelings for her. What man would learn a skill to give a woman a gift if he did not love her and want to meet all her needs?

Curled up in her lap was a little girl, just two years old and pretty as a doll with tumbling sandy-brown curls and sweet blue eyes. Those blue eyes were closed tight for the moment as the little girl napped, tuckered out from a day of running around outside in the snow with her older brother.

Estella paused in her sewing to rub her daughter's back. "I love you, Ada," she murmured.

Ada was her first child with Christopher, of course, named after the cousin who was indirectly responsible for bringing the two of them together. She was a prim and proper little one, fond of frilly dresses and rarely without a ribbon in her hair. She was also curious and full of energy, always following Cody around and asking him questions in her bell-chime voice.

Estella strongly suspected she was with her second child, though she was not yet fully certain and hadn't told Christopher yet. But it seemed like his dream of a ranch full of nippers was on its way to becoming true.

In some ways, raising Ada had been easier than raising Cody, especially when it came to feeding and care in those early days. In many other ways, it had been harder. Plenty harder. There were times when she had questioned everything, even if she was a good mother.

When she had those doubts like that, Vera was there for her. So, too, were Clementine and Jackson, now married and with a baby of their own.

And Christopher was there for her, always. When she needed time to relax, he would take the children and play marbles with them. If she wanted to talk, he lent her his ear. Should she only want his embrace and comfort, he was eager to provide. In return, she kept his house clean, his belly filled, and his heart as happy as she could.

They did not want for anything. Christopher's horses were sought after by cowboys across the whole state. He had an entire list of folks all waiting for their turn to buy one of his well-trained animals.

A few times a week, he went into town to sell pieces of furniture he had made and to help out at the blacksmith's.

And Estella had started her own business with Clementine, selling custom gowns through the mail.

Everything was as it was meant to be. Not perfect, but full of wonder and happiness.

The front door of the house flew open, and Cody rushed inside. Now five, he was a lean and energetic boy who abhorred the slowness of walking. He ran straight to Estella and clambered up into her lap, jostling his sister.

"Careful, now," Estella laughed. She put her sewing aside and stroked her son's wild hair. "What's got you all helter-skelter, my dear?'

Cody pointed out the nearby window. "I saw a man. He's comin' this way, Mama!"

"A man?" She stroked his hair again, smoothing it. "What sort of a man?"

"A gray man!"

"A gray man," Estella echoed, not understanding. She wondered if he was playing some sort of game. "Where's your father, Cody?"

"Mama?" Ada sat up, blinking and rubbing her eyes.

There was a knocking on the door. Cody gave Estella a look, asking silently if she believed him now.

When it comes, it all comes at once, she thought, amused.

She stood, holding Ada in one arm. Her daughter curled against her, laying her head on her shoulder.

With her other hand, Estella took Cody by the shoulder. She walked to the door with her children and opened it.

In an instant, she understood what Cody had meant by gray man. The person standing outside in the thin layer of snow that had fallen last night was certainly gray. His hair was too long and in need of a trim, a drab, limp fish-belly shade of silver. His skin was pale and lacking in color except for a red flush on his cheeks and the tip of his nose. A face-scrunching odor of whiskey exuded from his stained, rumpled clothes.

Estella pressed Cody behind her, her heart beating faster. She had no idea who this person was or what he could want from her. Over his shoulder, she could see Christopher coming, which was good.

"Can I help you?" Estella asked the gray man.

The man looked at her with bloodshot eyes. His cracked lips peeled apart. "I lost the tailor shop," he said.

"I don't..."

...*know what you mean,* was what she started to say, and then realization hit her right in the stomach.

She looked at the man again and saw him as he had been more than five years ago when he had stood before her, scowling, righteous in his fury as he refused to bury her cousin properly.

"Uncle Luther?" Estella gasped, covering her mouth. He used to be such a tall and lean figure. Something, a series of somethings, had turned him into this hunched, flabby shadow of his former self. He was all softness, with a gut rounded from too much drinking.

"What's goin' on here?" Christopher demanded, striding up behind Luther. He stepped inside and put his arm around Estella.

She looked at him and gestured at Luther. "This is...my cousin Ada's father. My Uncle Luther."

Christopher lowered his head with a growl. "And why is he here on my ranch?"

Luther held up his hands; at some point, he had lost the tip of his right thumb. "I lost the tailor shop," he repeated, sounding confused. His eyes ticked around aimlessly. "I had to sell. I was packin' up and found some old letters Ada had sent with this address. And I got to thinkin' about her. My...my girl."

Estella squeezed Christopher's arm, silently asking him to back off. She wanted to hear what Luther was saying, to know why he had come after so much time had passed.

Tears leaked from Luther's bloodshot eyes, a pitiful sight. "I realized that I failed my only daughter!" he blurted out. "I done kicked her out when I should have loved her harder. I'm...I'm so sorry. I wanted to come and see my grandson."

Estella knew Cody was peeking around from behind her, staring at this man he didn't know, who was saying things he didn't understand. He didn't know Estella wasn't his birth mother, that Christopher wasn't his real father. They had decided to tell him when he was a little older and could more properly understand.

"Is that him?" Luther croaked. He pointed at Cody, who hugged Estella's leg tightly. "Is that my grandson?"

"It is," Estella said. She reached out to the man, touched his shoulder. Christopher stiffened at her side. For once, she ignored her husband and patted Luther on his shoulder. "His name is Cody."

"Cody," Luther echoed. He wiped his face on a filthy handkerchief. "He sure is handsome. You done good by him, Estella."

Estella looked at that disgusting handkerchief stained with a myriad of dark substances, and something turned over inside of her. She wanted to be angry at her uncle for sending Ada away when she needed her family to support her. No, she *was* angry.

But five years had dulled the anger. She had seen and experienced so much more since then, and she understood now that sometimes people acted irrationally when they were hurt. She knew that simple mistakes could grow rapidly into terrible situations.

Luther had done what he thought was right, even though he had been very, very wrong. He could be blamed, but he could also be understood.

And he was here now, with an apology, with tears and a desire to see his grandson.

I can't turn him away, Estella thought. And her resolve solidified.

"Luther," she said, gentle but firm. He looked up at her, still dabbing his eyes, leaving stains from the handkerchief on his cheeks in the process. "Are you stayin' in town?"

He nodded.

"Why don't you go back to your inn?" she suggested. "Get some rest. You can come back tomorrow, and we'll talk more. But you must be so tired right now."

"I am," he said. "I am tuckered out. Plumb tuckered."

"You need any tin?" Christopher asked, surprising Estella. She shouldn't have been, really. He was lending her his support with the offer.

Luther waved his hand. "No, I-I got money. If I do go...can I come back tomorrow? Can I? I'd like to see more of my grandson. And hear about what you've been doin' here. When I asked about you in town, seemed like everyone nearby had praise for you."

Estella clasped Luther's grimy hand in hers. "Yes, you *can* come back tomorrow *if* you get some rest and wash up."

Her uncle looked down at himself and laughed slightly as if only realizing right then how filthy he was. "Shame on me, comin' here like this. Alright. Yes, I'll come back. Thank you."

"Of course," Estella said. She knew she was going to be busy making him a new handkerchief that night.

Luther gave Cody a final look and then walked away from the house. He had no horse with him. He trudged under his own power, head down, feet kicking the ground.

"Mama?" Cody peered up at Estella. "Why was that gray man so sad?"

"He realized he made a mistake," Estella told her son. "Why don't you go on and play with your marbles, dear? Your father and I need to talk."

Always eager to play marbles, Cody needed no further convincing and trotted off.

For a moment, Christopher and Estella stood there in silence, their arms around each other. They each took a little time for their thoughts before voicing them.

"What did you make of that?" Christopher asked, breaking the quiet first with his deep grumble. "An old fool down on his luck and feelin' sorry for himself. He came here as a last resort to feel better."

"Maybe so," Estella said. She leaned her head on his broad shoulder and breathed in his scent of horses and golden straw. "Maybe so, but if it's all he's got left to cling to.... We know what that's like, don't we, my love?"

"You got a point there." Christopher squeezed her and sighed. "You're goin' to forgive him, aren't you?"

"I already have." She laughed slightly, a little amazed at herself for it. But what choice did she have? If she were Luther, she would want to be forgiven. She would *need* that absolution in order to survive.

Estella said, "If he comes back here tomorrow in better shape, we'll have dinner. Get to know each other. We'll see how it goes, and hope it goes well. Alright?"

"Alright." Christopher nodded and kissed her cheek. "He *is* Cody's grandfather. He's got a right to know him. We'll do it."

"Thank you." Estella turned her head to catch his lips with hers.

As always, there was no real way to know what tomorrow would bring them.

As always, as long as they had each other, they would get through it.

THE END

Also by Ava Winters

Thank you for reading "**Christmas on His Doorstep**"!

I hope you enjoyed it! If you did, here are some of my other books!

My latest Best-Selling Books

#1 An Uninvited Bride on his Doorstep

#2 Once upon an Unlikely Marriage of Convenience

#3 Their Unlikely Marriage of Convenience

#4 An Orphaned Bride to Love Him Unconditionally

#5 An Unexpected Bride for the Lonely Cowboy

Also, if you liked this book, you can also check out **my full Amazon Book Catalogue at:**
https://go.avawinters.com/bc-authorpage

Thank you for allowing me to keep doing what I love! ❤

Printed in Dunstable, United Kingdom